DEADLY WHEN DISTURBED

DEADLY WHEN
DISTURBED

D. M. BARR

LEVEL
BEST BOOKS

First published by Level Best Books 2025

This novel is entirely a work of fiction. The names, characters and incidents portrayed in it are the work of the author's imagination. Any resemblance to actual persons, living or dead, events or localities is entirely coincidental.

First edition

ISBN: 978-1-68512-831-9

Cover art by Level Best Designs

This book was professionally typeset on Reedsy.
Find out more at reedsy.com

To true friendships, and the many wonderful people in my life who've been there through thick and thin, especially Martha Rubenstein, who was taken from us far too early.

Praise for Deadly When Disturbed

"Two women. Friends? Hardly. They're both after the same thing. And as the stakes get higher, the mind games get uglier, until—*well, I'm not going to give away the killer ending*. D. M. Barr's latest domestic thriller is a total rush. It's like being back with Betty and Veronica all over again—only this ain't high school, and these women (like the title says) are *Deadly When Disturbed*."—Marshall Karp, #1 *New York Times* bestselling author of the *NYPD RED* series

"Who's the hunter and who's the hunted in this taut domestic thriller? Don't even try to guess. Just relax, enjoy, and hang on as *Deadly When Disturbed* takes you on a wild ride."—Brad Parks, international bestselling author of *The Boundaries We Cross*

"Tense, well-written, and surprising—Liane Moriarty meets Gillian Flynn by way of John Lutz in D.M. Barr's latest domestic thriller, *Deadly When Disturbed*. Gaslighting and suburban intrigue abound in this carefully crafted tale, guaranteed to keep you in suspense all the way to the final chapter. Put this one at the top of your to-be-read pile!"—Richard Helms, Thriller, Macavity, and Shamus Awards-winning author of *22 Rue Montparnasse*.

"*Deadly When Disturbed* is a superb dark thriller that offers a brilliantly written bizarro take on the classic *All About Eve*. Shifts in reality and twists of the plot keep the reader on edge until the stunning and unexpected climax. Fasten your seatbelt and hang on. It's a great ride."—S. Lee Manning, award-winning author of *Trojan Horse, Nerve Attack, Bloody Soil*, and *Deadly Choice*.

i

"In this electrifying psychological thriller, D.M. Barr masterfully weaves a tale of deception and deadly ambition. When successful realtor Dara Banks meets the seemingly perfect Merry Rafter, their carefully constructed facades begin to crack, revealing the darkness beneath polished veneers of suburban success. This sophisticated reimagining of the *Single White Female* scenario creates an atmosphere of mounting tension where every gesture of friendship masks a threat. With razor-sharp prose and devastating twists, *Deadly When Disturbed* builds to a shocking conclusion that will leave readers questioning everything they thought they knew."—Emilya Naymark, Sue Grafton Memorial Award nominee, author of *Behind The Lie* and *Hide In Place*.

"*Deadly When Disturbed* by D.M. Barr is a clever psychological thriller reminiscent of The Hand That Rocks The Cradle, updated for today's culture and with a superior narrative.... With a steady and increasingly intense pace, [it] is a hypnotic read of insanity and wretchedness that will stay with you long after the last page."—Gaius Konstantine for Readers' Favorite

Prologue

Samantha Ellingsworth stood at her dining room table and calmly fingered through the cardboard box, double-checking that the paperwork was in chronological order. Even now, no one could accuse her of being anything but organized and precise. For nearly forty years, it had been both a gift and a curse.

First the letters from Harry, professing his incendiary ardor during their abbreviated law school courtship. The GIA certificate for the diamond, his glittering promise of passion extending through eternity. The deed to their Upper West side condo. A copy of her resignation from Davis & Milliker, where she'd been on the fast track to partner. The birth certificates for her daughter, dated a year later, and the surprise twins, ten years after that.

Next, the children's coveted acceptance letters from Harrison—Manhattan's most elite private pre-school and elementary—followed by every one of the glowing report cards she'd worked with them so diligently to earn. Campaign flyers she'd created for Harry's run for state senate. Her passport opened to the page containing the stamp from that fateful trip to Aruba. The letters she'd written, refuting everything he'd accused her of—all unopened and marked "Return to Sender." The prescription for Prozac, unfilled, as if any pharmaceutical could rescue her from this pit of depression. Finally, the divorce papers she'd received a few weeks back, still unsigned.

A lifetime of aspirations, misunderstandings, and betrayals, all encapsulated in a pile of paper less than three inches thick. She affixed the cover to the box and took a long, wistful look at the "perfect" apartment they'd been so ecstatic about buying, beating out several competing bids thanks to the lingering cachet of the Ellingsworth name and its clout in political circles. Confident that the condo was spotless, with everything in its place, Samantha slowly donned her hooded sheepskin coat, grabbed the box, and headed out.

The elevator operator nodded when she entered, but Gloria from the floor above murmured a curt hello and diverted her gaze as they descended from the seventh floor. Samantha had grown used to this frostiness over the past few weeks. Did the other tenants fear it was catching, that if they inched too close, their spouse and children might abandon them, reducing *their* lives to rubble? Whatever.

She trudged southbound through the early morning wintery mix, package still cradled to her chest like a newborn. Frigid raindrops grazed her eyelashes before cascading downward and stinging her cheeks as she passed the signs in Zabars' windows, reminding patrons to purchase their Thanksgiving turkeys while they lasted, the holiday drawing close. Thanksgiving. The irony did not escape her.

Shivering as much from the weather as from what lay ahead, she descended the subway staircase at 72nd Street, pushing against the horde headed toward the sidewalk. She had someplace to go too, and nothing—not crowds nor apprehension—was going to delay her.

Today was the day, a chance to finally make him understand.

Samantha tapped her phone against the OMNY reader to pay her fare, pushed through the turnstile, and headed toward the stairway leading to the uptown train. She positioned herself close to the opening of the tunnel and stood by the edge of the platform, resummoning her fleeting courage as the crowds swelled behind her. Commuters, too involved with their phones to notice the determined woman beside them whose breathing had quickened and whose face had grown hot. She hugged the box even tighter to her fidgeting body and waited. And waited.

The loudspeaker announced that the next train was going out of service and wouldn't be stopping, eliciting a collective sigh from the throng. She saw the light in the distance and heard the clunk-de-clunk and whirl—a deafening gale descending onto the tracks, drowning out the murmur of the passengers. Her ride to the most important meeting of her life. And it was the number 2 train. How appropriate. Just like her, relegated from number one.

Timing was everything, the oncoming gleam only yards away. She tightened her grasp on what she had left of her world, recalling the face of the bitch who'd laughed as she'd stolen the rest away. Then she took one last breath and jumped onto the tracks.

I

Dara

Chapter One

Five Years Later

D ara Banks had murder on her mind.

First, there'd been Ava's morning meltdown. Despite the January cold, she'd spent an hour refusing to wear anything but her tattered Cinderella costume to her second-grade class. The battle left Dara with a pounding headache and late for the first of five dismal job applicant interviews, which she had to endure without her usual Caffe Americano.

But since you can't be angry at a stepdaughter with autism, Dara directed her ire toward Kylie, her departing assistant, who had decided, rather abruptly, that a future of cleaning up poop at the local doggie daycare was preferable to sticking address labels on real estate solicitations. Kylie was someone she could legitimately daydream about killing off, though in truth, it was her own fault for hiring a teen straight out of high school. Then again, even the more mature assistants never stayed. Was it her fault that juggling a mountain of responsibilities left her with no patience to coddle the incompetent?

In the end, Dara set her homicidal sights on the stream of unqualified candidates who insisted on wasting her time with their drivel when all she wanted was to concentrate on that night's fundraiser. The first applicant wanted to know if vacation leave would cover her impending trip to Tahiti, two weeks away. The next needed an hour off at precisely 10:00 am each day for an aqua aerobics class. The third warned that while she was willing to work as an assistant, Dara had better watch out because she intended to get her license and eventually take over as Rock Canyon's leading Realtor.

At 2:15 pm, Kylie sashayed in with the last of the jobseekers—a blonde Grace Kelly wannabe in her late thirties wearing a black Dior suit awkwardly adorned with a blingy pin that undermined the elegance of the outfit.

Dara invited the applicant to sit, but before she could say more, her phone rang. She glimpsed at the screen with a scowl. The last thing she needed was a call from her caterer, and any communication this close to the event couldn't signal good news. She turned toward the window, wincing as a frantic Emily spewed a torrent of apologies from across town.

"Ms. Banks, I'm so sorry, so sorry. We just found out. We can't deliver the cake."

An atomic bomb detonated inside Dara's skull.

"What the hell are you talking about, Emily? We discussed this months ago. I have five hundred guests who paid $1,000 apiece to Autism Vanguard, expecting cake at the end of their dinner. What do you mean you can't deliver?"

"The pastry chef finished the cake. It was incredible, truly. And on the way to the hotel, a speeding truck t-boned his delivery van. The driver is okay, thank God, but the van flipped on its side, and the cake along with it. Unsalvageable, I'm afraid. And with a design as intricate as the one you requested and with so little notice, I can't find a substitute. Again, I am so, so sorry..."

Pushing back a wave of nausea, Dara disconnected the call and squeezed her eyes shut, a steel door slamming down between her consciousness and the mental Siberia where she exiled all unwelcome news from "Celeste" until she could figure out a way to cope. Celeste was her counselor, her staunch protector—but cloaked in a vortex of panic and destruction. Over the years, therapists had trained Dara to imprison her psychological demon, but during moments of great stress, Celeste managed to dislodge those barricades and often made Dara do things she later couldn't recall.

Dara counted to ten, willing logic to override Celeste's fury. She could always tell the guests the truth about the delivery truck. But why not capitalize on an unfortunate situation? Perhaps say that Autism Vanguard donated the money earmarked for dessert to the cause? Or that they were purposely skipping dessert to spotlight how sweets negatively affected autistic children's sugar levels...

"Excuse me, Ms. Banks?"

The soft, shaky voice jerked her back from her ruminations. Even Celeste took momentary cover. Dara spun around to face the job candidate she'd forgotten was in the room. She just couldn't, not right now.

"I'm afraid this isn't the best time for an interview. Leave your resume and I'll call if I think it's a good fit."

"I couldn't help but overhear. I think I may be able to help you," said the woman, unperturbed.

Dara blinked and focused on the applicant for the first time. In a less gender-conscious era, people would have characterized her as a handsome woman, with a face that was pleasant enough to look at but fell short of pretty. Her expression was earnest, so Dara decided to hear her out. It was, after all, a gutsy move to offer to help a prospective employer during a job interview.

She glanced at the resume, desperate for a name.

"Ms. Rafter. Meryl, I—"

"Everyone calls me Merry."

"Merry, then...I appreciate your offer, but I have a fundraiser for a packed ballroom of guests starting in less than four hours and have just discovered we have no dessert to serve. How could you possibly help?"

"I have an idea...you said it had to serve five hundred, right? Any particular theme?"

Dara's eyes widened with incredulity. "The fundraiser is for Autism Vanguard. We're holding it at the Astor Hotel downtown. The caterer planned to cut the original cake into three hundred small pieces, since many people skip dessert altogether. The decorations always convey a message of hope, that you can do anything if you set your mind to it. If you can deliver that, I'll reimburse you double what it costs you. But I doubt that—"

Merry smiled and stood to leave. "Don't worry, I'll be there with the cake in plenty of time."

"But how..."

"No time to waste with explanations. Just relax. I've got this."

* * *

Five hours later, it was go-time. To Dara's relief, the hotel staff had decorated the opulent gold and crystal ballroom just as she had requested. The animated chatter of elegantly clad donors rose above the clinking of forks against porcelain, guests polishing off their roasted quail or lollypop lamb chops. Dara always gave her speech right before dessert. A dessert she had yet to see, due to her handling of other minor crises occurring beyond the kitchen. Nor did she truly expect to see it. Having little faith over anything she couldn't personally control, she'd settled on the sugar-sacrifice-as-reminder explanation as a fallback position.

While the waitstaff removed the dinner plates, Dara slipped off to the ladies' room to compose herself. The mirror reflected the sophisticated and poised persona she'd strived hard to perfect, not one hair of her strawberry-blond pixie cut out of place. But her insides were jelly. Addressing crowds had never been her strong suit. Despite years of practice, she still interpreted the audience's polite stares as daggers, seeking to gut her, expose her as the shy, submissive introvert of her youth. She wondered if these self-doubts would shadow her for the *next* forty years.

One pep talk later, she emerged from the restroom and approached the podium. Her friend and fellow volunteer, Brooke, offered an upturned thumb and an encouraging smile from her seat at the front table. The gesture tamped down Dara's burgeoning existential crisis, but it wasn't until she spotted the caterer wheel the cake into the ballroom that her worries completely dissolved.

Six tiers, ranging from small to large, were covered in elegant white frosting, with green plastic figurines—were they soldiers?—scaling the sides, holding onto a rope that connected them. On the top, three figurines who had obviously made it to the pinnacle held up their tiny arms in triumph. *Perfect.* A frisson of excitement raised goosebumps on Dara's bare arms.

The crowd applauded and the social influencers ran up to photograph the dessert before the staff returned it to the kitchen to cut and serve. Dara surveyed the room to offer Merry her thanks but couldn't locate her among the crowd. She took a deep breath and leaned into the mic.

"Ladies and gentlemen...friends...I'll keep this short. I just want to thank you once again for your generous donations over the past year to Autism Vanguard. With your help, AV has raised $600,000 for AVa's Place, our sanctuary for those with invisible disabilities. We've rented a floor of a building downtown, and your dollars will cover the creation of our low sensory room, where children with sensitivities can relax and play without bright lights, crowds, and loud noises."

Dara paused until the applause died down. "You have also helped fund twelve months of 'Birthday Parties for All' or BPA. We all know how much it hurts when neurotypical children exclude our neurodivergent kids from their parties. BPA will celebrate every child's birthday and guarantee them a wonderful, sensory-sensitive event. As importantly, we will extend an invitation to those parties to every child in our database, regardless of their abilities or social skills. Please give yourselves another round of applause for funding this vital initiative."

She raised her glass. "Please join me in a toast...to Autism Vanguard. To AVa's Place. And to you, for making this all possible! Enjoy tonight, because tomorrow, I'll be back on the phone, asking for your help for next year."

When the roar of a second ovation devolved into chatter, Dara carefully stepped down from the podium, eager not to undermine her message by tripping over her new blue satin Manolos. Though the most stressful part of the evening was behind her, she still longed to strip off her gown and spend quality time soaking in her tub. Tomorrow, it would be back to the grind: taking real estate listings, attending closings, and, of course, making a slew of fundraising calls. Right now, she deserved a moment to rejoice, to imagine the looks of joy on the children's faces—children like her Ava— when they arrived at their first inclusive birthday celebration, slated for

June.

She headed to the bar, tastebuds primed for a glass of Gavi di Gavi, her favorite Italian white wine. The bartender apologized profusely, explaining they were out. "Are you kidding me?" she spat out, a bit too loudly, causing those around her to turn. Dara shot them an apologetic smile, tamped down her fury, and grudgingly opted instead for a chardonnay. While she waited, she watched her co-chair, Brooke Barnes, work the tables, thanking guests for their donations. Brooke's wavy blond tresses graced a perfectly fitted lavender gown over an incredibly toned body. *She hasn't changed a bit since college*, Dara thought, her admiration tainted by a tad of jealousy.

She tipped the bartender a twenty and took one long swig, inviting potential inebriation to transport her to a less fraught state. Then, as she walked the perimeter of the now-crowded dance floor back to her table, she spotted Merry. Her cake savior was sipping champagne by the kitchen entrance, clad in a black sequined Givenchy gown spoiled by garishly large rhinestone-hoop earrings. Dara made a detour, eager to make amends for her earlier rudeness.

"You did good—and I love your gown. Oscar de la Renta?" Merry asked with an engaging smile as she and Dara clinked glasses.

Dara nodded, swallowing a jolt of discomfort. She still berated herself for spending money on designer dresses and shoes, even for events such as this. A throwback to her parsimonious upbringing, no doubt.

"You really think it went okay? I practiced that speech for two hours last night...and still I was shaking." A rare admission of vulnerability that shocked even her. Maybe it was the chardonnay at work.

"No one could tell. You were great." Merry gave her arm a brief squeeze.

Dara didn't quite know how to react to this overture, coming from someone she hardly knew, but chalked it up to Merry being naturally gregarious and, considering her gaudy earrings, perhaps unaware of the boundaries that existed in polite society.

"I must apologize for my rudeness before... I'm not good under pressure. I can't thank you enough for coming through with dessert."

"I totally understand. No apologies necessary."

"Tell me, Merry, how did you do it? And what do I owe you?"

Merry smiled playfully and winked. "You can repay me with a second chance at an interview. Will tomorrow work?"

Chapter Two

Friday greeted Dara with none of the challenges of the previous morning. Ava dressed herself without a quibble—the norm as long as her outfits involved no zippers—and her stepson Khai offered to walk her to school, something he hadn't suggested since he'd entered his rebellious teens. Even Jason was less short-tempered than usual, managing to lift his fork without assistance by wedging it between his mangled fingers and then scarfing down his veggie omelet without complaint.

Rock Canyon Realty was deserted when she arrived, typical for any real estate office at 8:30 am. Her colleagues typically didn't crack an eyelid before ten, but perhaps that's why Dara had quickly risen to Triple Diamond status. She sipped her Caffe Americano while she scanned the resume Meryl Rafter had left the day before. To her surprise, it contained no mention of college and a dearth of the job experience Dara expected from someone she estimated to be in her late thirties.

She glanced at the day's agenda: Cold calls, more interviews, a meeting with Brooke to assess the previous night's event, a listing appointment. Then, her usual Friday three-hour stint volunteering at the local women's shelter before picking up or ordering dinner for the family.

Life would be so much easier if Jason could still cook—she certainly didn't have the time—but glass shards from a job accident hadn't only sliced through his hands' tendons, rendering even the simplest finger functions nearly impossible, they'd severed his desire to even try. Everything changed from that point forward. He lived in sweats, lacking the fine motor skills he needed to manipulate buttons and zippers. They'd even had to swap out all their house's door knobs for levers. He often needed someone to feed him, leading to frustration and embarrassment that had reduced their social outings to nil.

Despite surgery and physical therapy, his hands remained stiff and gnarled, and while doctors insisted he could regain some semblance of normalcy with ongoing therapy, the ability to manage something as simple as holding a pen continued to elude him. After repeated disappointments, he'd just given up. It broke her heart that Manhattan's once leading architect no longer had the will to relearn to open a can or turn on the stove.

Two candidates arrived before Meryl's appointment, with each interview lasting less than fifteen minutes. Dara simply couldn't tolerate the sense of entitlement. When someone's first questions targeted sick days, vacation time, and internet access instead of the requirements of the job, she showed them the door. In her world, work ethic would always trump self-indulgence.

Dara's cell phone distracted her from the paperwork she attempted to complete before Meryl showed up. She glanced at the Caller ID. Great, just what she needed right now. She took a deep breath and summoned an upbeat tone.

"Hi, Mom, what's up?"

"Good morning, Da. I wanted to know how the fundraiser went last night."

Never "How are you?" or "How are the kids?" Always about the charity. And why was that surprising? Even her name was derived from the Spanish verb "Dar," to give. And her nickname, Da, was Russian for "Yes." That was her mother's view of Dara's role in the world: to give of herself and never refuse a request.

"It was a sellout. We probably generated north of a half-million."

"Good work, darling. That's truly where your talents lie. You should devote yourself to the cause and forget about this real estate nonsense. The needy and disenfranchised demand the help of people like us."

In other words, nothing you do is ever good enough.

"Mom, we've talked about this. I told you, what I do *does* help those in need

I always reduce my fee for clients with lower incomes. Plus, with Jason still not working and Ava's mounting therapy bills, we need my commissions more than ever."

"Nonsense Dara. You and I both know Jason could work if he put his mind to it. He could hire an assistant to do what he can't use his hands for anymore. Draw up blueprints, whatever. He could be a rainmaker... and free you up to be home more with his children when you aren't volunteering."

"Uh, Mom? They're now my children too."

"Same difference. They need a mother. No matter how many causes your father and I supported over the years, every night, I made sure there was a homecooked dinner on the table."

"The difference being, you always had me, along with seven or eight foster kids to help out."

"Speaking of which, you know what tomorrow is, right?"

How could she forget? "Yes, Mom, of course. I have the candles ready."

"All these years gone, and I still think about them every day..."

"Me too. But anyway, the point is, you always had support. Right now, it's just me at home...and Khai, whenever he deigns to show up after school."

"That's another thing, you really need to put your foot down with that boy—"

"Mom, I'm sorry, I'm in the middle of interviews, and I really don't have time to discuss the improbability of teenage boys listening to anything they're told."

"Interviews?"

"Yeah, my assistant is leaving at the end of the week. So, if you could excuse me..."

"You know, if you gave up the real—"

"Gotta go, Mom. Bye."

Dara disconnected the call before her mother could provide additional unwanted career advice, all of which she'd heard a thousand times before. *Why work when Jason's parents have millions? Raise your family. Volunteer, help others. Repeat.* Why couldn't her parents be more like Jason's family? They came from old money, too, but hadn't let guilt over their inherited millions propel them into a spiral of relentless philanthropy. How she yearned for her mother and father to treat her with the benevolence they extended to the rest of the world or see the value of her work…or of anything besides incessant altruism.

Ironically, much of their philosophy had rubbed off on her, for better or for worse. It had been the only way to curry her family's affection and attention when young, and as she aged, it influenced her every decision, from the causes she supported to her choice of husband.

The only thing in her life not inspired by goodwill was real estate. Sure, she'd taken it up after the accident so they wouldn't dip into their savings. But she found out early in her career that she enjoyed the competition, the moment of triumph when a homeowner selected her from the horde of rival agents to list and sell their home, or to help them select their next one. It was wonderful when clients recognized and rewarded her skill, as opposed to her willingness to give.

Her office phone rang and with no one around, she put the call on speaker. It was Vivian Hunsicker from 83 New Mill Road, where Dara had recently made a listing presentation. Hunsicker was a hoarder whose congested Colonial teemed with everything from antique doll collections to empty pizza boxes. Of course, she wanted an unrealistically high price. Still, a listing was a listing.

"Vivian, I'm so glad to hear from you. I can swing around and put a lockbox on your front door later today. I think we should list the property as 'Coming Soon' to create some buzz and—"

"Dara, I don't mean to interrupt you, but we've decided to go in a different direction."

Dara definitely didn't like the tone of her voice—and Celeste certainly didn't—but she rarely encountered an objection she couldn't reverse.

"A different direction? Does that mean you'd prefer to go right to market so we can get the house sold this week?"

"No, I'm afraid we've decided to list with another agent."

Oh no, you're not.

"I see. Have you signed the contract yet?" Dara's saccharine tone could make a listener's teeth hurt, but it successfully belied the bolt of anger, causing the vein in her neck to throb uncontrollably.

"No, he's sending it over today electronically. He said a few clicks here and there, and we're set."

"Well, that's fine, Vivian. I can always bring you the buyer. Tell me, who will you be listing with, so I'll know who to call to make an appointment."

"I don't know if I should say—"

"Really, it's okay. Just give me a name so I can ask him or her when it's going to come on to the market and get my buyers lined up."

"It's Ruben. Ruben Bockelman."

Dara purposely paused as the less altruistic, more mean-spirited Celeste took over. "Ruben? Well, I think that's wonderful, Vivian. He's a top agent...and he really needs the support these days, so it's great you'll be helping him keep his mind occupied."

"I don't understand. What do you mean?"

"Oh. I guess he didn't mention it. Let's forget I said anything."

"No, Dara. Please. What did you mean about Ruben?"

"It's just his kidneys. He found out about a month ago. Dialysis, three times a week, four hours at a time. Why does it always have to be the good guys who suffer?"

"Oh, I didn't know."

"Vivian, not to worry. I'm certain he's hired a team who'll be available to help you when he's indisposed. Even if they're new, I'm sure they can explain away your buried underground oil tank, monitor the radon testing, conduct the well inspection, counter any lowball offers, all of that. It shouldn't be an issue."

Dara shut up and waited. She heard muffled chatter between Vivian and her husband while they considered how an inexperienced team could never be as effective as a lead agent, especially when more complicated issues arose. It was a shame to use Ruben's affliction against him, but maybe next time, he wouldn't use a hospital where the gossipy aides happened to be Dara's past clients.

"Uh, Dara, Noah and I just talked, and maybe it would be better if you oversaw the sale for us. Could you send over your paperwork today?"

Dara mentally patted herself on the back. "I'm on it, Viv. Expect the contracts in the next hour or two. And don't worry about Ruben. I know it's an awkward situation, so I'll give him a call after you sign the documents and let him know you've gone in a different direction. You've made a good decision. I'm going to get you top dollar for your home." The throbbing in her neck subsided, and she imagined Celeste giving her an imaginary thumbs up.

"We're sure you will. Thanks, Dara." *Click.*

"Wow, you really *are* a killer."

Dara looked up with a start to see Meryl standing in her doorway, this time wearing a black Alexander McQueen blazer over a white, way-too-short linen pencil skirt and carrying a large duffle bag.

"There was no one at reception, so I found my own way back. Hope that's okay."

"That's fine," Dara said with a more welcoming smile than the day before and invited her to sit.

"Again, I can't thank you enough for coming through for me yesterday." She rescanned Merry's CV. "Your actions show a resourcefulness I respect in the people I work with and expect of those on my staff. I'm just a little confused by your resume…under 'experience,' you list an on-again, off-again stint as a "staff member" with a company called Extras Special. What exactly is that?"

Merry leaned forward as if to share a secret. "Before I was married, and then again afterward, I worked as an actor. Extras Special places performers in locations where we're most needed."

"Such as…?"

"Judging by the crowd at the fundraiser last night, you have a large and supportive sphere of friends and acquaintances, which is wonderful," Merry began. "Unfortunately, that's not true for many people, and that's where Extras Special comes in. They supply bridesmaids or groups of guests for weddings, or additional mourners for funerals where the number of grievers might be less than the family would have preferred. And, of course, we were

15

there for gallery openings, political rallies, that sort of thing, where the media might judge the success of an exhibit or campaign on the number of attendees it attracts."

Dara squinted, her mouth agape. "So, your product was ego massage?"

Merry laughed. "I suppose you could call it that. But I prefer to think of it as having used my talents to provide comfort and support to the emotionally needy."

Dara reached for her coffee and took a long gulp. Helping people was certainly something she knew about, having practically been breastfed on it.

"Merry, what did you talk to these people about? How did you convince them you were actually a friend of the bride or groom, or someone who knew the deceased?"

Meryl winked. "I've learned two truths in life when it comes to communication. First, people love to talk about themselves; it's their favorite topic. So, I'd ask them questions before they asked me. And second, so much of life is illusion. People believe what you want them to believe...if you're persuasive enough. Like last night—everyone believed the cake the servers rolled out was real, right?"

Dara arched an eyebrow. "Yes...were they wrong?"

Meryl reached down, unzipped her duffle bag, and drew out a large Styrofoam circle. "Yes and no. The cake I delivered last night was composed of several different-sized cake dummies like this one, stacked on top of each other. Bakeries usually decorate them and use them as window displays. I have a friend who provides these cakes for weddings, one tier real and the rest fake. Saves the newlyweds a ton of money. She had a cake ready to go for a client who isn't getting married until next week, so I borrowed it. Just added the soldier figurines I picked up at Walmart, along with the sheet cakes the caterers fed your guests. No one noticed the difference; they never do."

Dara leaned back, astonished but also impressed. Meryl's life hacks, no more or less unscrupulous than what she herself had just pulled with Vivian, would make her a capable assistant. Yet, the holes in her resume remained concerning.

"Merry, I appreciate how quickly you think on your feet... There's just a huge gap here, with no work listed between Extras Special and now. What have you been doing recently?"

Meryl's expression clouded over while she squeezed the Styrofoam circle back into her bag. "I'm coming off a couple of bad marriages. The men were wealthy, though, and I really didn't have to work. I spent most of my time volunteering—food kitchens, suicide hotlines, and fundraising for my pet project, Neglect-Thee-Not."

"I'm not familiar. What's Neglect-Thee-Not?"

Merry's face brightened again. "NTN rescues neglected animals from uncaring owners and rehomes them. Dogs living outside and chained to fences, cat hoarding situations, that kind of thing. Once, we raised nearly a million to rescue a dolphin who was living on its own as an attraction in a two-bit theme park. He spent his days tossing around one blow-up toy, no other stimulation, dying of depression. It was heartbreaking. We bought him and donated him to SeaScapes, a park where he's now part of a family of dolphins and trainers who keep him busy and happy."

The story tugged at Dara's heart. "You went out and physically rescued these animals? I mean, not the dolphin, but the others?"

"No, it's too gut-wrenching for me to see neglected pets, ones powerless to save themselves. I fundraised and made large anonymous donations of my own every year. I still do."

"I see. That must have involved clerical skills, right?" said Dara, searching for any reason to justify the hire. She liked how Meryl wasn't some wide-eyed kid smack out of college, but rather, a woman with seasoning and street smarts.

"Oh yes," responded Merry. "But I have always had an interest in real estate. As you can see, I did earn a certificate in home staging from Stage For. I imagine that could be helpful, yes? Let you spruce up listings without dishing out money for an outside stager. And I'm quite willing to get my real estate license if you need someone to cart around buyers, give you more time to go after new listings. Just put me to work, and I promise, I absolutely promise, that I'll go above and beyond. You won't be sorry."

"You do realize it's mostly grunt work. Filing, answering phone calls, managing my social media, sometimes picking up my lunch and drycleaning…"

"None of the glamour of attending strangers' funerals, then?" Merry asked, straight-faced.

There was a pause, and then they both burst into laughter.

Dara wasn't normally an impulsive person, but there was something about Meryl that she liked and trusted. Her work ethic, shrewd thinking, and propensity for helping others made Dara believe she may have found a kindred spirit, a mini-me.

"I do have one last question, Merry," she said, handing her a packet with employment forms. "When can you start?"

Chapter Three

The next morning, Kylie taught Merry the intricacies of the job. Dara left her door ajar, half-listening to the targeted questions Merry asked, pleased that her hire picked up new skills quickly. By noon, Merry was already calling buyer agents to request feedback on showings and seemed unperturbed by Kylie's final departure that Friday.

The next few weeks went by uneventfully, satisfying Dara that despite her impulsivity, she'd made a good hiring decision. Merry cheerfully arrived each morning on time, competently completed her tasks, and ensured Dara's coffee was always on her desk by 8:30 and her salad picked up at noon. During her free time, she watched webinars on various aspects of real estate.

It was a relief. Instead of wasting time correcting Kylie's errors, Dara solicited prospective AV donors, volunteered more often at the women's shelter, and arrived home early enough to read Ava her favorite bedtime story—always Cinderella, no deviation allowed.

She even grabbed lunch with Brooke, where they rolled around ideas for next year's fundraiser. Hanging out with her oldest friend was a treat because, truth be told, Dara rarely socialized. Interactions with her fellow agents at Rock Canyon Realty didn't count; even if they invited her to lunch or dinner, the hosts would always remain rivals who feigned undying friendship to get inside information or a competitive edge. She and Jason didn't venture out much; his physical disabilities and Ava's invisible ones made any excursion trying at best. Even when she'd drop Khai off at one of *his* friend's houses when he was younger and try to start a conversation with the boy's parents, they'd remain aloof, no doubt thinking she was only lingering to convince them to buy, sell, or invest. So, any time spent with Brooke was a welcome interlude in a day filled with home sales and evenings of strained domesticity.

"She's a treasure," Dara confided over their Cobb salads. "No pushback; everything done as requested."

"Sounds almost too good to be true."

Brooke's sarcastic tone didn't surprise Dara. Her friend was the sharpest woman she knew. Through smarts and grit, she'd made it out of a bad neighborhood with a full scholarship to Syracuse. Part of those smarts included never taking any person or situation at face value. Her observations were usually entertaining, but this time, Dara failed to see the humor.

"Not everyone has an agenda, Brooke. Some people are just grateful for an opportunity. She was on the outs. You know how hard it is for a woman with no college education pushing forty to get a job. I saw hiring Meryl as a way to help."

"Help her, or help you?" Brooke downed the remainder of her Merlot.

"Can't it be both? Anyway, she promised I wouldn't be sorry, and so far, I'm not."

"Well, I'm waiting for the other Jimmy Choo to drop."

Dara put down her fork and pursed her lips. "What exactly is your problem with her?"

"Da, I spoke to her at the fundraiser while she was waiting for the caterers to roll in the cake. She was all 'I've organized charity events double this size. I've saved the day with the dessert, I, I, I.' She's overly impressed with herself. Me, not so much."

This was unexpected information, but it didn't dissuade Dara from coming to her assistant's defense. "Maybe she was just nervous. New crowd, worried I wouldn't like the cake; there are a million reasons why she may have been overcompensating, not been herself."

"Fair enough, Da. Just keep your eyes open, okay?"

"I always do, hon. I always do."

She wondered if Brooke's reaction had more to do with jealousy than with keen observation. The past few years, she'd been Dara's right hand on the Autism Vanguard fundraising committee. Then, out of nowhere, Merry popped in and saved the day.

About a month in, though, an incident caused Dara to wonder if Brooke had been right after all.

She woke up early to give herself extra time to get to work, a lingering nor'easter threatening delays from downed trees and power lines. But Ava, with her limited verbal abilities, kept shoving a pad under Dara's face, yelling "Car-Net, Car-Net," her way of requesting drawings of the Cartoon Network logo. That was her thing now, an insatiable desire to see television logos drawn off-screen.

At breakfast, Jason engaged in his usual passive-aggressiveness. He sighed deeply but wordlessly at the toast, cream cheese, and marmalade Dara set in front of him, her omelet-making time cut in half and therefore skipped, thanks to Ava's logo perseveration.

She finally arrived at her potential client's home at 8:45 for an 8:30 listing presentation. Drenched and thrown off her usual game, Dara was quick to bluntly point out the home's flaws—older windows, outdated bathrooms, and worst of all, smoke damage on the kitchen wall—evidence of a recent grease fire—which left her completely rattled. She closed for the listing but was unsurprised when the seller insisted that she'd have to "think about it." The final straw came when she arrived at the office at ten and found Merry's desk empty and her assistant absent, the last thing she needed to exacerbate her already foul mood.

Celeste took over, opining as she always did during moments of disappointment, tinging everything with negativity. *Taking advantage of the boss's morning appointment to arrive late? Unacceptable.*

Dara's stomach dropped at the thought of another bad hire. She rummaged through her purse for her cell, about to give Merry a telephonic dressing-down when her assistant hurried in, dripping wet, her duffle and Coach bag slung over one shoulder, a Starbucks cup in the opposite hand.

"Mrs. Creighton called screaming," she explained. "Her post toppled over last night in the storm, and she was livid. The sign guy said he was tied up all morning, so I ran to the hardware store, got a mallet, and went out to hang it up myself. Hope that's okay."

She set down the coffee on Dara's desk, hung up her soaked trench coat, and kicked off her mud-stained heels.

A jolt of guilt rattled Dara, ashamed of having assumed the worst. "Uh, no, it's great…Thanks for taking that initiative."

"Hey, anything's better than an unhappy client, right?"

Merry pulled out some envelopes to address, and Dara retreated to her office, silently swearing to never again allow Brooke's insinuations and Celeste's assumptions to tarnish her golden hire's glow.

To cap off a trying morning, it was time to call her husband's therapist. Thanks to Jason signing the consent forms, the doctor was free to discuss anything and everything with Dara. She prayed for good news because the situation at home was rapidly becoming untenable.

After three rings, the receptionist picked up and transferred the call.

"Good morning. Dr. Mitchell, it's Dara Banks. As usual, it's about my husband. I know you said by this time, he'd be getting better, but things are heading in the opposite direction. He's surly all the time now, even refuses to go to PT. What am I doing wrong? How can I help him?"

"Don't blame yourself, Mrs. Banks. These things take time."

"It's been over three years."

"I know, but chronic depression can be difficult to treat. He used to love to run, didn't he? No interest in resuming that?"

"No interest in *anything* physical." Their sex life had become a distant memory. In fact, little by little, the sweetness of their time together had devolved little by little over the months following the incident. She'd watched in dismay as every heroic attempt by Jason to return to work and regain his confidence was shattered by his inability not only to grasp objects but how much of his recovery relied on an optimistic attitude and perseverance. The last straw had been an abbreviated meeting when prospective clients made excuses and took off after glancing at his gnarled fingers. He'd remained stone-faced when she'd picked him up, then retreated to his den without a word, though she could hear muffled wailing from the hallway.

"Let me check on something," said Dr. Mitchell. The line briefly went quiet, "Along with the Zoloft, let's try Esketamine. It's a new nasal spray anti-depressant you may have seen advertised as Spravato. Some of my patients are reporting quick improvements. You'll have to monitor his blood pressure and watch out for nausea and dizziness. I'd also like to see Jason get involved with something physical, even if it's just a short walk inside the mall until the weather improves. Can you encourage that on your end?"

"I'll try anything, Doctor. Let me suggest that tonight. Thank you."

She hung up with a quiver of renewed hope, yearning for the Jason she'd initially met five years earlier. He'd been one of the most vibrant men she'd ever encountered. Tall, muscular, ruggedly handsome. When he wasn't working on his design for low-income housing—something sorely lacking in affluent Rock Canyon—he was holding fundraisers or attending other charity events to network with potential donors. They met at a silent auction for a homeless shelter, and there was an instant attraction. He'd been widowed young, his late wife succumbing to breast cancer and leaving him to raise two young children on his own. But his circumstances hadn't turned him sullen, something Dara admired. Hope in the face of adversity. He asked her to dinner, the first of many.

In the second year of their courtship, he'd been at a job site, admiring the view from an apartment balcony. Unbeknownst to Jason, his contractor had cut corners when installing the sliding balcony doors, substituting cheap regular glass for the safer, tempered type he'd ordered. When the door spontaneously exploded, the resulting accident changed their lives forever.

At first, he remained unfazed, enthusiastic about his projects and his recovery. Dara knew he'd need help, especially with his children, and suggested they marry. Looking back, she wondered which had motivated her more: love or a sense of duty.

Regardless of the impetus, the union hadn't turned out as she'd expected. Dara never dreamt that his physical therapy would falter, leaving her to raise the children, handle all the household chores, and become the family's sole breadwinner. They'd hoped a settlement would cover the cost of a nanny, but their contractor skipped town before they could sue. Even that wouldn't have mattered if depression hadn't engulfed him, changing his personality so dramatically. If she could do anything to bring back the original Jason, nothing would stop her.

Encouraged by the doctor's suggestions, Dara turned her attentions back to work. She contacted the newest expired listings to offer her services, then decided to listen in as Merry solicited feedback from last Sunday's open house visitors. It was vital that her assistant had the scripts memorized but could still make them her own.

Meryl: "...Mrs. Xi, it was smart of you to visit 45 Demarest during that first open house because it's doubtful we're going to have another. Five offers already—can you believe it? I can't say I'm surprised, though; there are a lot of people out there who are savvy when it comes to real estate investment. We knew there'd be a bidding war, being on *that* street and in *that* school district. I only wish I had the funds to buy it myself."

Dara stifled a laugh. There had been no offers. The home was an overpriced wreck, the worst house in a top neighborhood. It seemed structurally sound but needed at least $100,000 in cosmetic updates. Dara had listed it only to put a sign on the lawn and get exposure. She'd priced it at $750,000—the sellers' price, not hers—and hoped someone might offer $600k.

Mrs. Xi: "It's not really our style; it needs a ton of work. How low were the other bids?"

Meryl: "Unfortunately, MLS rules preclude me from disclosing the other offers... Let's try this. Why don't you mention a number, and I'll let you know if you should go higher or not."

Mrs. Xi: "If we were interested—and again, taking into consideration all the work the house needs—I couldn't think we'd go higher than...$650,000."

That's being overly generous.

Meryl: Oh no, we're way higher than that. We have offers from contractors who know how simple it would be to make a few easy updates."

Easy updates? A new kitchen and all new baths at a minimum.

Mrs. Xi: "Really. I hadn't considered that. Hold on."

The buyer half-covered the receiver as she conferred with her partner.

Mrs. Xi: "The highest we'd consider is $775k."

Dara's heart skipped a beat. *$775k? No way.*

Meryl: "That might put you in the running...but we'd need a strong downpayment. Could you put half down? And send proof of funds? I'm sure you realize this would be an 'as is' deal, so any inspection would be for informational purposes only."

Where the hell had she learned that?

Mrs. Xi: "Well, I guess..."

Meryl: "Great. I can't swear your offer will make the cut, but you sound like such a nice lady. I'll have Ms. Banks present it to the sellers and get you an answer as soon as I can. You're sure you can only do 50% down? The other offers are a little higher; sixty percent down might put yours on top."

Good going, Merry, getting the buyer's ego involved.

Mrs. Xi: "Um...can you guarantee we'll get the house then?"

Meryl: "There are no guarantees, but I'll push hard for you. Please email us a copy of the bank statement showing funds of at least...$465,000. I'll get back to you as soon as I hear. I'm excited for you and think you've made a wise choice."

Mrs. Xi: "Well, thank you. I'll keep my fingers crossed."

Mouth agape with both excitement and admiration, Dara set down the receiver and hurried to Merry's desk.

"How did you know to do that? No way Kylie gave you any of that script."

Meryl blushed. "My first husband and I used to dabble a bit in real estate investment. He'd wrangle down the price, fix up the place, and flip it. Everyone wants a bargain, and often, they let that cloud their better judgment. You're okay with what I did?"

"Yes, of course. We call it the auction effect," said Dara.

"I don't have a problem letting people's bad mistakes boost up your sales price if you don't. If I ever overstep, just let me know."

Dara recognized an opportunity when she saw one. This woman was a diamond salesperson in the not-so-rough. "Well, if you're going to negotiate deals, you need to be licensed. There's a 75-hour course, starting next week, that the board gives on nights and weekends. I'll cover the cost. Interested?"

Merry grinned widely. "I'd love that, thanks."

"Great. When you've finished the rest of your calls, lunch is on me."

* * *

The pre-licensing course took four weeks, three hours on Monday, Wednesday, and Thursday evenings and five hours on both Saturdays and Sundays. Dara had Merry work during the days but gave her free time to study. She could tell her assistant appreciated the gesture. Whenever she went out for coffee or a snack, she asked Dara if she could pick her up something as well. Merry even volunteered to pick up her dry cleaning when a last-minute listing appointment prevented her from going herself. This was the work ethic Dara expected.

Life started to look brighter. Merry represented the first of a team that could operate on its own, leaving Dara free to concentrate on Autism Vanguard, her other charities, and her family. Once Merry graduated and passed her licensing tests, Dara planned to give her a raise. The extra profit from the Demarest deal would more than cover that. Now, if she could only get Jason to consider Dr. Mitchell's suggestion of Esketamine, she'd have a chance at a happy life at home as well.

Chapter Four

O n the March afternoon Merry went to Newburgh to take her licensing exam, Dara received an unexpected call from Burton Erickson, her husband's former partner at RC Architects and one of Rock Canyon's leading real estate developers.

"How's life going, Da? How's the big man doing?"

"Hey Burt. He's much the same, unfortunately. But I know that soon, we'll get him to turn a corner."

"You know I still want to come by and see him. Has he changed his mind on the visitor ban?"

"I'm afraid not, but I'm continuing to work on that." Dara frowned. Jason still refused to see any friends or colleagues from his previous life. Even the therapist from whom she'd sought advice over the past three years had run out of ideas.

"Well, ready for some good news, Da?"

"I'd love it."

"You know that abandoned brick factory up in Haversham?"

"I do."

"We just received the renovation permits and funding. We plan to transform it into a thirty-six-unit active adult condo complex, right on the water. We're going to call it the Fortress on the Hudson. And I want you to be our exclusive broker."

"You're kidding." Dara's pulse jagged into overdrive.

"Serious as a heart attack, Da. There's no one better than you. And you'll be happy to learn that fifteen percent of the condos will be designated as affordable housing units."

"That's fantastic!" *Something to keep my mother off my back.*

"There's one concern, though. I just want to be sure you can handle this on top of caring for Jason and the kids, managing your other listings, and your nonprofit work. You'll probably have to be onsite most days, especially during the renovation phase, guiding prospective buyers through the units. Steel-toed shoes, hard hats, the usual drill. You okay with that?"

"I appreciate your concerns, Burt, but Jason can get by at home on his own—Khai will just have to pitch in more—and I have a new office assistant who'll manage the grunt work. That'll free me up a lot. I'll be there for you one hundred percent. When do you want me to stop by with the paperwork?"

"Would Tuesday morning work? Around ten?"

"I'm writing it in my calendar now. Can't wait to see you."

"Ditto," Burton replied.

"And thank you. I can't tell you how much I appreciate your faith in me."

"Anything for you and Jason. You know that. See you Tuesday."

Dara disconnected the call, inhaled deeply, and speed-dialed Jason to give him the good news. He was quick to douse her enthusiasm with his patented brand of negativity masked as concern.

"How's that going to work, Dara? You're barely home as it is."

"Jason, we need the money." She ran her hand through her hair so roughly, her scalp ached. "Khai is only two years away from college, and I don't want student loans to saddle him with thousands of dollars of debt to pay off. If Ava finally gets into Attwood Academy, her tuition is going to be astronomical and climb even higher every year. Just like our property taxes. Where's the cash supposed to come from if not from my work?"

"Your parents—"

"Have earmarked every penny for the less fortunate. Sadly, they don't include us in that category. I've told you this over and over again: we can't count on them for support. And I don't want to lean on your parents or break into the trust because that's for retirement and for the kids after we pass. We can only count on me."

"And who can *I* count on?"

"Why don't we try the Esketamine we discussed? If it gets you into a brighter mood, you might be willing to go back to PT. And if PT helps you regain some of your hand function—"

"Do what you want. You always do. This conversation is over."

"Do what I want?" she yelled into the dead receiver. "When does that ever happen?" She pushed back her welling tears.

At that moment, Merry proudly strolled into her office, wearing a too-tight chartreuse mini-dress and waving her Pass certificate over her head like a beacon.

"Great job!" Dara plastered on a smile and shoved her phone deep into her bag, attempting to bury her upset along with it. "Let's get a drink to celebrate."

Chapter Five

212°F, Rock Canyon's hottest bar/restaurant (for the moment, anyway) was surprisingly quiet for a Thursday night. Dara grabbed an empty corner table, and the women were about to order two glasses of Chardonnay from the server when Dara thought better of it.

"Just bring the whole bottle. 2007 if you've got it."

Merry rested her chin on her hand while the server poured the wine. "I get the feeling this is about more than celebrating my license. You okay?"

"It's nothing, just a long day." Dara pushed Jason to the back of her mind and clinked glasses with her assistant. "Cheers to your success and your entry into the wonderful world of real estate."

Dara took a few sips, then launched into the speech she'd planned to give the following day. It was important to set boundaries early.

"Now that your status has changed and you're an agent, I want to clarify a few things, so we don't stumble over each other's toes. You're still on salary, which means you work for me. I need you to focus on my clients, not your own."

Merry listened and nodded without comment.

"You'll be able to take out buyers and show them properties, but I want to negotiate all offers," Dara continued. "On listings, you can field offers and speak with clients, but I make all final decisions, and any referrals you receive remain that: referrals. All listings go into the MLS under my name. As a bonus, you'll receive a ten percent commission split on any deals you close for me and twenty-five percent on any business you refer, but your personal listings and buyers don't get preferential treatment. We treat all clients equally. Are you good with that?"

"Seems more than fair, thank you," said Meryl. "I appreciate the opportunity and hope to make a real difference. But Dara, something's wrong. You seem off your game. What's up?"

Dara normally kept her personal life private, sharing anxieties with no one other than Brooke. But her second glass of wine broke down her usual reserve.

She stared at the table, avoiding eye contact. "It's my husband, Jason. No matter what I do, he doesn't appreciate it. I work and work, and all he does is complain."

Merry reached out and touched her arm. "It's not you. It's them. Men. I was the world's greatest wife, both times. No matter what they asked—in bed and out—they got it. With a smile on my face unless my mouth was otherwise occupied," she said with a wink. "So don't think it's you. You're a super hard worker. Your clients are so lucky to have you. And all you do for Autism Vanguard, it's amazing."

Dara looked at Merry with new, if slightly blurry eyes. Sure, her aide could be a bit crude, in spite of her designer clothes. Yet tonight, albeit with the help of alcohol, Merry appeared softer, kinder than before. Dara felt safe opening up.

"I try with the kids, you know. It can't be easy with their mom dying young. Breast cancer. I know I can't replace her, but I try to give them what they need."

Merry said nothing; she just patted Dara's hand and smiled empathetically. That's all it took; Dara's defenses caved, releasing years' worth of misgivings and self-doubt.

"Khai might resent me but he's fourteen, he resents the world. Hangs out with a bunch of kids...ones he should know better than to have anything to do with. Ava...Ava's a sweetheart, but her issues make it hard to break through. When she has her meltdowns, she can be uncontrollable for hours. But I try my best, I really do. Jason should appreciate that, even if I'm not always around to make dinner or monitor homework...."

"Of course not," said Merry. She paused to take another sip of wine. "I always made sure my family had three homemade meals a day, but then again, I wasn't working. And I love to cook. The homework, oh my God. That was the hardest part. My stepson from my first marriage was dyslexic. I sat with him, and we did his homework together every night. Met with the teacher every week. I was damned if he wasn't going to pass with honors. And he did, he did, my lovely Tobias. My stepdaughter from my second marriage, Lina? She was a veritable genius. But what a wild girl. I'd come home and catch her *in flagrante* with the neighbor's son. I thought she'd be the end of me. But now, look at her. Graduated top of her class at UConn. Got a fantastic job in pharma marketing. They don't need me anymore, but I call them every week. Always try to be there for them."

"Wow, Mother of the Year, eh?" Dara snipped. The budding warmth she'd felt for Merry quickly chilled as the woman used the pep talk to prop herself up at Dara's expense. Brooke's warning about her assistant's self-absorption came roaring back.

Merry appeared either deaf or disinterested in Dara's sarcastic tone. She blithely reached into her handbag and pulled out her cell, scrolling through until she found pictures that she force-fed Dara of a handsome boy with mahogany brown hair and soulful eyes, and a graceful girl in a black gown, long, blonde tresses capped by a graduation cap.

Dara retreated into her own wine-addled thoughts. Would Ava ever have the chance to attend high school, much less graduate college? Would Khai pull himself together, find his way? Would this new project be more of an irritant than the cash cow Dara had first envisioned?

"So why can't your husband pitch in?" asked Merry, pivoting back to Dara's dilemma. "If you're both working, you should either split the chores or hire someone—"

"Jason can't work," Dara interrupted. She described the accident and Jason's subsequent downward spiral. Recounting her fears for both him and their children compounded her growing despair.

When Dara finished, Merry grew quiet for a moment, then split what remained of the Chardonnay between them.

"I have a great idea. Next week is Easter. Do you celebrate?"

The unexpected question momentarily pulled Dara out of her funk.

"Er, no." She downed the rest of her glass. "We're not particularly religious people; bringing Ava to church and expecting her to sit through a service would be close to impossible. Jason's parents brought him up Catholic, and that's how he raised the kids until his first wife passed.

"My family belonged to an Episcopal church but attended less for the sermons and more because of their philanthropic efforts," Dara continued. "To be honest, we never formally celebrated anything, just spent holidays serving up food in soup kitchens, or distributing gifts to needy kids on Christmas."

"Well, I'd like to invite your whole family to my place for Easter dinner. I have no one to cook for, and I really miss it." Merry's voice quivered with anticipation. "I'll make a feast—leg of lamb, glazed ham, sweet potatoes—it'll be amazing."

Dara hated to bring down the hammer and squash her assistant's excitement.

"That all sounds wonderful, Merry, and you're so sweet to offer, really. But that's not going to work. Jason won't leave the house, Khai will probably be with his friends, and Ava isn't good in new surroundings..."

"None of that is an issue," Merry insisted. "Spring is about rebirth. This can be a new beginning for your family, and I want to be a part of it. What are everyone's favorite foods?"

Dara paused for a moment, questioning the motivation behind Merry's offer. Loneliness? Job security? Or maybe good, old-fashioned empathy? Anything was possible. Truth was, it would be good to get out for a change.

"Well, Jason used to love pastitsio. You know, Greek lasagna with bechamel sauce. Khai practically inhales steak whenever I have time to make it. Ava— that's easy. Peanut butter and jelly sandwiches."

"Well, that settles it. We'll have a very nontraditional Easter dinner, and it will be fantastic. I have a wonderful pastitsio recipe with lamb and cinnamon. Steak? I'll make filet mignon, covered in the most delicious béarnaise sauce, and if Khai wants to bring a friend or two, that's fine, we'll make space. PB&J sandwiches, no problem, but I also make an incredible peanut butter and jelly cheesecake. It's to die for. And you, what's your favorite dish?

Celeste's suspicious nature reared its head. Did she really want Dara to be beholden to her assistant for anything?

"I'm fine with all that, but really, I don't think—"

"Nonsense, this will be great. What's your go-to, can't-live-without entrée?"

"I like shellfish, but—"

"Lobster Thermador for you. You're going to love it. One last question: what's your family's favorite movie?"

What a ridiculous exercise in futility, thought Dara. Her family was never going to go for it. Jason couldn't hold a fork easily, so either she or Khai fed him, or he leaned forward to grab food from the plate with his mouth. That was not something he'd want to display in front of people outside the family. But clearly, the only way to extricate herself from this conversation was to go along with it. Later, when Meryl settled into a calmer, less inebriated state, Dara could explain the obstacles more clearly.

"Before the accident, I remember we all went to the theater and saw *Black Panther*. Even tiny Ava sat through it, wide-eyed and smiling. It was a really nice evening out."

"That's it then. After dessert, we'll stream *Black Panther*. It will be fun for them but, most importantly, a way for the family to bond. And a chance for you to relax."

Dara let out an exasperated sigh. "You don't have to do this, Merry."

"Of course not, but I want to. Just ask them. Tell them I have no family, and it would be like a gift to me. Maybe that will make the difference. Please, let's see if we can make this work. I think it will be incredibly special."

Chapter Six

Dara insisted on a family powwow the next evening. Ava sat at the dining table in her Cinderella costume, repeatedly swiping her dark hair from her Cadbury-colored eyes as she stacked, demolished, and restacked her pile of dominos. Khai, a striking boy with high cheekbones and his sister's soulful expression, scowled and spewed expletives under his breath over having to cancel plans with his friends. Jason at least made an effort to be pleasant, perhaps because Dara had come home early to prepare dinner, rather than ordering out.

Halfway through their Chicken Francaise, Dara cleared her throat and launched into her prepared speech, fearing the worst. "As you know, we haven't been out together as a family for a long time. I'd like to remedy that. My new assistant, Merry, has very kindly invited us to Easter dinner. She's agreed to make everyone's favorite foods and even encouraged Khai to bring along a friend. Ava, maybe we'll get you a new toy bunny to share Easter with us. You'd like that, right?"

A moment of silence ensued, punctuated only by the sound of her family chewing. Dara wondered if she'd speed-rapped her speech so quickly, no one had understood what she'd said. Then Ava smiled, nodded, and momentarily set aside her domino play in favor of a bite of her PB&J sandwich.

Encouraged, Dara pushed forward. "Anyway, I think we should use this as an opportunity to start doing things together as a family."

She braced herself for an onslaught of negativity, but to her surprise, Jason leaned forward and murmured, "Easter used to be one of my favorite holidays."

"Remember when Mom would dress up in that bunny costume and hand out the eggs she'd spent all week decorating?" Khai asked his dad. Ava nodded vigorously.

Jason smiled, an unusual occurrence these days, and added, "She'd always stash away the chocolate bunnies and crème eggs. Khai, you'd tear across the house, throwing the cushions off the couch, rummaging through coat pockets hanging in the closet, making the place an absolute mess until you'd found them all, and then share half with your sister."

"Wow, I just realized I haven't had crème eggs for years," said Khai.

Heart leaping, Dara sensed this could be her best chance to heal her family and make things better again.

"I know it won't be exactly the same, but I'd be happy to dye eggs and hide chocolates around the house. Let's savor those happy memories and build on that tradition. Can I tell her yes?"

Jason shrugged. "Sure, why not? What's the worst that could happen?"

Many terrible outcomes flashed through Dara's thoughts, but she refused to give them airtime. "Okay, great, I'll tell her we'll be there."

* * *

Later that evening, as Dara reviewed some purchase offers in her home office, Khai peeked in and asked if she could spare a moment. It was rare that he came to her for anything. Dara knew she was still an interloper in his eyes, and she didn't want to blow the opportunity to deepen their shaky relationship. She set aside her papers and invited him to join her on the loveseat so they could speak more intimately than if she had remained behind her desk.

Khai was clearly nervous, fumbling for the right word. She reached out and put her hand on his. She felt him tense, but to her relief, he didn't pull away. "It's okay. You can say anything to me. I won't judge, I promise."

"Err," he said, his voice wavering, "I just wanted to say…how much I liked what you said before. About Easter. And the crème eggs. You usually spend so much time at work, and when you're here…you really never acknowledge

Mom and the fact we had a life before she..." He stopped and sucked back a whimper. "And I get that. This is all probably pretty hard for you, too...and I know I haven't made it any easier...but you trying to revive a tradition...it meant a lot. So, thanks."

She squeezed the top of his hand. "I realize I can never replace your Mom, Khai...and I know that, between your sister's condition and your father's accident, I haven't been able to give you the attention you deserve...but I'll try to do better. I promise."

Her words may have evoked some long-buried memories. Khai's eyes glistened, and he looked down at his lap, pulling his hand from hers to wipe away evidence of his unease. "I used to be able to come to her whenever I needed anything. Once, she spent a whole half-hour trying to get me to take cough medicine because I'd spit up every dose, but she wouldn't give up..." He glanced back up at her with an expression of hope. "Do you think that after Easter, maybe we could all go away together? I mean, nowhere far, but maybe a weekend at an indoor water park or something?"

"A getaway...?" Dara tried to maintain her smile and ignore the visions of disaster that flooded her brain. The challenge of dividing her stress between keeping Ava from drowning in the pool, Jason's embarrassment as she fed him him dinner in front of strangers, and worrying about whatever was happening with her clients at work overwhelmed her, and her expression did not elude Khai, who rose abruptly.

"Forget it. It was just a stupid thought..." he said, bolting toward the door.

"I didn't say no," Dara protested, but it was too late. He was gone, and with him, her earlier victory.

* * *

The next morning, Khai left the house before Dara could explain away her previous evening's reaction. She tried to set aside her anxiety as she drove to Brooke's condo to start formalizing plans for AV's first Birthday Parties for All event. As always, food helped drown her feelings. Brooke served salad with some of the vegetables and herbs she'd grown in her building's communal garden, and Dara raved over the tomatoes.

"How did you get them so red and sweet?"

"Don't tell anyone, but over the dark web, I got a hold of some paraquat granules."

"Really? Didn't I read something in the Times about the government banning that herbicide?"

"In many countries, yes. Here, in the U.S., it's only sold to commercially licensed users, but who can afford professional pest control? Hence, the dark web. Nothing I've tried works as well. As long as you're careful with it, it keeps all the insects away and allows my plants to grow beautifully."

"Huh. Well, these tomatoes are delicious. Maybe you should do BPA's catering." Dara lifted her fork as if she were toasting her friend. "Speaking of catering, I guess we should get down to the meat of it, eh?"

Dara tried to concentrate on the logistics—finishing the build of their low sensory room on time, what to serve that would take all the children's needs and food allergies into account, how to publicize the event. But she could barely contain her excitement over her family's plans for Sunday afternoon.

"I can't believe Jason agreed to go," Dara said while they reviewed possible menus. "This could be the restart of his recuperation. The mental one. The doctors said even now, with repeated physical therapy, he might still regain some use of his fingers. I'd be happy if he'd go back to work and hire someone to essentially be his hands. Or consider amputation and agree to robotic prosthetics. They're the newest thing. Up to now, he's been opposed to all of that. This dinner could be the first step to opening up his mind and getting him to consider the possibilities."

"Or it could just be a dinner...hosted by an overstepping employee. Please don't get your hopes up, hon." Brooke pushed a plate of macarons toward her. "Try these. Esther picked them up in Paris, and they are amazing."

Dara resented Brooke's insistence on dousing her dreams with cynicism. Why shouldn't she have hope? Why couldn't this be a turning point? Far better to switch the topic of conversation to her friend's far younger spouse.

"Paris, huh? How did she find time to get away from the station house?"

"The RCPD owed her about six weeks' time off and she told them that this year, she was actually going to take part of it. There was a suspense writers' retreat in Lyon, and you know Esther's plan: graduate from research assistant to crime analyst, put in her time, and become the next Sue Grafton after she retires. Anyway, she figured the officers could manage their own research for a change while she dabbled in her hobby."

Dara nibbled on a macaron and let the sugar momentarily transport her to a more relaxed state. Brooke's next diatribe yanked her right back into reality.

"Da, Meryl Rafter isn't a family therapist. Far from it. Didn't you tell me a while back that she was twice divorced? And let's face it. An assistant's home is not a 'safe space.' If Jason loses his shit, or Khai insults her, or Ava has one of her epic meltdowns and breaks something valuable, it could impact your work relationship. And frankly, now that she's licensed, any of those very realistic events could provide her with fodder to turn potential clients against you if she ever goes off on her own. I can hear it now: 'Oh, you don't want to list with Dara Banks. Her family life is so fraught with drama; you never know when she'll be too busy with their antics to market your property effectively or vet your offers.' You know what agents are like. Dara—you, better than anyone. And it's not like she's signed a non-compete or lifetime agreement to remain your assistant. When commission money is up for grabs, everyone turns into a shark."

Incensed, Dara pushed her chair back. "Brooke, where are you getting this stuff? Meryl Rafter has never done anything to hurt you or me. She's offering me the opportunity to bring my family together. Why can't you give her a chance?"

Are you jealous that she's horning in on our friendship? That maybe now, I'll have two friends instead of one? It was a leap, but certainly a valid one, considering how often Brooke went after this new woman in Dara's life without provocation.

Brooke seemed unflustered by the outburst. Then again, Dara rarely saw her frazzled. No matter what happened to those around her, Brooke remained a refuge. Which was why Dara was so stunned by her overreaction. She walked to the Keurig before Celeste had her say something she'd regret later.

"Listen to me," Brooke continued as Dara, back turned, poured herself some coffee. "Merry might be a nice person with very innocent intentions. I'm just trying to temper your expectations and warn you of the ramifications that could arise from turning employees into friends. Listen or don't. It's up to you."

Dara kept her back turned as she added stevia and skim milk to the brew. "You've made your opinions known. Consider your conscience clear. I suggest we change the subject back to BPA and decide what date we're going to hold the first party in June. Are we agreed?"

* * *

Easter Sunday finally arrived, and despite Brooke's warnings, Dara's hopes remained as high as a pothead at a Grateful Dead concert. She'd called ahead to ask about preferred attire, and Merry had assured her that casual was the way to go. She'd worn jeans and a pink silk blouse, nothing too fancy. So, naturally, she was quite surprised when Merry answered the door of her apartment in full makeup, coiffed hair, and an apron worn over a designer black and tan cocktail dress. As usual, she had inappropriately accessorized the ensemble, this time with a black pillbox hat and fascinator, its mesh gracing the left side of her face.

In response to Dara's look of incredulity, she explained, "Well, as the host, of course, I needed a little something extra, but you all look great."

Dara handed Merry a bouquet of flowers and a bottle of wine, the enticing aromas wafting from the kitchen, suggesting Merry's ability as a skilled chef. Then she took in the décor with her Realtor's eye, at least what she could see from the foyer.

The living room was spacious, with cranberry wallpaper over beige Berber rugs that accentuated gleaming hardwood floors. The contemporary furniture, covered in burgundy and beige upholstery, so perfectly matched the other colors in the room that it had to be custom. Contributing to the room's cozy vibe were elegant pale-yellow vases, table lamps, and throw pillows that added splashes of accent color. In fact, the room's elegance was in such sharp contrast to Merry's garish choice of accessories, Dara surmised she'd brought in a decorator.

"You must be Jason; I've heard so much about you," squealed Merry. She immediately embraced him and then helped him off with his coat. Dara expected him to pull back or at least wince, but to her shock, he accepted the overly effusive display of affection.

"We've heard a lot about you, too," Jason lied, adding, "It's so nice to finally put a face to the name."

It was the old Jason, exuding a charm Dara hadn't seen in years. *See Brooke? This was a great idea.*

Merry led Jason to the living room couch opposite a seventy-five-inch Sony broadcasting the Hawks playing the Magic. Then, she returned to greet the remaining members of the party.

"This handsome boy must be Khai. Welcome. Who's your friend?"

"Uh, this is D'Andre." Khai fidgeted from foot to foot. "Dara said it would be okay to bring a friend…."

"And, of course, it is!" More hugs all around. "Boys, if you go into the den, you'll find a PlayStation with the latest version of *Call of Duty.* Go enjoy, and I'll call you when dinner is ready."

"You have a PlayStation?" Khai's wide eyes reflected his disbelief.

"I do now." Merry winked.

Before the boys could bolt, Dara interjected, "Actually, Merry, it's a lovely gesture, but we don't allow Khai to play *Call of Duty.* It's a little too violent."

She hated being the bad guy, but she and Jason had made a point of instituting that rule at home, and consistency was important, especially for a kid who was constantly hanging with a questionable group of thug-like friends, D'Andre excluded.

Merry's fervor deflated like a three-day-old helium balloon. "I'm sooo sorry. I never meant to create an issue—"

"Dara, this one time won't turn Khai into a serial killer," Jason called from the living room. "It's a special occasion."

"Yeah, Mom, pleeeease?"

Khai almost never called her "Mom," and coupled with his imploring tone; her resolve collapsed from solid ground into quicksand. Maybe Jason was right; maybe she shouldn't be so inflexible, especially considering how infrequently they went out as a family.

"I guess…"

Without waiting to hear the rest of Dara's retraction, the boys scurried into the adjoining room, and Merry knelt beside Ava, who was normally aloof around new people. Not this time. The eight-year-old stood, mouth open, in awe of this ebullient stranger.

"And who is this beautiful princess?"

"Ava. Ava. Ava," the little girl chanted excitedly.

Score another point for Merry, thought Dara, always joyful to hear the child utter even a single syllable.

"Well, Ava, I have something special for you too. Wanna see?"

Merry straightened and gestured toward what Dara assumed was her bedroom. A jumping Ava kangarooed her way down the hall in pursuit of her host. Dara heard a shriek of delight and hurried in to see what had caused the commotion. There sat Ava, wearing a toy tiara and peering into a giant, three-story plastic playhouse.

"My Lina had one just like this." Merry directed the explanation to both mother and child. "She loved it, and I had the feeling Ava would too. You're always welcome to come over and play with it any time you want."

Precisely how did she know what to buy? Celeste prodded at Dara's suspicious nature. Dara shushed her guardian, eager for a successful afternoon. Maybe she'd guessed; maybe she'd googled what captivated teen boys and little girls. How they'd gotten here seemed immaterial. It was the result that counted.

Once Ava was quietly engrossed in rearranging dollhouse furniture, Merry looped her arm around Dara's and led her out of the bedroom.

"Time for us to do some arranging as well. You can help me set the table. I wasn't sure who would want to sit next to whom."

"Really, Merry, there was no need to go through all this trouble."

"Dara, how often do I get the chance to entertain my boss and her family for the first time? And on such an important occasion, too. Not only is it

Easter, but a chance for your family to heal and grow together. Just being a part of it makes me shiver." The tremble in her voice convinced Dara of her sincerity. "Anyway, you're the one who did the real work. You got everyone here. That could not have been easy."

It actually had been simpler than she'd imagined, but why spoil Merry's image of her? Healing, helping, charity was Dara's jam. Her identity. She reveled in others noticing the good she did, the ways she brought positive change to people's lives. That's what she always argued during her mother's weekly harangues. Just like running Autism Vanguard and volunteering at a homeless shelter, her real estate work helped change people's lives for the better. Did its lucrative nature make it any less beneficial to those she helped buy, sell, rent, or invest?

As she laid down the china and flatware, her mind wandered back to performing the same task at her childhood home in Locust Valley more than twenty-five years earlier. She, along with her foster brothers and sisters, used the chore to vie for her parents' approval. The fosters didn't have to do much to win Quincy and Angelica's praise; their very survival earned them places of honor in the eyes of the home's matriarch and patriarch. But since she'd been born into privilege, Dara needed to exceed expectations by astronomical measures to attract their attention, much less their accolades. As they constantly reminded her, it was her duty to give back and keep giving back. A perfect report card? Ho hum, we demand nothing less. Earned ribbons in Track and Field? What a waste when you could be volunteering at the local nursing home or animal shelter after school. Don't even mention the prom—that was the time you worked behind the scenes to put on a "mock prom" at the local orphanage or senior center.

Her parents paid for Syracuse only because she'd agreed to major in Nonprofit Management, and that had been an eye-opener. It's where her roommate Brooke, who'd come from a meager but close-knit family, explained that love and happiness were attainable even without donating every second to others or attempting to outshine a seemingly endless stream of strangers who'd taken up residence in her parents' house and heart. It's where teachers commended her for *her* academic efforts, and students in the stands cheered as *she* crossed the one-hundred-meter finish line. Best of all, it had taken her away from her parents and the dolor that had engulfed them since the fire.

"Earth to Dara. hon, the glasses go to the right of the plates. Here, let me do that for you." Merry gently pushed her to the side and rearranged her work, even refolding the napkins. Dara stared in disbelief, silently reproaching herself for screwing up the one job Merry had assigned. She skulked back into the living room to check on Jason.

"How are you doing?" she whispered, nestling next to him on the couch.

"Shhh...Hawks are winning, so there's that." His eyes remained glued to the screen. From the other rooms, Khai and D'Andre's laughter over the violence befalling their avatars, coupled with Ava's happy chanting, signaled the children were both occupied and amused, and Dara's ministrations were unneeded.

She leaned back then forward again, unable to get comfortable, stretching her fingers, stiffened from tension. This cozy domestic scene should have imbued her with joy and satisfaction, but instead, a strange hollowness made her wonder if she'd arranged for her own obsolescence.

That's crazy. You're just letting Brooke's paranoia get under your skin. You've waited three years for things to get back to normal. Cheer up and enjoy it while you can.

A few minutes later, Merry emerged from the kitchen, announcing dinner was served. Leaving Jason to make his own way to the dining table, Dara headed to the bedroom to retrieve Ava, who, despite extensive cajoling, did not want to interrupt her routine of arranging and rearranging miniature bedroom furniture. Only when Merry appeared, brandishing a Play All Day Elmo toy, did she look up from the playhouse. Merry tossed it from hand to hand, causing Elmo to squeal, and Ava screeched right along. Together, the four of them made their way to the dining room, Elmo's animated mutterings leading the way.

Jason sat at the head of the table, flanked by Khai and D'Andre. The men were already feasting on their steak, pastitsio, and corn pudding at a table laden with crescent rolls, various vegetable side dishes, and the bright floral arrangement they'd gifted. Dara froze when she entered, stunned that Jason was managing to eat without her, his steak and pastitsio precut into bite-size pieces, which he stabbed with a fork attached to a wrist brace on his right arm. She couldn't ignore a pang of hurt. She'd tried to get him to use a similar apparatus right after the accident, but he'd refused, insisting on just leaning over his plate and using his tongue and teeth to grab the food.

"I…uh…was afraid you might have forgotten yours, so I had one at the ready," said Merry, following Dara's line of vision.

Again, Celeste tugged at her paranoia. *How did she know?*

Jason looked up. "This works great, sweetie. Let's reimburse Merry for this one and bring it home. I feel almost normal."

"We have one…don't you recall?"

"Da, I'm disabled, not brain-dead. I think I would have remembered."

It wasn't worth the argument, especially not in her assistant's home. Dara swallowed her pride and sought out her seat, which was at the opposite end of the table, facing Jason. Ava sat to her left, and Merry's empty seat was to her right. It seemed odd to be seated at the head of the table at someone else's house. However, less odd than had Merry placed herself next to Jason. *Sit down and relax, Dara, and be grateful for the deferential gesture.*

Merry emerged from the kitchen with a plate topped by an opaque plastic dome, which she placed in front of Ava. With a flourish, she pulled off the cover to reveal not one but two peanut butter and jelly sandwiches, accented by colorful plastic Easter eggs on one side and Cadbury Crème Eggs on the other. Once again, Ava howled with delight. Dara's first reaction was to pull the crème eggs away—too much sugar normally threw Ava into a manic state—but before she could say anything, the girl had already started unwrapping the treats. *What's one more sleepless night? At least my family is having an enjoyable time.*

Dara scooped white rice onto her plate, followed by a dollop of lobster Thermador. It smelled divine, but she waited until Merry sat down before diving in. She brought a lobster chunk bathed in cognac sauce to her lips. Of course, it was luscious. Merry was a great cook. In fact, was there anything Merry didn't do well? Other than accessorize, of course. She

45

pondered the question with a twang of envy and a large helping of self-doubt, thanks to Celeste, waving from the depths of her consciousness, eager for an opportunity to join the party.

Go away, Dara silently told her protector. *This is a good day. You have no place here.*

"Merry, where did you learn to cook like this? It's really delicious," asked Jason, mouth half-full of pastitsio.

"I'm so glad you're enjoying it. In my younger days, when I was acting and modeling, I spent weeks at a time in Paris. The runway shows, you know. And while I was there, I took classes at Le Cordon Bleu. I actually had quite a wild time, as I recall…"

Dara stifled a laugh. Though her body was enviable, Merry was only five-foot-two, with a face that would never sway any haute couture designer to add her to his lineup. The idea of her working the Paris Fashion Week was ludicrous.

"Aren't models, like, six feet tall?" Khai asked, putting voice to her apprehension.

"Oh no, I wasn't modeling on the runway." Merry pivoted without missing a beat. "I mean, I *was* a model for the company, but I did specialty modeling. Hands, feet, showroom work. But during Fashion Weeks in Paris and Milan, the company brought everyone along to help out, get the models dressed and undressed quickly, that kind of thing."

Well, that seemed much less delusional, but why had she excluded it from her resume?

Jason certainly bought in, nodding vigorously as their host launched into an animated tale of how she'd taken the City of Light by storm in her late teens. With mixed emotions, Dara observed her holding court, enjoying the audience, throwing in a joke here and there. She couldn't remember when her own family paid her this much attention. Merry stopped only when it was time to clear the table—with Dara's help—and then pulled out the PB&J cheesecake for dessert.

The afternoon's only low point of the afternoon came after dinner, when Dara, who had paperwork waiting, started making noise about having to head home. Ava was having no part of that. Fueled by her sugar high, she wailed ceaselessly until Dara allowed her to drag them back into the bedroom for another dollhouse play session. That gave Khai and D'Andre time for a bonus *Call of Duty* battle and left the rest of the party in the living room, where Jason's occasional laughter punctuated Merry's unceasing chatter.

Close to an hour later, Ava's jonesing had been satisfied to the point where Dara could get a coat on her, but only because she promised they could come back another time. Then she realized she didn't have her purse.

The whole family went on a scavenger hunt seeking the missing bag, though Ava used it as an excuse to revisit the doll house. Finally, Merry located and delivered it.

"You're always leaving that bag everywhere, Boss Lady," she said with a laugh. "Maybe you should get a GPS and sew it into the pocket."

Another thing you can't manage to do right, Dara.

They boarded the Odyssey, Jason's car which they'd barely used since the accident, and took off for home, Ava preoccupied with Merry's Elmo gift.

"That Meryl is really something," said Jason, in a spirited tone a world apart from the curmudgeon he'd become over the past few years.

"Oh? How so?" Dara waited for the string of accolades that were sure to follow, hoisting her assistant high on the same pedestal her parents once used to celebrate the fosters.

"She just tries way too hard," he said, causing her mouth to drop. "I mean, yeah, she's a good cook, and yeah, it was really nice of her to invite us all to her home, but the separate meals and the gifts for Ava? And do I really believe she happened to have a PlayStation with the latest games lying around for her own amusement? She's bucking for a raise, Da."

"Oh, I doubt that." Dara suddenly found herself in the awkward position of defending her assistant when she tended to agree with her husband over Merry's excessive fawning. "She's clearly got money. She just needs people to see her value. And hey, she gave us the first really nice afternoon we've had in a long time."

The car went quiet while Dara maneuvered through the windy streets, courting an epiphany. Maybe that was it, she thought. Merry might try too hard, but perhaps not to show Dara up—that was her own self-doubt talking. No, it's probably because she's terribly lonely, having been on her own for so long. She's already admitted how much she misses her family, especially the stepkids she lost through divorce. She needs to feel appreciated. That was something Dara could understand. A trait they definitely had in common.

Befriending Merry would be a perfect way to help her. And considering Dara's own dearth of companions, it could also be a wonderful way to help herself.

Chapter Seven

The following Sunday's open house at 26 Carnaby Street was a mob scene. Family after family flooded in to see the four-bedroom, two-bath high ranch Dara had purposely underpriced to encourage a bidding war in spite of the home's outdated stucco walls, shag carpeting, and green-and-pink floral wallpaper. Dara normally marketed properties through appointment only, but the owner, desperate to show off her supposed decorating prowess, insisted on attracting a horde. Asking Merry to share the work, as well as the buyers, had been more of a necessity than a favor.

They took turns leading tours through the house and by four o'clock, they'd received five offers that Dara believed more than compensated for their sore throats and aching feet.

"This calls for drinks and a celebratory dinner—my treat!" Merry announced.

"Yes to the meal, no to you paying," said Dara. "Especially after all you did at Easter. This one's on me."

"How about Poisson?"

Dara nodded, and the two ladies drove their cars down to the waterfront. When it first opened, Poisson had been the "in" place for romantic seafood dinners. But then, the restaurant owner had fallen on tough times and sold out to an investor with deep pockets and a love for pop culture. The joint now catered to singles as well as couples who enjoyed walls covered in ichthyological paraphernalia ranging from films like *Finding Nemo* and *Jaws* to *A Fish Called Wanda*.

The only free table was one with four seats by the fireplace, empty, no doubt, because the blaze left the area uncomfortably hot. Dara agreed to the spot, despite her unease over the flames and the memories they evoked, opting for the seat with her back nearest to, but facing away from the fire. It left her fidgety but with an excellent view of the pick-up action at the bar. The ladies grabbed the server's attention and ordered two *Aquaman Specials*—vodka, Midori, a spritz of seltzer, and a celery spear. Dara asked for hers to come extra strong, anything to soothe her nerves.

"Do you come here often?" she asked her assistant.

Merry shrugged. "Probably more often than I should, but the drinks are potent, and there's great eye candy."

She gestured with her head to a pair of twenty-something bodybuilders chatting up the mermaid-clad female bartender between downing tequila shots. "What shall we talk about? I'm up for anything other than real estate— I'm all Realtored-out."

They started out discussing trivial topics, but as the norm when brokers get within three feet of each other, the conversation drifted to new listings, deals gone awry, buyers who were liars, and sellers who were storytellers. It wasn't until after their third drink, and they'd ordered two swordfish steaks that the conversation floated to more personal topics.

"Let's talk about you," suggested Dara, finally relaxed but a bit bleary-eyed when the server set down a basket of rolls in the shape of sailboats. "When did you first decide to study acting?"

"You have to understand; I grew up the older sister of the Chosen One. My brother Ricky was the golden boy, the child my mother always wanted and kept trying for after being saddled with—gasp—a girl. She relegated me to the number two position, even during my two-year stint as an only child. When he came along, it was Ricky this and Ricky that. The only time my mother showed any interest or pride in me was when I got a role in the school play. It gave her something to brag about to her friends."

Dara nodded. She knew the drill far too well.

"When I finally got out of there, there being the dregs of Syracuse—"

"Wait, you grew up in Syracuse?"

50

"Well, the suburbs, yeah."

"Small world. Brocke and I went to college there."

"Brooke—the woman I spoke with at the gala?"

"The very same."

"Then you know—it's a city that looks best from your rear-view mirror. I escaped at seventeen and hit Manhattan, looking for my big break. Me and every other ingenue who sang "Tomorrow" in their junior high's production of *Annie.*"

Dara noted Merry's bittersweet tone and attempted to turn the conversation more upbeat. "It must have been exciting, taking off on a big adventure, living on your own."

Merry sighed. "It had its moments."

"Speaking of acting, now that you're licensed and an official member of the team, we need to add your picture to the website. Maybe one of your old acting headshots would work. Save you on hiring a photographer.'

Merry paused. "Is that really necessary?"

"It's not absolutely required, but potential clients worry about getting scammed. If they're previewing homes online, they're more comfortable if they can see the agent's face."

"I can appreciate that, Dara, but I've worked really hard to keep my face off the web for a similar reason. Scammers can take those photos, and suddenly you're their fake face on dating sites and who knows where else. I've stayed off social media for the same reason. I don't mind being online with an avatar and posting as your unnamed assistant, but I really don't want an Internet presence if I can avoid it. You understand that, right?"

Dara nodded, too buzzed to argue. She'd never met anyone, especially a salesperson, who had an issue with receiving free media exposure online. But then again, as an extra, Merry must have taken on several personas—as false bridesmaid, mourner, political candidate supporter— that she wouldn't want to come back to haunt her later. It made sense. She'd find an avatar to substitute for Merry's smiling visage.

They ordered dessert and two coffees apiece, buying them time to sober up before venturing out. Dara watched with surprise as Merry scooped three heaping scoops of sugar into her cup.

"How do you stay thin with so much sugar in your diet?" she asked.

"It's my only weakness. I love the caffeine but can't stand the bitterness."

Once their inebriation waned, they headed out, Dara feeling she understood her assistant far better than when they'd arrived.

That evening was the first of several outings the two women enjoyed over the next few weeks at Poisson—Dara always insisting on a table far from the fireplace, one night even waiting fifteen minutes until the server found them an empty table. Merry once questioned her about her fireplace aversion, but she waved her assistant off and quickly changed the subject.

The evenings were a welcome respite following long days of work with Dara listing new sellers, Merry taking out buyers, and immersing herself in the real estate business. Dara was surprised at how quickly her assistant acclimated to the grind, as if she'd been an agent for years. She was equally delighted at how close the two had grown the more time they spent together.

She remembered Brooke's warning not to poop where she ate, how friendships with a subordinate always led to trouble, especially when you needed to pull rank and discipline them. But Dara didn't care. She rarely enjoyed friendships with women other than Brooke, seldom had the time to invest in cultivating close connections. This one had grown organically, thanks to the hours they'd spent working together, considerably longer than the time she spent with her family each week. Sometimes they took in a movie after work, other times a gossip session over lunch. Anything to decompress. They were more of a team than boss and assistant, and Dara took comfort in having conversations with someone other than her troubled and disabled family.

Dara and Merry were back at the restaurant a few weeks later, downing martinis while comparing notes from another set of Sunday open houses, when their server interrupted, delivering a third round.

"I'm sorry, we didn't order these," Dara said.

"Compliments of the gentlemen at the end of the bar."

Dara looked over. Two balding, middle-aged men in grey suits with loosened ties smiled hopefully. One twiddled his fingers in a mini-wave.

"That's okay, we're not interested," Dara said coolly. "Could you please bring our entrees?"

"Wait...why not let them come over?" said Merry. "It could be fun. I bet you haven't flirted in years."

Dara hadn't enjoyed flirting even when she was single. But the alcohol had dampened her desire to argue, and as the married one, who was she to ruin Merry's chance at a new romance?

"Fine...but when the entrees arrive, they leave. Agreed?"

"Whatever you say, Boss Lady."

As Dara tried to decide if she liked that moniker or found it overly familiar, the two men pulled out the empty chairs at their table and plopped themselves down. They introduced themselves as Warren and Lee, local insurance sales associates who'd just come from attending a weekend conference at the Astor.

"So, ladies, what brings you to Poisson? *Fishing* for companionship?" asked Lee, whose smug smile—a testament to how proud he was of his own pun—told Dara everything she needed to know about the man. Time to shut this down, and quickly, before she saw black and Celeste took over.

"Gentlemen, I don't think you know who you're talking to," said Merry before Dara could launch into a self-righteous rant about how women like her didn't view fancy restaurants as pick-up opportunities. "If you knew anything about Rock Canyon, you'd know that this is Dara Banks. Not only is she the town's leading real estate professional, she's also the driving force behind Autism Vanguard and all the good they do for children on the spectrum. And I...am her assistant."

Dara found amusement in Merry's tone and the dramatic pause she took before announcing her own ancillary status, actually making her role sound more important than Dara's. Whatever. At least her words had some effect. Both men's eyes opened wide, and they quickly pivoted from their pickup routine.

"I apologize, Ms. Banks," said Lee with a wince. "I didn't mean anything by what I said. In fact, my brother's kid has autism. I remember you now. Didn't you give a talk a year or so ago about how to travel with these kids, how to prepare and such? I know it helped my sister and her husband a great deal."

Dara retracted her hackles and relaxed. "Well, thank you. It's always nice to hear that what we do helps."

Lee leaned close and launched into a long description of his nephew's adventures in autism—from his diagnosis at age three when he remained nonverbal, all the way through their fights with the school board for special services. He tried to keep it light with little jokes about coping, and she smiled along with him, but it was all a bit much for Dara's alcohol-addled brain to take in.

She occasionally glanced at Merry, who cozied up next to Warren, periodically touching his upper arm, laughing a bit too loudly at whatever lame joke he was sharing. As usual, she tossed around her "expert" opinions on the *super best* book she was currently reading and the *absolute* most thought-provoking movie currently showing at the cinema. To any outsider, this would have looked like a double date. As the evening progressed, along with her wooziness, she heard longer snippets of conversation involving Warren's warnings about inadequate insurance coverage and Merry emphasizing the importance of knowing the current value of your home. *Hell, if she can get a listing out of it, why not let them stay for dinner?*

Warren called the waiter over and asked for menus. Merry gave Dara an imploring look, and she shrugged her acquiescence. The men asked what would take the shortest time to prepare so their entrees could come out at the same time as the ladies' and settled on two orders of cioppino, which the server explained was premade and only needed reheating.

Yes, by all means, let's speed this up. Her new project, The Fortress on the Hudson, was finally opening to potential buyers, and Dara had to be on-site to conduct tours first thing in the morning.

Over dinner, Merry and Warren were uncharacteristically quiet while Lee pressed for tips about how to get his house ready to sell. Dara tried to respond coherently but was half-asleep, the effect liquor normally had on her, though usually not after only three glasses. Odd. The swordfish didn't improve the situation, and by the time the server removed their plates, Dara suggested they say their farewells.

"You're in no condition to drive," Merry said, her speech slurred. "Let's leave your car here. I'll drive you home tonight, and then in the morning, I can give you a lift to pick it up."

"You've both been drinking," said Lee. "I've only had soda tonight. Let's get her out of here before she collapses at the table. I'll drive you both to get coffee. That'll give you time to sober up. Then we'll drop Dara off at her house before swinging back here for you to pick up your car...and Warren, I reckon. Sound good?"

"That's very gentile of you, hon," Merry responded, perhaps a tad too eagerly.

Burton...Haversham...Fortress," Dara mumbled, and with her arm across Lee's shoulder, he led her to the front seat of his Honda and strapped her in. Merry jumped in the back, and Warren ducked his head in to say he hoped to see Merry real soon, followed by a lascivious laugh.

"What's the address?" Lee asked Merry, who'd stretched out in the back seat.

"42...Linconssshire..." slurred Dara in her haze.

They pulled out of the parking lot and headed west, Dara fading in and out of consciousness to the hum of flirtatious chatter. They stopped at the first Dunkin' they saw, and after a cup of hot coffee, Dara felt a bit better. When they arrived at the house, Merry insisted it would be more appropriate if she were the one who brought Dara inside. Lee agreed to wait in the car. Wobbling a bit, the two women finally made it to Dara's front door.

Khai answered the bell. "Wow, we were getting worried...are you okay, Mom? Wait...are you drunk? Hey, Dad, get in here. Your wife is plastered! And it looks like some strange guy drove her home."

The two staggered into the foyer, Dara leaning on Merry's left shoulder.

"Khai, honey, that's very disrespectful," Merry said, giving the teenager a reproachful look. "Your mom was only drinking because it was a stressful day, and she needed to relax. She works way too hard—as you well know. That stranger happens to be a future client."

"Hello, Merry," said Jason as he entered the foyer and eyed his wife's condition. "Between cooking for us and helping us out, we're going to have to put you on our personal payroll." He put his arm around Dara's unsupported shoulder. "What do we have here? Honey, are you okay?"

"Yeah...just a bit...tired...thirsty..."

Merry went into the kitchen and fetched her a glass of water, while Jason held her upright.

"Wanna help me bring her upstairs?" he asked after Dara downed the glass. Dara leaned on them both as they navigated the stairs and then collapsed into her bed. Through her haze, she watched Merry remove her jacket and heels and say goodnight, before closing the door behind her.

"Wait a minute. I'll see you to the door," Jason called out after giving her a kiss on the forehead.

"Haversham...9 am..." mumbled Dara before she finally dissolved into sleep.

Chapter Eight

Awakened by the sound of her husband rummaging through dresser drawers, Dara sprung awake with a pounding headache. Sunshine streamed through the half-opened curtains—not a good sign. Panicked, she checked her watch. 9:30—already thirty minutes late for her meeting.

"Why did you let me sleep?" With eyes half-open, she peered curiously at her husband, sitting on the corner of the bed, donning his Kisik slip-on running shoes for the first time in years. "And what are you doing?"

"To answer your first question, I thought after last night's bender, it was best to let you sleep off whatever you were drinking so enthusiastically. And because it's a beautiful day, I thought I might go out for a run."

"A run..." Dara let the words sink in. "I mean, that's great. You must be feeling better."

"Yes, it's about time I pulled myself together. I called Dr. Mitchell the day after Easter and asked her to prescribe Esketamine. I have to admit, I was wrong—it's been a life changer."

"Why...why didn't you tell me?"

"I didn't want to get your hopes up in case it didn't work." He strode to her side of the bed, where he leaned over and gave her the first kiss she'd had in months. "You've been so good about everything. I want to get back to being the man you married."

Despite her hangover, she felt a stirring in a spot that, after years of matrimonial neglect, she'd written off as fossilized. A warmth radiated through her chest, a quiver of hope. But once Jason left the room, reality set in, and she bolted out of bed, searching frantically for her purse and, in it, her cell phone. She vaguely remembered Merry helping her into the foyer and fetching her a glass of water before heading up the stairs. She ran down, then exhaled with relief at the sight of her bag sitting on the kitchen table. She downed a bottle of water, then rummaged for her cell, grimacing as she placed the call.

"Burton, I'm so sorry I'm late...I can be there in thirty minutes," she promised once he came onto the line.

"Dara, Dara, it's okay. We're fine. Merry's here. She told us about the food poisoning and volunteered to handle the tours, so we're good. Why don't you take the day to recover?"

A wave of relief cascaded over her. Food poisoning? Merry had come to her rescue yet again. This was becoming a habit...but one she could grow accustomed to. It was wonderful living with a safety net.

"I'll come by, Burton, but a little later this morning, if that's okay with you."

"Whatever works, but really, we're covered here."

Dara set down the phone and returned upstairs when the doorbell rang. Her first instinct was to reach for a robe, but then she remembered she was still in the previous night's clothing, well, all except for her jacket and heels. She ran back down, but before she could reach the landing, she heard the voices of three men—Jason, Khai, and...*what the hell?*

She hung back, trying to catch the gist of the conversation, but they spoke in muted tones, followed by the click of the door closing. She contemplated retreating upstairs, but when Jason rounded the corner and saw her standing there, he made her decision for her.

"Who was that?" she asked, feigning ignorance.

Jason held out a business card stuck between mangled fingers. "This was your friend from last night. Lee Something-or-other. Said he was stopping by to see how you were doing and also to discuss real estate. Said he didn't catch your agency's name, but since he knew where you lived..."

Dara couldn't decide if Jason's expression and tenor conveyed curiosity or disgust. Probably a combination of both. She could explain...but was there really anything to add?

This had been an innocent encounter. Yeah, she'd had a few drinks. Considering the stress levels at home and at work, who was more entitled than her to a boozy night out? Chin lifted high, she plucked the card with a quick thank you, and headed back upstairs. She pondered how long it would take for his gaping jaw to close.

A quick shower and change of clothes later, the hangover had subsided, and Dara felt ready to take on the world. She took and Uber back to Poisson, picked up her car, and sped off for Haversham, taking a moment during a red light to ask her car's Bluetooth to dial the number she read off Lee's card. She debated whether to chide him for stopping by her house and decided it wouldn't be necessary since she'd make sure he now had the office address.

He answered on the second ring.

"Lee, this is Dara Banks. I wanted to thank you for bringing me home last night. I understand that you wanted to discuss real estate."

"Are you alone, Dara? Can I speak freely?"

She pursed her lips. What an odd question. "Er, yes. I'm on my way to an appointment, but I have a moment to chat."

"I was surprised to run into your husband earlier. I had no idea you were married, but hey, that's okay. No biggie. I just wanted you to know, what went on last night? That stays between us. I don't want you to worry about that. My mouth is like a tomb. Nothing gets out...well, except my tongue." He chuckled softly.

Huh? "Lee, you must have me confused with someone else. This is Dara. The Realtor from dinner last night? We spoke about real estate?"

"Okay, okay, if you want to play it that way," he snickered. "We *talked*. About *real estate*. So, when can we get together and talk about *real estate* again? I'm free after five tonight—"

His insinuations tempted her to smash her car into the nearest tree.

"This conversation is over. Please don't contact me again."

She disconnected the call and pulled over to the shoulder until she could catch her breath. She fought to think over the pounding of her pulse. The man was delusional. Should she call the police? She knew nothing happened, but stalkers—convincing ones, anyway—could make nothing sound like something. And she *had* been inebriated. She couldn't swear to what she had or hadn't said.

Wait, I have a witness. The realization slowed her heartbeat to just double its normal rate. She signaled left and started to pull off the shoulder when the phone rang again. His number. *Oh God.* She let the call go to voicemail, his calm voice dripping through the speakers like sulfuric acid.

"Dara, a word to the wise. Don't *ever* hang up on me again. I'll be in touch, Babycakes." *Click.*

Without thinking, she erased the message so no one could ever use it as evidence of supposed adultery. As if on cue, the wall slammed down, and Celeste appeared, whirling like a dervish, and laughing while singing out, "You screwed up. You screwed up again! At least I'm here to protect you, set things right."

When Celeste took over, she blocked logic and rational thinking, preventing Dara from calmly and clearly recalling the previous evening's events. Instead, she was an instigator of chaos, a provocateur of rage.

With a death grip on the wheel, Dara hit the gas, driving like an automaton to The Fortress on the Hudson. Parking at an obscene angle that occupied three spaces and unwilling to wait for an elevator, she charged up the stairs, gasping for breath as she flung open the door to the leasing office.

"Dara, are you okay? You look like you're on the warpath." Burton put his arm around her shoulders and led her to the couch.

"I…need…to…speak…to…Merry. Is…she…here?"

"Sure, sure, calm down and take a deep breath. She's showing prospective buyers around the place, but hold tight, I'll call her right now."

Burton dialed Merry and summoned her back to the office immediately. Then he poured Dara a glass of water and implored her to take a sip.

Dara drained the glass in five gulps and squeezed her eyes tight, forcing Celeste back into isolation. Having a friend like Merry nearby depleted some of her power, dulled her influence. By the time her assistant showed up, hardhat over a burgundy suit, Dara's breathing had returned to normal, her thoughts unimpeded.

"She ran in here as if she were being chased by a pack of rabid dogs," Burton explained. "All she wanted was to speak to you. Why don't I take any new visitors out for a tour and leave you two ladies alone." He headed into the hall, closing the door gently behind him.

Merry sat beside Dara and put an arm around her, drawing her close. Having anyone touch her felt suffocating. She pushed Merry away, jumped up, and began pacing the floor.

"Be honest with me, Merry. Last night...did anything happen?"

A blush brightened Merry's cheeks. "Well, for me, yeah, but I doubt that's what you're asking about."

Dara stopped, stared at her assistant, and frowned. "No, I meant between me and Lee. Did I say or do anything questionable? Flirtatious?"

Merry jerked her head back in surprise. "You? No, of course not. You acted in a perfectly respectable manner...I mean as much as I saw."

"What do you mean? You were there the whole time."

Merry cast her eyes downward. "Well...I was mostly there. At one point Warren and I stepped outside."

"Wait, what? Why?"

Merry shrugged. "We went to his car for a bit. For a little privacy. We couldn't have been gone for more than a half hour."

Dara vaguely remembered a period from the night before when she could only hear herself and Lee talking. "Really, was that necessary?" The edge in Dara's voice sounded more like Celeste. Her guardian had discovered a crack in the wall and was wedging her way through.

No! Get back!

Merry blinked. "I'm sorry, but I'm a grown woman, and I wasn't on company time. If I want to get in the back of a car for a little something something, I'm not about to ask permission..."

Tears of frustration welled in Dara's eyes, forcing her to look away.

Merry continued in a more compassionate tone, "Look, I'm sorry I snapped. You're clearly upset about something, and it's not about my tryst with Warren ...how can I help?"

Dara focused on a spot on the other side of the room. "Lee showed up at my house today. He left his card with Jason and said he wanted to talk about real estate, When I called back, he implied that we'd been intimate, and he wanted a repeat performance. I hung up, outraged, he called back and..."

Dara envisioned her world crumbling around her. In a rare exception to her normally stoic nature, she collapsed onto Burton's couch and accepted Merry's embrace, soaking the shoulder of her suit jacket in a torrent of tears. Merry said nothing, just squeezed her tightly until the downpour dissipated and Dara steadied her breathing.

"It'll be okay," Merry whispered. "Maybe Warren told Lee about our night together, and he just assumed you were as uninhibited and available as I am. I'll have Warren talk to him. In fact, I'll call him right now. Will you be okay if I leave for a second?"

Dara nodded, and once Merry left the room, she drew her knees up to her chest and cradled them, gently rocking back and forth. She rarely encountered a situation she couldn't rescue herself from, either through quick thinking or common sense, but this was unexplored territory. Having momentarily banished Celeste from her consciousness, she was at a loss to know what to do.

Merry called Warren from the hall, but the muffled sound of raw language, delivered in a pointed tone, drifted back into the office.

"What the f—I don't care what he thought...mumble, mumble...a leader... mumble, mumble...not some adulterous slut...mumble, mumble, no, not an apology, just never call...mumble, mumble...JUST DO IT."

Merry slipped into the office, and hope slowly seeped back into Dara's psyche.

"It's done. Lee won't be bothering you again. And if he does, you call me, and I'll take care of it."

Dara spluttered, a laugh escaping her lips. "You're five-foot-two and thin enough to fall over if he breathed on you too heavily. I appreciate the thought, but exactly how are you going to sway him?"

Merry raised one eyebrow and gave Dara a look cold enough to freeze time. "I'm not. But trust me, I know 'people' that will. People armed with an excess of firepower and limited respect for the law. If he's smart, he'll never call again." She paused and added, "Hmm, I wonder if any of those 'people' need a new home."

Dara shivered with shock, causing Merry to fly into unrestrained peals of laughter. "Oh brother, you bought that hook, line, and sinker. Don't you think I know better than to hit people up for business who make offers that can't be refused?"

Dara wasn't so sure. Leaving bars to fool around in cars with strangers? Hanging out with people she implied were mobsters? What did she really know about this woman?

Merry had again come to her aid, but for a moment, Celeste suggested that her assistant might be the one from whom Dara would ultimately need to be rescued.

But then Dara remembered Merry was an actor, one prone to hyperbole and dramatic speeches, with an addiction to being the hero of the hour. With that realization, Dara's momentary apprehension faded, and logic triumphed over Celeste's meddling. Merry was a resourceful assistant, not a gun moll. And one of the few people she could almost call a friend. Hopefully, Lee was out of her life for good and she could return to worrying about her usual concerns: family, work, and charity.

Chapter Nine

Dara heard nothing more from Lee the following week and figured Merry's stern warning, conveyed by Warren, had put the situation to rest. More brownie points for Merry.

That Sunday, she agreed to do an open house at The Fortress on the Hudson. Unfortunately, it looked like she'd be doing it solo. She had Merry holding an open across town at a new listing, and none of the newbie agents at Rock Canyon Realty were available to shadow her. Even her usual cadre of vendors eager to meet buyers at these events—real estate lawyers, mortgage brokers, decorators—all had previous engagements. Dara suspected those "engagements" were with suntan lotion and loungers because the forecast was for an unusually warm, cloudless May afternoon with eighty-degree temperatures. But the joke was on them because a storm system rolled in, turning skies dark except for sporadic flashes of lightning.

Rather than the crowded event she had anticipated, the weather shift turned the Fortress into a barren wasteland that afternoon. Though normally unflappable, Dara cringed as her four-inch heels echoed through the hallways, past eerie stretches of scaffolding and unpainted sheetrock, fragrant with the lingering scent of chemical sealants. She decided to sequester herself in the leasing office and restrict tours for any visitors that *did* show up to the four model apartments on the same floor.

Seizing the opportunity to play catch-up, Dara was in the middle of seller update calls when she was startled by what sounded like a pack of black bears awakening from hibernation. Once she realized the rumblings were only the antique elevator, its operation extra jarring due to the shaft's proximity to the leasing office, her heartbeat slowed a bit. But it returned to high alert when the car clattered past the fifth floor and stopped above her on the sixth.

Celeste intoned, "What kind of moron buyer ignores a sign on the front door that clearly states the location of the agent on duty?"

Dara forced herself to ignore Celeste and waited for the elevator to descend one level once the buyers realized their mistake. But the building remained silent, causing her skin to prickle. She debated climbing up a flight to sort out the situation. Wasn't there an intercom system she'd seen Burton use? Or had he communicated solely by cell phone?

She searched the walls and the desk for evidence of a communications device. Nothing. It was clear that unless she wanted aimless buyers to walk the halls for eternity, she needed to head upstairs.

"Miss?"

The strange voice caused her stomach to jump into her throat. She swung around to find a silver-haired gentleman and his frumpy wife patiently waiting for her attention.

"Oh my God, you scared me. I didn't hear the elevator return to this floor"

"We didn't trust that deathtrap, so we walked down one flight," said the man matter-of-factly. Dara stared at their feet. Rubber-soled sneakers and slow movements explained why she hadn't heard them on the stairs.

"We're in from Pennsylvania, and we're thinking of relocating to be closer to our kids and the baby. What are the starting prices here for a one-bedroom?"

Dara recited her sales pitch, attempting to regroup. "Uh, when it's completed in the fall, the condos will all be brand new, with hardwood floors, granite countertops in the kitchens and bathrooms, and top-of-the-line, stainless steel appliances. There are four different floor plans ranging from 750 square feet up to 1,200 square feet, and prices run from, uh, $350,000 up to a half-million."

The wife's smile devolved into a grimace. "$500,000 for this neighborhood? It's so seedy outside. We figured these would be going cheap."

Dara forced herself to remain upbeat. "The Fortress on the Hudson is just the first of many projects down here. The riverfront is undergoing a huge transformation. Developers investing tons of money, determined to raise this area to Rock Canyon standards. Think South Street Seaport in Manhattan or even Faneuil Hall in Boston. By getting in on the ground floor, you are guaranteeing yourself a high return on your investment. In five years, you won't be able to touch any real estate in this part of town for under three-quarters of a million."

The man remained dubious. "We could get mugged and burglarized several times over those five years. I'm not paying a premium for that kind of treatment. Thanks for your time, miss. We wish you luck." They turned to leave.

Dara's killer instinct took hold, wiping away any earlier trepidations. "Understood. What are you looking to spend? I cover the entire lower Hudson Valley. Why not sit down for a free, no-obligation consultation? I'm sure I can find you something that would fit both your tastes and your budget."

The couple agreed to listen, and by the end of her sales pitch, the rickety elevator had delivered more potential buyers who'd braved the weather for tours. The open house ended more successfully than it had begun, and when Dara walked through the underground parking garage, she had two signed contracts in her satchel and an appointment to show the skeptical Pennsylvania couple less expensive condos in a 55+ community later in the week.

The garage contained a handful of cars that Dara assumed belonged to shoppers who'd given up on finding street parking and were willing to take their chances leaving their vehicles in a construction zone. And it was quite a chance they'd taken. The overhead lights flickered like a squad car, and there were potholes every few yards, a hazard that could cause someone to twist an ankle or worse if they were walking without paying close attention. Dara zigzagged to avoid them, but when she witnessed one large enough to swallow a tire, she put down her satchel and pulled her cell from her purse. She was so engrossed in typing a note to Burton, urging him to have the holes filled before they got hit with a lawsuit, she totally tuned out her surroundings.

Before Dara could react, she heard a nearby car door open and rapid footsteps. Suddenly, two strong hands grabbed her from behind, causing her to drop her phone. One arm covered her mouth, silencing her scream; the other wrapped around both of her arms and held them tight to her chest so she couldn't lash out. She twisted back and forth, desperate to get away, but the arm just crushed tighter, compressing her lungs to the point where it became difficult to breathe.

Her muffled attempts to shriek only made her assailant laugh while he dragged her to the hood of a nearby car and bent her over, her chest and cheek pressed against the cold metal. Using his own chest to hold her in place, he ran his free hand up her leg and under her skirt. She smelled the liquor on his breath, the hardness of his erection against her backside.

"If hanging up on me made me angry, you can imagine how being told to stand down by my co-worker made me feel," he snarled. "Now, Ms. High and Mighty, I'm going to make sure you feel it too."

Each of the words Lee spit out were tiny hypodermics, injecting terror. Dara sought to remain lucid, to fight through her panic, and when Celeste stepped in and took over, she was, for once, a welcome companion. A calmness swept over Dara, and with it came a memory from a Realtor self-defense class she'd taken years earlier. When her attacker pulled back to grasp and lower her panties, she seized the opportunity, realizing this might be her only chance to escape. She bent her knee and slammed the full force of her four-inch heel right into Lee's foot. She thought she heard bones crack, followed by the satisfying sound of Lee's howling. He took a step back, but before he had completely disengaged to tend to his injury, she repeated the move with her right foot.

Lee collapsed on the ground, pulling his left foot to his chest, the right leg outstretched. Celeste pointed out he was in the perfect position for what she suggested next: a sharp kick to his balls that was nothing short of Ronaldo-esque. Dara ignored the temptation to jam her heel directly into his scrotum; that seemed like overkill, even for Celeste. Instead, she studied the bawling, injured, would-be rapist, now curled into fetal position, and smiled. Then she retrieved her phone from where she'd dropped it, undamaged thanks to its sturdy casing, and walked serenely to her car.

Pulling out of the garage, Dara considered calling the police and reporting the rape attempt, but Celeste reminded her of how women often became the ones blamed for such encounters. She had no intention of going through that ordeal, especially considering her standing in the community. Looking like a victim, even a heroic one, could cost her clients. Instead, Celeste prompted Dara to speed dial Merry's cell phone and then did all the talking.

"He came back." She spat the words out like artillery fire. "Please speak to your people and have them do whatever it takes so I don't ever have to see him again."

She disconnected the call before her assistant had a chance to respond.

Chapter Ten

To celebrate the June opening of AVa's Place, Autism Vanguard held its first BPA or Birthday Parties for All event in their new low sensory room. Dara, Brooke, and the entire volunteer staff had been working towards the debut for nearly a year, mostly funded by the proceeds of AV's past two galas.

Before the guests arrived, Dara took a moment to admire what she and her team had accomplished. She walked through the main floor into the low sensory room, where children could relax in dimmed lighting and walk silently over the plush carpeting or roll their wheelchairs on vinyl-covered pathways. She ran her hand against the acoustic wall fabric that would spare her guests from the jarring noise of outside traffic. She visualized the children enjoying gluten-free meals at long wooden tables and then lounging in their choice of couches, beanbags, and rocking chairs. There were even cots with weighted blankets for those exhausted from all the excitement. And everywhere she looked were sensory-friendly decorations and toys meant to calm and delight.

Out of their compiled list of thirty-two children with June birthdays and 150 potential guests, forty-seven had RSVPed for the June event. Dara was certain low prices and a pay-what-you-can policy for those short on funds had boosted attendance. Ava was not on the guest list, however. Dara had opted to leave her home with Jason so she could concentrate on ensuring everything ran smoothly. Even Merry had volunteered to help.

With their team of ten spread throughout key areas of the floor, Dara, Brooke, and Merry positioned themselves in the foyer, greeting children with an effusive "Happy Birthday, all!" until the last of the guests trickled in.

"I so love this group and its mission," gushed Merry. "I would love to play a bigger part, join the board."

"It's...a thought." As resourceful as Merry could be, Dara wasn't positive she wanted Merry insinuating herself in every aspect of her life. Brooke quickly put an end to the awkward pause.

"Why not join me in Treasury?" she suggested with a tight smile. "I could certainly use the help."

Merry beamed and walked off to serve food and chat with parents who, if they didn't need to remain close to their children in the sensory area, could watch them on an oversized LCD screen from an adjoining room through the aid of Kid Cams.

"As much as I'm on the fence about your assistant, at least in Treasury, I can keep an eye on her and make sure she doesn't do too much damage," said Brooke once Merry was out of earshot. "Today's turnout is amazing. You must be walking on air. What a wonderful thing you've done here."

"What a wonderful thing *we've* done," corrected Dara, smiling broadly. "You've been a huge part of this. Ordering equipment, keeping us on budget, managing the books—that's all stuff I don't have time for, and I'm so grateful you were willing to take it on." She put her arm around Brooke's shoulders and squeezed her close. "I don't know what I'd do without you."

"I've got things under control here if you want to go schmooze the parents and maybe pick up a few listings."

Celeste stirred, excited by the prospect, but Dara quelled her inner mercenary demon. "These folks deserve a little respite from everything today, including solicitation. They know I'm a Realtor. If they seek me out, fine. Otherwise, I'm just a special needs parent, like everyone else here."

"I know, I know," Brooke said with a wink. "You merely consult on creating sensory-friendly spaces, for free no less, and casually let it be known that you can help them find larger or more conducive housing if needed. You are the most ethical and altruistic real estate shark I know."

"Well, I never," said Dara with mock outrage while Celeste took an imaginary bow. "I guess I'm ahead of the game. At least you didn't call me a piranha, like people refer to the rest of the agents at Rock Canyon Realty."

Dara peeked into the Sensory Room, where the party was already in full swing. Under the watchful eyes of four volunteers, curious children gathered by the bubble tubes, entranced by their calming effect, while others pressed on the musical wall boards to see their changing colors and music. Several sat quietly with headphones on, listening to MP3s. She sighed as a rush of satisfaction enveloped her. No meltdowns. Not yet, anyway.

With everything going so smoothly, Dara decided to take Brooke's suggestion and venture into the adults' room, more to gauge their reaction to the party than to ply her wares. She smiled while she watched parents capitalize on their break from 24/7 caregiving to grab a snack, down a mocktail, and commiserate with others in similar circumstances. Then she noticed Merry out of the corner of her eye, speaking to a couple as she scrolled through her cell phone feed. *What the...?*

She drew closer and caught snippets of the conversation.

"Great backyard...finished basement would be perfect for a playroom... redone kitchen..."

Masking her fury, Dara strolled over and joined the threesome.

"I'm sorry to interrupt. Are you having a good time?"

Both parents nodded enthusiastically.

"Wonderful. Would you mind if I borrowed Merry for a moment? There's something we need to discuss."

They signaled their assent, and Dara led Merry out to the less-crowded foyer.

"Exactly what were you doing?" she asked softly. "These people are here to relax, not hear a real estate spiel." Her words came out harsher than she intended.

Merry's eyes opened wide, visibly confused by the admonishment.

"They came over and asked me where you were," she said, her voice shaking. "I wasn't sure, so I asked if I could help them. They said they were interested in moving to a larger house and I thought, rather than bother you since I knew you were busy, I'd whet their appetites with our new listing over on Sandusky. Was that wrong?"

"It's just that I go out of my way to keep work and philanthropy separate," said Dara, backing down a bit. "But if they approached you…"

"They absolutely did. But next time anyone asks questions like that, I'll be sure to make an appointment for you to speak with them sometime after the event."

"That would be excellent, thank you." Dara turned to leave, but Merry touched her on the shoulder.

"While I have you," she said so quietly, Dara had to lean in to hear, "That thing you asked me to do? It's taken care of."

"Thing? What thing?"

"You know…Lee."

"Oh." She vaguely recalled Celeste asking Merry for something after that frightening encounter. The request remained a blur in her memory, which frustrated her, but that's how Celeste operated—clear at the time, hazy in retrospect. "Can you be more specific?"

Merry still had her phone in her hand and scrolled to a local news story in the online Rock Canyon Gazette.

"Here," she said, handing Dara the phone. "See for yourself."

The story featured a photo of an overturned, burnt-out vehicle and the headline, "Charred Remains of Local Residents Identified." Dara's stomach sank. She scanned the story of a blue Honda Accord that, in the wee hours of the morning three days prior, had somehow flipped over a barrier on the deserted parkway. According to the report, the car landed on the train tracks below, whereupon it burst into flames. The paper speculated that the driver had lost control of the vehicle, but there were no witnesses to concur. Dental records helped identify the bodies of two men found in the charred wreckage as Warren Feder, aged forty-six, of Stony Cliffs, and Lee Eastwick, forty-five, of Westminster. Both men were insurance agents with Freedom Mutual and were married, with young children.

"I…I…I don't remember hearing about this accident…" said Dara, her knees jellifying.

"I think we're inundated with so much news every day, it all becomes noise," said Merry with a sigh. "I'll email you a copy. It's a shame Warren had to go too because we had a little thing going, but I guess he knew too much..."

"Knew too much..." Dara echoed. AVa's Place disappeared, and with it, all the children, parents, and noise, all the cake and presents. Celeste had stranded her in a vacuum, a vast plain of incomprehension while she struggled to make sense of what she'd just read.

"It's what you said you wanted," Merry added when Dara failed to respond. "No way you can be traced to it."

"Traced to it..." The comment snapped Dara back into coherence, outraged at the insinuation. "Are you suggesting that I am in any way responsible for the death of these two men?"

"Well, I certainly didn't do this on my own. I liked them. Warren was a fun lay, though I felt some little blue pills could have helped..."

Merry's voice became muffled as Celeste's entreaty came flooding back into Dara's consciousness.

"I said I wanted Lee out of my life. I figured your friends would threaten him, break a bone or two. I never meant..."

Merry's eyes narrowed. "You said, and I quote, "Please speak to your people and have them do whatever it takes so I don't ever have to see him again.' I know because I still have the recording on my phone." She paused for a beat. "I record all my calls. That way, there's never a misunderstanding later. Like with clients who suddenly change their minds."

The foyer began swirling and Dara reached for the wall for support. What had she done? What had Celeste made her do? Hadn't she learned better than to listen? And now, Merry had this recording, implicating her in these deaths, these mob hits. Bile, its sourness laced with remnants of the turkey sandwich she'd eaten earlier, raced up her esophagus.

"I'm going to be sick—" Dara doubled over and spewed vomit onto the beautiful new stone floor installed only two weeks earlier.

Curious families, either walking between the Sensory Room and parents' area, or on their way to the restrooms, formed a semi-circle to observe the two women. Merry remained by Dara's side and texted Brooke a

Code Red request to come to the foyer immediately with a glass of water. Brooke delivered the drink, quickly assessed the situation, and launched into damage control. Citing food poisoning from dinner the night before, she handily ushered onlookers back to the parents' area so the acrid scent of vomit, along with the disinfectant they'd need to use for cleanup, wouldn't create a sensory meltdown for the party guests. Other volunteers rushed in with paper towels, a bucket of water, and sponges.

"Are you okay?" whispered Merry.

"You just told me I ordered a hit on two men who are now dead," Dara moaned, too low for anyone but Merry to hear. "Men with families, with children. I may never be okay again."

"No one will ever know. We're *friends*. And *friends* never tell."

Dara heard Merry's words, but all that sunk in was their underlying threat. *Stay my friend...and my employer. Or else.*

Chapter Eleven

Dara returned home shellshocked from the BPA event, collapsing on the living room couch and remaining there undisturbed until the evening when Jason's parents drove him and Ava back from a visit to their home. She knew she couldn't confide in him about what Merry had done—or rather, what Celeste had instructed Merry to do. She hadn't even told him about the assault, essentially because after it occurred, she'd blocked it from her memory. That was until Merry brought it all whooshing back with her declaration of murder accompli.

Jason was actually humming when he and Ava returned, a happy sound that had been absent from their home for years. He had been that way since Easter, thanks to his daily runs and nasal spritzes of Esketamine.

He had even re-entertained the idea of amputation, replacing his hands with robotic prosthetics thanks to articles he'd received from Merry regarding advances made in equipment and procedure. "Good going finding her, Da," he'd said. "She's a keeper."

Great, a "keeper" who'd started an email communication with her husband behind her back. Now, Dara had no choice but to "keep" her unless she wanted to go to prison.

It wasn't as if Merry had threatened or blackmailed her. Such actions may not have even occurred to her. Dara questioned whether her imagination was working overtime. Maybe the best course of action would be to treat her assistant as she always had, amicably and with respect, and throw all her attention into Autism Vanguard and her real estate business, just like always.

And that plan would have worked out great if a detective hadn't come snooping around Rock Canyon Realty the following week.

She and Merry were in the conference room, going over a Comparative Market Analysis for Merry's first listing presentation. Dara was suggesting different comparable properties when Judy, the receptionist, knocked and popped her head in.

"Dara, I didn't want to put this over the loudspeaker, but there's a homicide detective up front, and he's asking to see both of you." She lowered her voice to a whisper, causing Dara to strain to catch the kicker: "He said he's investigating a possible murder."

Dara's breath hitched before she caught herself. It was essential she appeared nonchalant.

"Well, Judy, of course he is, murders are what homicide detectives investigate. I have no idea how we might be able to help, but naturally, we'll be happy to speak with him. Here in the conference room might be best; there's more room than in my office."

She and Merry exchanged glances, and Dara quickly conjured up a game plan while awaiting Judy's return.

"I've got this. Follow my lead," she told Merry. "You can agree with me, but please don't offer any extraneous information, okay?"

Merry nodded.

Judy ushered in the visitor and introduced him as Detective Frank Contardi of the Rock Canyon PD. A striking man in his thirties, he wore a dark navy suit that accentuated his straight dark hair and piercing light blue eyes. Dara silently prayed Merry would know better than to engage in flirtation at such a tenuous time and perhaps let on she knew more than someone who had merely read the news story in the paper.

"Detective, a pleasure. Please have a seat. I'm Dara Banks, and this is my assistant, Meryl Rafter. How can we help you?" She smiled warmly as the visitor pulled out a chair and sat down. Judy closed the door to ensure their privacy.

"It's genuinely nice to meet you both, especially you, Ms. Banks. You're like a legend in this town, with all your good works. I'll try to keep this brief as I know your time is valuable."

"I appreciate that, Detective."

"I'm sure you've read about the two insurance agents who died in that car crash the other morning. Warren Feder and Lee Eastwick?"

"Yes," said Dara, determined to get ahead of the story. "A dreadful business, especially since we both knew Mr. Feder and Mr. Eastwick, at least briefly. But you must have known that, or you wouldn't be here. My question is, why is a homicide detective investigating a traffic accident, awful as this one might have been."

Detective Contardi leaned forward, elbows on the boardroom table, scribbling into his notebook. "I'll get to that, Ms. Banks, I promise." He looked back up. "How did you first meet the two gentlemen?"

"Lee and Warren sent over drinks when we were dining at Poisson a few weeks back," she responded. Obviously, there had been witnesses, not to mention a credit card receipt, which is why he'd sought them out. She could gain nothing by lying.

"We were recovering from a particularly crowded open house," Merry piped in. Then she leaned back, as if realizing she'd overstepped by embellishing unnecessarily.

"The men sent over drinks and asked if they could join us, so we said okay."

The detective paused. "Is that something you would typically do?"

Dara shook her head. "It's something I never do. But we probably had already had one too many and weren't thinking clearly."

"To be fair, it was my idea, Detective," said Merry. "I'm single, and I didn't see the harm in a little chat." She winked, and Dara bristled.

Detective Contardi tapped his pen vertically against his lips. "So, what did you all chat about?"

"This and that. Small talk. It's all a little hazy because, as I just said, we'd been drinking," said Dara.

"Did either of them mention they were married?"

"No, not that I recall, but then again, it's not the sort of thing people discuss when they're sending drinks over to strange women in bars, is it?"

He turned toward Merry. "Is your recollection any clearer?"

"I hold my liquor a little better, so yes, I remember the evening fairly well. They didn't mention the marriage part. We talked about movies and books at first, you know, really inconsequential stuff. As the evening went on, Warren tried to sell me insurance, and I tried to sell him real estate. I guess the more we drank, the more mercenary we became."

"Is that how you remember it?" he asked Dara.

"To be honest, by that time, I was half-asleep. As I recall, one of them helped me to Lee's car, and then Lee drove the two of us to my house. Merry brought me up to my room, and I fell asleep. I'm sure my husband can corroborate that."

The detective nodded. "And was that the last you heard from them, Ms. Banks?"

Dara hesitated and decided that with phone records so easy for the police to commandeer, it was best to disclose at least part of the rest of the story.

"No, Mr. Eastwick showed up at my front door the next morning to check on my condition and discuss real estate. He spoke to my husband and stepson. Again, they can confirm that. And later in the morning, I called to thank him."

The detective raised an eyebrow. "You called him?"

"Yes. As I said, he'd given me a ride home and then came to my door the next day to discuss real estate. He'd left his number, so I figured he was in the market. Though, I'm sure if I hadn't called, he would have called me. My number is on over fifty For Sale signs and billboards around Rock Canyon. I'm not exactly anonymous."

Detective Contardi must have noticed the strain in Dara's voice because his next question had a less accusatory tone. "So, what did you discuss over the phone?"

"He had the impression I was interested in him in a less-than-professional manner. I set him straight and told him never to contact me again."

"That's probably my fault," Merry interrupted for a third time. "I was far friendlier with Warren. At one point, we went out to his car to...get to know each other better. After we dropped Dara off, Lee doubled back to Poisson so I could meet up with Warren, and we could spend the night together So, Lee might have gotten the impression that Dara was as...open-minded as I am."

Goddammit, Merry. Why don't you just get on the floor and spread taose Prada-stockinged legs of yours?

The detective let out an embarrassed cough and turned back to Dara. "And did you? Hear from him again?"

She shook her head no. She'd checked with Burton—there were no cameras in the parking garage. They were on order. There was no way anyone could have known about Lee's attempted assault unless he'd told them, and what were the chances of that? Unless, of course, he'd gone to the doctor to set broken bones in his foot. Surely, he wouldn't have admitted how he'd gotten those.

The detective turned back to Merry. "And you, Ms. Rafter, how many times did you see Mr. Feder after that night?"

"Once or twice. And he spent the entire night at my apartment, so I never had reason to suspect he was married. Of course, I never asked. It wasn't like I was looking for a long-term relationship. I prefer to keep things light and breezy." She winked. Again.

Merry was so like the outfits she wore, thought Dara. Elegant clothing, always destroyed by some element that didn't belong. Now, spewing sexual innuendo unbefitting of someone who worked in a professional field. What was it they said about making a silk purse out of a sow's ear?

"And the last time you saw him?"

Merry shrugged. "I don't know. Maybe two, three weeks ago. I knew it wasn't going to go anywhere, Detective. He was a bit...abbreviated...if you know what I mean."

Detective Contardi's expression grew slack. "Come again?"

She giggled. "That's exactly what he *couldn't* do, the little bugfucker—"

"Can you tell us why you're asking all these questions, Detective?" Dara interrupted before Merry could elaborate further.

The detective cleared his throat. "We have reason to believe someone tampered with the brakes of the Honda the men were driving. We're speaking to everyone who had anything to do with Mr. Feder and Mr. Eastwick. If I have further questions—"

"Please don't hesitate to call." Dara pushed back from the conference table and stood, determined to end the interview before Merry could say anything else stupid, flirtatious, or that thrust their innocence into question. "Let me see you out."

When she returned to the conference room, Merry commented on how well she'd thought things had gone. It was all Dara could do not to bite her head off, but she remembered her precarious situation.

"Let's just hope that's the end of it. Do you know if your guys left any loose ends?"

Merry let out a snicker. "They're professionals. Even if evidence implicated them, they have enough 'friends' in the department to have the whole investigation aborted."

"As long as Detective Contardi plays along, you mean."

"Dara, my friends are serious men with a long reach. People don't argue with them. I'd relax if I were you."

Dara wasn't sure if that was a compassionate suggestion or a threat. "How did you even get involved with people like that?"

A sly smile spread across Merry's face, and her braggadocious side took over. As Dara had witnessed in the past, her assistant could never pass up a chance to expound upon her wild youth as a desirable Manhattan femme fatale.

"When I came to New York City to break into Broadway, there weren't many parts available. Somehow, down there, starring as Velma in a Syracuse high school production of *Chicago* didn't count for much. So, I got a job waiting tables and did a little dancing while waiting for my big break. Ever hear of Brazen? Heavy hitters—quite literally—spent their nights drinking there, and I became *friendly* with the more affluent and influential regulars. Thanks to their help, I moved to a better neighborhood and could afford to shop at Bergdorfs. And thanks to my help, they went home to their wives with a smile on their face."

Dara remembered reading about the scandals the celebrity-ridden, upscale strip club had endured over the years. What she couldn't fathom was why Merry suddenly felt so comfortable relaying intimate and seedy aspects of her life to her boss.

Oh, that's right. Dara couldn't fire her without risking being implicated in what had evolved into a homicide investigation. She was cornered, screwed. Merry was free to brag about her sordid past without reproach, and she obviously reveled in the attention. Dara only prayed that her assistant's bravado would die down soon and that she wouldn't need to go to Celeste for her special brand of assistance.

Chapter Twelve

Dara spent the next several months waiting for the proverbial other shoe to drop. The detective never returned; however, either his curiosity had been satisfied, or those higher up had satisfied it for him. Merry refrained from mentioning the incident again. Instead, she continued helping Dara with grunt work without complaining about the monotony of fact-checking MLS data and sticking labels on envelopes. When she showed homes, many of her buyers ultimately made offers and closed. She even met with Brooke every other week to go over the Autism Vanguard budget and help plan each month's Birthday Parties for All.

After observing Merry's behavior with the detective, Dara checked with clients and with parents attending BPA; there were no reports from either camp about the type of flirtatious language or demeanor Merry had exhibited around the detective. By November, Dara felt comfortable enough to let her guard down a bit.

If she had one complaint, it was that Merry invited her family to Sunday dinners every other week. She'd agreed to the first one only because, at the time, she was still raw from Lee's death and from what she'd assumed to be Merry's veiled threat. She couldn't risk retaliation if she refused.

Jason and the kids loved Merry's cooking as well as their royal treatment, commencing from the moment they crossed her threshold. Her assistant always presented Ava with a new stuffed animal and Khai with the latest video game, and their delighted reaction pushed her into accepting the next invitation Merry extended. It was a pleasant change from take-out, she conceded, though it put a constant spotlight on her own domestic failings.

It was two weeks before Thanksgiving, and the two were reviewing which For Sale by Owner listings had lingered on the market long enough to be ripe for solicitation when Merry brought up the topic of the upcoming holiday.

"I bet you do a huge dinner for Jason and the kids with all the trimmings," she mused.

"Actually, our family tradition, if you can call it that, is to go out for Thanksgiving at Restaurant Rex. We have a standing reservation. They have a great buffet, and everyone can select exactly what they want, plus go back for seconds and thirds." Dara paused. "Merry, you've been so generous with your invitations this year; why don't you come as our guest?"

Merry curled her upper lips into a sneer. "That's kind of you, but...out on Thanksgiving? I've always seen it as a homecoming, an opportunity to relish the company of family and friends. A restaurant seems so...impersonal."

Dara suspected what was coming next, but she had no interest in having her assistant host their annual holiday dinner.

"Have you been to Restaurant Rex?" she asked.

Merry shook her head.

"It's set in a historic house, dating back to 1745, originally owned by Rex Brayden's great, great grandparents. It's warm and cozy with lots of nooks and crannies, kind of like everyone's childhood home."

Merry narrowed her eyes. Dara could tell she was unconvinced but pressed on. "It's settled then. I'll change our reservation to a party of five. You're going to love it."

A few evenings later, Dara and Jason enjoyed a rare romantic moment, snuggling on the couch in their living room, her head pressed against his shoulder. Ava had gone to sleep early, and Khai was out with friends. It was the closest they'd been in... Dara couldn't remember how long.

"I finalized the date with the surgeon for the operation." Jason kissed her on the forehead. "These robotics are incredible. Some even restore sensory feedback, and many of the devices under development are mind-controlled."

She nodded and mentally calculated that she'd need to sell twenty-two luxury homes to cover the cost without dipping into their savings or his trust. That constituted a sizable portion of her projected earnings from The Fortress on the Hudson. Money well spent.

"I was discussing the possibilities with Burton, and he doesn't see any reason why I can't return to RC Architects once I get through rehab. And I owe it all to you, my love."

He slid one finger under Dara's chin and lifted her lips for a longer, more intense kiss.

"I'm so happy this is all coming together for you," Dara murmured. "I think getting back to work is going to make you so much happier."

"Not that it's been bad, staying home with the kids. Ava's really improved with all the one-on-one I've been able to give to her lately. But now that Attwood Academy has found a place for her—well, as long as they agree she'd be a good fit—I really won't be needed here as much."

"We're lucky someone on their waitlist dropped out," Dara replied. "The public school's special needs teachers clearly can't give Ava what she needs. If Attwood can get her talking on a regular basis, it will be worth every penny of that tuition. And you know, with it being so quiet here during the day, you might want to consider splitting your time between RC and your home office, keep a presence here."

"And you as well," said Jason, brushing a lock of Dara's hair behind her ear. "Now that you have Merry in place, and she seems to be working out so well, there's no reason you can't join me at home sometimes. I could use the help of an assistant, someone working…under me."

He waggled his eyebrows suggestively. Dara winked and laid her head back on her husband's shoulder. Staying at home wasn't an enticing prospect, even with the promise of an occasional afternoon delight. Being out in the fray, making presentations, negotiating deals—that's where she felt the greatest draw.

"Speaking of Merry, I meant to mention I added her to our Thanksgiving reservation at Rex's. I thought it was the least I could do, considering how many times she's fed us over the past few months."

He squeezed her a little tighter. "Actually, I called yesterday and cancelled those reservations."

"You what?" Dara jerked herself up and faced him. Restaurant Rex sold out months in advance, especially for holiday dinners. Those spots would be impossible to replace.

"I had no choice. Merry called and asked...well, practically begged us to come to her apartment for Thanksgiving. She never mentioned you'd invited her to join us at the restaurant. With all she's done for us, how could I refuse? The kids were so excited when I told them." He reached up and stroked Dara's cheek with the back of his gnarled hand. "There'll always be next year at Rex's, I promise. Or if it's that important to you, we can all eat there the day before the holiday. Or the day after."

"When exactly did Merry call to invite you...I mean, us?"

"Yesterday. I was in the middle of reviewing a Social Story with Ava so she'd be ready for her school interview tomorrow when the phone rang."

Dara's face flashed hot. Yesterday was two days after Dara had unequivocally turned Merry down. *How dare she go behind my back?*

It was an impossible situation. She didn't want to go to Merry's. Again. Since the Lee incident—probably because of it—she'd wanted to enforce stronger boundaries between her work and personal lives. But if she refused, everyone would be angry with her, including Merry. She couldn't risk her assistant and would-be host lashing out and sending an anonymous tip to Detective Contardi.

"I guess we could go to Rex's next week. But after this, I'd really like to start cutting back on the Merry visits. I'll make more of an effort to be here in the afternoons to cook for the family. I will. I promise."

She hated cooking. It reminded her of dinner prep back at her family's estate on Long Island, where she would fight with the fosters over who would do what, competing for Quincy and Angelica's approval. No matter how often she pitched in or how hard she worked, she usually earned her parents' admonishment instead.

Now, Dara needed to put those bad memories aside and return to the kitchen. Home cooking was clearly something her family valued, a place where she could help. She'd have to heap more onto Merry's shoulders, so she'd have time to shop and prepare, but in a way, by orchestrating this

Thanksgiving fiasco, her assistant had brought that additional work upon herself.

Jason chuckled and pulled her back to his side, kissing her head again. "Dara, it's okay. I know cooking isn't your strong suit. Spend the time where it makes you happiest, at the office."

His comment, though well-meant, felt patronizing. Before she had a chance to object, Ava wandered out of her room holding a plastic cup, her way of asking for water. Dara swallowed her ire, as she always did, even back on Long Island with the fosters, and silently walked her child to the kitchen. Celeste, however, was less inclined to let the matter drop. She added another item to her mental list of reasons why, ultimately, Merry had to go.

Chapter Thirteen

When Merry greeted the Banks family at her front door on Thanksgiving afternoon, Dara's shock almost caused her to drop her corn pudding casserole. Their host had cut her hair into a pixie cut and dyed it the same strawberry-blond color as Dara's. Ava took one look, yelled, "Mama!" and hugged Merry's waist, a wide smile spreading across her face. 'Mama' was one of Ava's few words; to hear it wasted on Merry threw Dara into a deeper funk than being forced to betray their annual Restaurant Rex holiday tradition.

"Oh my," Merry exclaimed, slowly extracting herself from Ava's grip and kneeling down to speak to the child on her own level. "I'm flattered, Ava, but I'm not your mother. I'm your Aunt Merry."

She spun Ava around to face Dara. "See, darling? That's your mom. No one could ever replace her."

Ava stomped her foot and then turned and pushed past Merry, bound for the apartment's master bedroom to reconnect with her playhouse and see which new presents were waiting.

Dara hadn't realized how stupefied she appeared until Jason put his left arm around her and squeezed.

"Come on, Da, don't be upset. You two look alike now. A real estate powerhouse team." And then, to Merry: "I find the cut very flattering. And dinner smells incredible."

Dara pasted on a smile and followed Jason and Khai into the flat.

"I've always admired Da's look, and now that we're working together, I thought it would be fun to do a 'twinsy-type' marketing thing," Merry explained. *As if she's now head of our marketing department.* Then she blithely yammered on, awakening Celeste's wrath. First, the secret invite, then the hair, and now, calling her Da. It was all a bit much.

Merry directed Khai and Jason to the living room couch where she'd moved the PlayStation, accompanied by the newest first-person shooter games, even though Dara had expressed her misgivings about violent video series like *Call of Duty* back at Easter. She suggested the men alternate between the video games—which only Khai had the dexterity to play—and watching the Giants battle the Cowboys while she and Dara took care of dinner prep in the kitchen.

Lash out! Stand your ground! Celeste prodded. But Dara held back, unsure of how Merry might react. Safer to keep her anger in check until she figured a way out of this mess.

"Please put the casserole in the microwave." Merry pointed above the stove. "I just have to baste the turkey again, leave it in for a bit longer, then heat the corn along with the stuffing, and we'll be ready to go. A time-honored, traditional meal."

Dara blinked. "Actually, haven't you ensured that this year, all traditions got tossed out the window?"

"Oh, please, Da, don't be like that. Your husband and children deserve a home-cooked Thanksgiving dinner, and I knew you'd be too busy to prepare it. What's the harm of me taking that on for you? After all, I take care of all the things you don't have time for in the office. And now, with this haircut, I can do even more. Say you can't make it to a listing appointment or property showing. I could substitute. If they don't look too closely, they might not notice the difference. Wouldn't it be a wonderful way to free up your time? Now be a love and help me set the table. We'll need settings for seven."

Dara swallowed her indignation over being told she and her assistant were interchangeable and instead asked, "Seven? Who else is coming?"

"Well, you know how well Brooke and I are working together on BPA. I thought it would be nice to invite her and her partner to join us as well."

Dara smiled for the first time all day. At least she'd have two friends at dinner, confidants who could agree that Merry was way out of line. Maybe there'd be a way to confide in them, get their opinion on how to disentangle herself from the web Merry had spun. Then again, with Esther working as an Investigative Assistant for the RCPD, that might not be the smartest course of action. She couldn't reveal any information about what leverage Merry held over her, lest it get back to Detective Contardi, who might work in the same squad room.

"There *is* something I need to discuss with you...oh wait, there's the door. It must be them. The other thing can wait."

Merry left to greet the last of her guests with her usual effusiveness. Dara watched from the kitchen doorway, waving hello.

"Welcome, ladies! This must be Esther; a pleasure to meet you. And what an absolutely gorgeous coat. Is it fox? I must have one. Where did you get it?"

Esther Okoro, a stunning, tall Black woman in her mid-twenties with a colorful Gele, or head wrap, and a lilting Nigerian accent, hugged the coat to her body.

"It was a gift from a secret admirer." She nodded toward Brooke. "I love it. I never want to take it off."

"I keep telling her I didn't send it. On my salary, it would really be an impossibility. But she won't believe me," said Brooke with a laugh. "So apparently, my wife has a secret admirer. I am appropriately jealous."

"Sure you are," said Merry, playing along. "You can wear it through dinner, Esther, but I think you're going to get a little hot."

"Nah, you can take it, but just hang it where I can see it. I'm still unconvinced it's not an illusion that will unexpectedly disappear. Now, Da, where are those kids of yours so they can give their Aunts Esther and Brooke a proper hello?"

"One's in the bedroom, and the other's on the couch with Jason. Help yourself. I'm on table-setting duty."

Carting in a wooden chest containing seven sets of flatware, Dara couldn't help but admire how Merry had set the dining room table. She had outdone herself: beige linen tablecloth adorned with gold piping and matching napkins, gourds running down the center, each holding a mini arrangement of matching flowers. Even Waterford crystal wine goblets. But when Dara noticed the nameplates in front of each table setting, she nearly dropped the chest onto the floor. Her tag was at one end of the table, flanked by each of the children, and Jason's was at the opposite end—with Merry by his side. Celeste wanted to pull the tablecloth out from under the settings, sending the china, the gourds, and the glasses careening to the floor. Instead, Dara tamped down the impulse and rearranged two of the cards.

Esther was the first to return to the dining room and give Dara a big hug. "You look less than thrilled to be here," she said in a low voice. "Frankly, we're surprised too, but she practically begged us to come. Brooke explained how Merry needs to feel loved by everybody she meets, and that's why our attendance was so important to her. Since Brooke has to work with the woman, I said okay."

"Brooke Barnes is a wise lady. I'm so glad you're both here. How's life at the station?"

She was dying to ask if they'd closed Lee's case, but the last thing she needed was Esther wondering why she cared.

"Always hopping. I've been spending my spare time with some of the detectives, studying what they do. I'm hoping they'll promote me to crime analyst one of these days. I'll work those cases, switch out names and dates, and become the next best-selling writer of police procedurals."

"Michael Connelly, watch out."

"Exactly. I hear Jason is going to get the surgery?"

Dara nodded. "It takes a while to get all the approvals in place and customize the equipment, so we're looking at mid-spring to early summer. He's almost like his old self these days. Things are finally getting back to where they were before the accident."

Merry's voice rang out from the kitchen. "Dinner's ready. Could everyone please carry a side dish into the dining room and take a seat while I carve? Jason and Khai, I bought extra legs for you. I hope you like dark meat."

Once the buzz of the electric knife died down, Merry swept into the room carrying the turkey platter, ready to hold court. Then she glanced at the seating pattern, and her expression soured. Dara noted her dismay with a ripple of triumph.

"I hope you don't mind, Merry, but I switched around the place settings. While it was so sweet of you to put me at the head of the table as host, you truly deserve that honor, and I need to be next to Jason to cut his turkey. That's not a problem for you, right?"

Merry's face stiffened into a frozen smile. "No, of course not."

As usual, during dinner, their host regaled the table with stories of the wonderful parties she'd held while married to each of her ultra-wealthy husbands, whom she referred to as Creep One and Creep Two, and how wonderfully her two stepchildren were doing out in the world. Dara and Jason exchanged side glances. They already knew the drill; listening to Merry's hyperbole was the cost for a delicious meal, and they didn't attempt to interrupt.

Dara could tell by their muted laughter and dazed expressions that Brooke and Esther, new to that afternoon's performance of *Meryl Rafter Live*, were bored by her unending blather. They trumped up an excuse to depart prior to dessert, a choice of chocolate pecan pie or apple cinnamon-topped cheesecake, except for Ava, who received fresh fruit salad.

As per Merry's suggestion, Khai and Jason enjoyed their dessert in front of the television. Ava returned to playing with her new toy in the bedroom, a crystal ball that misted and lit up to reveal a magical furry pet. That left Dara and her assistant in the dining room to finish their dessert before clearing the table and loading the dishwasher.

Dara scraped turkey bones into the trash, searching for any alternative to her host's next round of self-validating clamor. "So, what did you want to tell me earlier, before we got interrupted?"

Merry positioned the plates in the lower drawer of her dishwasher "It's more of a confession," she said, looking up. "I'm afraid I screwed up the accounts at Autism Vanguard, but I can't locate the error. I could have sworn we collected around $6,200 in cash donations at the last BPA event, but the account total is short by around $3,700. I brought home the books so we could review them together and correct the math."

Dara frowned. "Isn't that something you should discuss with Brooke?"

"Of course, you're right, but I don't get the feeling Brooke likes me much—that's one of the reasons I invited her and Esther here tonight, to get on her good side. Anyway, the last thing I want is for her to deem me incompetent and regret having asked me to help her in Treasury. I really love the birthday events and the good we do for the community. I don't want you to throw me off the board."

Merry seemed legitimately upset, and Dara appreciated she wasn't hiding her mistake or brandishing the Lee incident as a bargaining chip. "Sure, leave them with me," Dara handed her assistant the plate she'd just cleared. "Accounting isn't my strong suit, but I'll work out what I can. And I won't mention anything to Brooke."

Merry heaved a deep sigh. "Thank you. I owe you. How about another piece of pie?"

Chapter Fourteen

Thanksgiving evening was quiet at the Banks' house. Sleep overtook Ava as they drove home, and Jason carried her up to bed before taking a nap himself. Meanwhile, Khai made plans to hang out with his buddies. With the prospect of uninterrupted time alone, Dara carried the Autism Vanguard ledgers into the den, donned her reading glasses, and tried to make sense of the figures.

Merry was right; the totals didn't add up. Where was it off? She brewed a pot of coffee and settled in with her calculator for a long night, comparing cash donation receipts against deposit totals.

By three am, she'd found her answer but was too upset to join Jason upstairs. She'd gone back a full year, even before the BPA events, when the galas, along with cake sales and pocketbook bingo, had been their primary fundraising tools. Someone hadn't logged in the cash receipts correctly. It wasn't every entry, but sporadically, there'd be $50 left off of this amount, $100 left off there. In the end, they were indeed short by $3,752.

At first, Dara aimed the finger of blame directly at Merry, who'd obviously concocted this scheme to make Brooke look bad so she could take over more of a role at Autism Vanguard. But then she realized the discrepancies predated Merry's arrival at AV by months. There was no way she was involved, at least not at the beginning. It had to be Brooke. Her mouth grew sour with the notion that her best friend would cheat her and her charity.

This was so out of character for Brooke, one of the most giving people Dara had ever known. They had roomed together freshman year. If it hadn't been for Brooke and her sense of adventure and fun, Dara might have spent her entire college career with her nose in her nonprofit management textbooks. But Brooke drew her out, forcing her to attend film festivals, keggers at frat houses, and weekends gambling the little spare change they had on the slots at The Turning Stone casino in Verona.

In her sophomore year as a social work major, Brooke came out. Dara celebrated her and her lifestyle, joining her at gay bars and pride events, and helping her drain the Smirnoff bottle after every breakup. Now, when she wasn't helping out at Autism Vanguard, Brooke was part of the staff at the women's shelter where Dara volunteered, helping battered and mentally abused women find work or apply to college and trade schools.

Brooke had gotten by on her wits since she was a poor high schooler living in New Haven, working hard to earn the scholarship that allowed her to escape. Why would she start stealing now? And if she were pocketing cash donations, why invite Merry onto the treasury committee and risk getting caught? Was it with the hope of pinning the embezzlement on a scapegoat if anyone ever discovered the inconsistencies? Dara wasn't sure what the story was, but she was determined to find out.

Celeste rumbled in the back of her brain: *No one steals from me.*

* * *

The next morning ushered in a truly Black Friday. Dara texted and asked if she could stop by the condo before Brooke left for the shelter. She arrived carrying the ledgers in a satchel so her friend wouldn't instantly get defensive. While Brooke poured water for tea, Dara sat at the dining table, trying to maintain her cool by making designs with her spoon in the sugar filling the Limoges bowl she'd given the couple as an anniversary gift.

"So, what was so urgent that it couldn't wait until Monday?" She set down two mugs and sat opposite Dara.

"Merry came to me after dinner last night, apologizing. She thought she'd messed up the books for Autism Vanguard." She kept her voice low, controlled.

"Oh." Brooke ran a hand through her hair, scrunching her brow. "It's not surprising, I suppose…she's always so busy telling tales of her grand adventures or cataloging her qualifications for World's Best Stepmom, I doubt she has the bandwidth left to concentrate on minor details like accurate accounting. I'll take a look at it over the weekend and fix what I can." She hesitated. "I know this is a touchy situation, her working for you at the agency and all. Would you like me to be the one who lets her go?"

Dara looked her friend in the eye, torn between anger and loyalty for all the ways Brooke had been there for her over the years. "No…the thing is…I already took care of that. I was up until practically dawn wading through the donation receipts and comparing them to deposits. I couldn't make it work."

Brooke's eyes narrowed. "So, you're saying she's stealing from us?"

"That would have been the easier conclusion, except the shortages started months before she joined the board. Brooke, why don't you tell me about the coat?"

"The coat?" she echoed, her voice strained. "We don't know who sent it…"

"Don't play me. No one anonymously gifts fur. The gratitude sex is too enticing to pass up. You bought her the coat with AV's money. I want to know why."

Brooke faced the floor to hide her quivering lower lip. "I fucking begged her not to wear that coat last night. But she insisted she had to show it off. I knew this would happen."

"I would have figured it out, even without the coat. What I can't fathom is why. You've always been…resourceful…but never to the point where it bordered on illegal. This is flat-out embezzlement. And from kids with autism. What were you thinking?" By that point, Dara's voice had gone from soothing to a snarl.

Brooke lifted her gaze but only made it halfway to Dara's eyes, concentrating on the locket around her neck. Tears welled in her pupils.

"I…I…Esther was going to leave me. I'm sure of it. There's this detective at the precinct who's closer to her age. She's been working later and later hours…and when she finally gets home, she's always laughing about something the woman said or did. I just knew I was going to lose her. I had to do something, anything…" She grew silent for a moment.

"Go on, I'm listening."

"I broke down one night while meeting with Merry. You know how she pulls you in, seducing you with stories of her miserable childhood and her brother being the prince of the family, all that BS? She mentioned she had a friend in a similar situation, working for a charity with cash donations, who started borrowing a dollar here and there…and no one was the wiser. I ignored it at first, but the more Esther came home talking about that f-king detective Candace, the more tempted I got…so I tried it, and nothing happened. So, I did it again…and again. It got out of hand, I know. What I never dreamt was that Merry would turn around and frame me, that cow."

She finally locked eyes with Dara. "I promise, I'll pay back every penny. Even if I have to take a second mortgage on this place, I'll make AV whole." Tears streamed down her cheeks; her voice wobbled. "Just don't notify the police, okay? And, please, oh please, don't tell Esther. She's a stickler about the law. She'll definitely take off if she knows."

Dara fidgeted, stiff-backed. If there was one lesson she'd been raised on, it was that you helped the poor, you didn't help yourself. And here was her best friend, helping herself to the money earmarked for Rock Canyon's most vulnerable. Even with years of friendship between them, she couldn't overcome the slight. Or rather, Celeste couldn't.

"That won't be necessary, Brooke. I deposited $3,752 of my own cash into the account on my way over here. We're whole," she said, surprising herself with the chill in her voice.

"Oh my God, thank you, thank you." Brooke grabbed a tissue, angrily wiping away her tears and clearing her nose. "I'll put in double time, triple time. Anything to make up for this."

"Thank you, Brooke, I appreciate that. But you have to understand, I can't let you work at Autism Vanguard any longer. It would be irresponsible of me to trust you with access to the funds after this."

"But…I love AV. I love the kids. I love working the birthday parties. Even if I can't remain as treasurer—and I understand why, I do—please let me help in any other capacity."

Dara pushed back her chair and stood to end this uncomfortable conversation. "I'm sorry, Brooke. If word ever got out that I'd uncovered fraud and then let you remain working for the organization, the scandal could sink AV. I'd lose my not-for-profit status, not to mention the trust of the families who rely on us. It would be the end of a charity that does so much for so many. I just can't." She turned to leave.

"Damn that Merry Rafter," Brooke spat, her contrition devolving into fury. "She's been trying to wedge herself between us since the day she arrived. She saw that coat the other day when Esther picked me up after our treasury committee meeting. I bet she figured if she invited us to Thanksgiving, you'd see it too. And then she just happened to bring up the books after a holiday dinner, knowing precisely how that money disappeared..."

"Brooke, the books show the money disappearing a few months before Merry even showed up."

Brooke jerked her head back. "What? That's not possible. I only started around the second BPA event."

"Would you like me to show you? I have the books right here."

"Da, if they show money missing before July, that's not on me. That's her doing. She must have cooked the books to make sure she wasn't the one accused of theft. Then turned me in. I'm telling you, Dara, she's trouble. I'm going to rip her a new..."

"You'll do no such thing," Dara interrupted. The last thing she needed was Brooke poking the bear and then Merry lashing out and letting any details over Lee's death anonymously reach Detective Contardi. Even if her assistant had participated in this accounting fiasco, Dara needed to keep tempers low. "Stay away from Merry. None of this is about her, and you know it. She might have given you a blueprint for embezzlement, but you're the one who followed it. This is squarely on your shoulders."

"I don't know why you're dead set on protecting her, Dara, but I'll find out." Hate seethed from Brooke's lips. "And then I'll make sure Ms. Meryl Rafter gets hers."

Chapter Fifteen

Two weeks later, Autism Vanguard held its December Birthday Parties for All celebration. Dara had considered cancelling; Hanukkah had just ended, Christmas was only a week away, and with all holiday activity going on, the party probably wouldn't be missed. Then she considered the record number of RSVPs, nearly sixty families—some commuting from as far as Manhattan—and she realized she had to go through with it.

The party went off without a hitch. She'd recruited additional volunteers to supervise the guests and Merry had cheerfully taken up the slack and filled in as co-chair. The parents were enthusiastic and grateful, the children excited to attend. But for Dara, the sparkle had vanished. Working on her pet project without her best friend was like going to a milkshake bar and ordering a glass of water. Whereas Brooke's smile and wit had inspired joy, Merry's constant babble fueled a throbbing headache that hampered her urge to mingle.

As the event drew to a close, Merry supervised the kitchen cleanup efforts, while Dara stood by the door, handing out parting gifts to grateful guests as they made their exit. She noticed a young brunette and her daughter clad in matching herringbone wool coats and hats, lingering apart from the crowd. When the last guest departed, the brunette asked if she could have a word.

"Maisie and I can't thank you enough for this great party," she said, "but I was a little surprised you had the cake lady here."

Dara cocked her head. "I don't remember you at the gala, but it's true, Merry delivered the cake that night. She was a lifesaver. But how did you know?"

"I'm not aware of any gala, Ma'am, other than my own. Six years ago, that lady ripped off me and my husband Xander for thousands of dollars, delivering a fancy wedding cake that turned out to be Styrofoam. After everyone left, the caterers told us that this Merry, if that's the name she's using now, was cutting up day-old sheet cake in the kitchen for them to serve. Then she scraped the frosting off the display cake and loaded the tiers back into her car. I didn't want to cause a scene by confronting her here, and I don't want her coming after me, so I'm letting it slide, but I didn't think a nice charity organization like yours could afford to be affiliated with someone like that."

The room started spinning. Merry had claimed a friend had designed the cake she'd brought to the gala. This stranger had no reason to lie.

The more Dara thought, the more sickened she became. First Brooke, and now this? Was everyone she knew committing fraud?

"I...I...I'm so sorry that happened to you. I truly am. I'll deal with it, I promise. Tell me, you said you didn't know her as Merry. What name did she use?"

"She called herself—"

The rapid click-clacking of high heels on the stone floor caused the woman to glance back and blanch. "I'm sorry, we have to go. Thanks again for the party." She pushed past Dara and made a hasty retreat without taking her gift.

Dara swung around as Merry rushed toward her, frantically waving her phone in the air. "It's Jason. He called me when he couldn't reach you—"

"I turn my cell off at these events, so I don't get distracted. What's wrong? Did something happen to Ava?"

"No, not Ava, not Ava." She forced out the words, her voice choked with tears. "It's Brooke. Oh, Da, I can't believe it. She's dead."

Chapter Sixteen

Dara raced over to Brooke and Esther's condo, thanking Merry for her concern but insisting she stay behind and finish the cleanup work. The ambulances and police cars made parking a challenge, but after three circles around the lot, she prevailed. To make up for lost time, Dara dashed up the five flights, too impatient to wait for the elevator to arrive.

The door was ajar, and inside, the condominium was buzzing with investigators and EMTs. Out of breath, she found Esther still sobbing on the couch in the living room and sat down beside her, squeezing her upper arm.

"Hon, what happened?"

Esther fell into her embrace and wailed. Dara remained silent until her friend cried herself out and was finally composed enough to speak.

"Oh, Da. I came home and found her slumped over the dining table. The detectives think she poisoned herself. They found a suicide note typed into the phone beside her. Something about feeling like the world had given up on her. First, that I was planning to leave her for someone at work. Second, that you let her go from Autism Vanguard. All her friends had deserted her, and there was no other way. Oh God, Dara, this is our fault. It's true I was tempted at work, and she must have sensed it, but I never cheated. She didn't tell me what went on between the two of you, but it must have been bad..."

"Just a misunderstanding about the way I needed the organization run. We agreed to part ways, but I never dreamt she'd take it this hard." Dara refused to sully Esther's memories of her wife by sharing the real reason she'd let Brooke go.

While she remained positive the firing had partially led to Brooke's depression, Dara was grateful not to carry the burden of her suicide alone. She'd contributed heavily, though, basically ghosting her friend since their meeting on Black Friday. That's all in the past, she told herself, allowing grief to drown her guilt.

"It's just…it's just not like her, Dara. I think something else went on here, which is why I called my squad in to investigate." Her eyes grew moist again.

"What could have happened?" Dara cocked her head. "Any sign of forced entry? Not that a random thief would necessarily come in and poison her. I mean, that's not the typical way burglars assault their victims."

"I know, but it doesn't make any sense. Just last week, they promoted her to assistant director at the women's shelter. We had plans to go to Cabo later in the year. Despite whatever went on at Autism Vanguard, she seemed happy. Then this…Maybe it had something to do with Merry's visit."

"Merry…was here?"

"Yeah, a few days ago. Brooke must have invited her. I heard them fighting when I came home from shopping. Merry ran out as I arrived, and Brooke wouldn't tell me what they were screaming about. She insisted I leave it alone. But maybe you have some idea…?"

Dara's pounding brain threatened to erupt and spew its gray matter throughout the apartment. She'd specifically told Brooke to stay away from Merry. If the argument had upset her…well, hopefully, Brooke's suicide would quell any inkling her assistant had for revenge.

Back to walking on eggshells for a while.

"I couldn't tell you, Esther. They never really got along. I know they tried, but the two of them were like chalk and cheese. Brooke always saw Merry as a rival for my affection, which was patently not true. Merry could never take Brooke's place."

Esther looked her dead in the eye, her face bathed in resolve borne of grief. "I don't trust her, Da. There's something that doesn't ring right. Brooke felt the same. I'm going to do some poking around."

Dara's insides knotted into a tumor of turmoil. She didn't want anything upsetting Merry, but at the same time, she'd just learned the woman was not merely an actor but a liar and a fraud. It wouldn't be a terrible thing for Esther and her police colleagues to dig up dirt on her assistant. The outcome might provide Dara with the perfect excuse to fire her, and the wrongdoings they dredged up could taint any accusations Merry later made to Detective Contardi, allowing Dara to disavow them, label them as retribution. She could finally disentangle her work, her charity, and her family from Merry's web.

"I don't think that's a bad idea, Esther. It won't bring our Brooke back, I'm afraid, but if Merry *is* involved, justice might help you find closure. Just be subtle, okay? I don't want my family or clients to be the recipients of her unhinged rage if she gets wind of your investigation. Please let me know what you discover, and if there's anything I can do to help, you know where to find me."

Chapter Seventeen

L ife went on, the pain of Brooke's absence in Dara's life fading from sharp jabs to lingering aches each day while she immersed herself in marketing The Fortress on the Hudson. Show condos, write up contracts, repeat. Long days stretched into the wee hours. On top of that, Ava was having a challenging time adjusting to her new school, and Dara often had to remain in the classroom for an hour or two after drop-off until the child relaxed enough for her to leave.

Despite her trepidations, she leaned heavily on Merry during those weeks. She couldn't afford to rock the boat, especially without knowing what had transpired between her and Brooke and the level of fury evoked by their argument. With any luck, Esther's investigation would turn up something juicy and allow her to ditch the woman from her payroll.

Meanwhile, in Merry. Dara had an assistant licensed and trained in her policies and procedures who appeared to relate well to both buyers and sellers. Dara checked in occasionally with her clients, asking if they were satisfied with Merry's performance. She received high marks across the board, and Dara decided, if it ain't broke, don't fix it. She endured the biweekly dinners and constant self-aggrandization in exchange for competent assistance.

About a month after Brooke passed, Esther held a private memorial service and dinner in her honor. She invited both Dara and her husband, but with Ava's more frequent meltdowns since she'd started Attwood, they decided Jason should remain home to babysit.

Esther begged Dara not to mention the service to Merry, whom she hadn't invited. The widow still believed Merry had provoked Brooke into taking her own life and was not interested in spending a moment longer with the woman than was absolutely necessary.

* * *

Only twenty mourners attended the service, held in a private room in a Mediterranean restaurant. The dinner featured all of Brooke's favorite dishes: chicken sauté, falafel, and moussaka, with baklava for dessert.

During the meal, each mourner stood and recounted what they remembered most fondly about their deceased friend. Esther began, explaining how she and Brooke first met. "We were part of the same tour of Greece, especially ironic since we lived within two blocks of each other in Rock Canyon. I had to travel close to five thousand miles to meet the girl next door."

Dara spoke of Brooke's vivaciousness, determination, loyalty, and joie de vivre. All the adventures they'd shared in college together. The work relationship that followed. The knot retightened in her stomach as she rattled on. She tried to disregard it, but it wouldn't relax and unfurl.

The service ended and Dara stood to put on her coat when Esther touched her on the shoulder.

"Could you hang around a moment? There's something I want to discuss with you, without the others here."

A chill crept up Dara's spine. Had Esther discovered the truth about her wife's firing? Or heard something about Lee's death at the station house? She willed her moussaka to stay down while waiting for the last of the mourners to depart.

Finally, Esther returned to her side, manila envelope in hand. "I told you I would keep an eye on Merry, and I have. I've been following her on and off since Brooke died. Last weekend, she went out of town, did you know?"

Dara scowled, stunned by this new intel. "Last weekend? I'll kill her. She told me she was ill and couldn't work my open houses. I had to recruit a pair of newbie agents to take over, and when I called buyers to gauge their interest, the feedback was not good. Where the hell did she go?"

"She spent the weekend in the city. I followed her every step, wearing dark glasses and a baseball cap. She never spotted me. And I took these."

Esther pulled a handful of pictures from the envelope and placed the pile in front of Dara, with only the top one showing. "Do you know any of these people?"

It was a photo of a dining table, she assumed, at a restaurant. A woman whose back was to the camera looked just like Merry, complete with the pixie cut she'd appropriated from Dara.

"She was facing the wall," Esther said. "I couldn't take a clear shot without getting noticed."

It was the smiling faces of the other three diners that stiffened Dara's muscles like the onset of rigor mortis. To Merry's right was the "late" insurance salesperson, Warren Feder—still very much alive. Across from her sat the miraculously resurrected corpse of would-be rapist, Lee Eastwick, the man on whom Dara had allegedly put out a hit. And to her right was no other than the homicidal investigator himself, Detective Frank Contardi.

Dara's anger, shock, and disgust fought for supremacy. She was furious that Merry had manipulated her so expertly, setting up a scam featuring what must have been a photoshopped newspaper article she'd never thought to verify.

Simultaneously, a giant boulder exploded from atop her shoulders. There was no "Lee incident." No exploding car. No dead bodies. She wasn't responsible for any crime Merry might use as a bargaining chip in the future. She owed the mob nothing. She owed Merry nothing. She was free!

Esther's voice jarred her back from elation to investigation. "Do you know any of these men, Dara?"

She looked Esther in the eye, determined to remain vague. "I've met each of them, always in Merry's company. Who are they?"

Esther turned the top picture over and spread the remaining photos across the table. There were three mug shots, one of each of the men in the original photo.

"Thanks to the wonders of facial recognition software, I can answer that." She pointed to the photo on the left, the one of Warren. "That's Carl Vonderman, also known as Carl the Copy. He served time in Westminster Correctional for petty theft and fraud, with a specialty in forged documents like passports, driver's licenses, and credit cards."

Her finger shifted to the middle photo, the one of the man Dara had known as Lee. "This is Jimmy Gordon. He was Carl's roomie at Westminster Correctional, convicted of embezzlement and various other white-collar crimes."

The photo of Jimmy brought back memories of Lee's threatening phone call and the subsequent attack in the garage. Dara struggled to keep from upchucking her lunch.

"And this third charmer is Tonino Randazzo, better known as Tony. Not only does he have mob ties, he's been repeatedly arrested but never convicted for luring women up to his hotel room and then sexually assaulting them. The women always drop their cases, no doubt after they're warned he's connected and very, very vindictive. Any idea why your assistant is all chummy with this group of losers?"

Dara shook her head. "How about Merry? Any mug shots of her?"

"Unfortunately, not. She's a crafty one. She looks down or shields her face whenever she's on the move, as if she knows people might be photographing her. I was hoping you might have a picture or two I could run through the system."

Dara thought for a moment. "She wouldn't let me photograph her for the website. But there must be one on her real estate license. I'll contact the Board of Realtors in the morning and get one to you."

"That would be great. Then I could pull up any criminal records."

"Actually, I doubt she has one. I believe they do a search before they give you your license."

"Well, that's only true if the name and social security number they were running actually belong to her."

Suddenly, Dara remembered something she'd forgotten in all the excitement over Brooke's suicide: the woman at the BPA event who'd known Merry as the cake fraud. She was about to share Merry's alternate name when she ran off.

"If that's not her name, I might have a way to find out who she really is. Esther, can you get me copies of these photos? I'm going to ask around, and they may come in handy."

"Sure thing, you can have these. I can make copies at the station house. Just...be careful, Dara. These are dangerous people. I don't want another death on my conscience."

Though she'd tried to project strength in the face of tragedy, the mention of Brooke's death caused Esther's eyes to moisten, as they had throughout the evening's tributes. Dara knew the investigation could only help Esther sublimate her sorrow so far before the memories again enveloped her. She gave her friend a hug, hoping to squeeze away some of her sadness.

"Esther, take care of yourself and don't waste any worry on me," she assured the investigator, channeling Celeste, and their joint percolating desire for revenge. "I'm going to be just fine."

Chapter Eighteen

Mentally attempting to unravel Merry's web of lies while navigating through snow flurries made Dara's drive home challenging. She remembered Merry had been the one who suggested Poisson the evening they encountered "Warren" and "Lee." Did she have this team of con men on speed dial, ready at a moment's notice? Did they have this plan in place all along to get her drunk, or more likely drugged, so she couldn't remember exactly what she'd said or done? Was "Lee's" parking garage assault pre-planned? Or had he just gone rogue, and then Merry found her leverage over Dara by improvising a fake death rather than insinuations of a romantic interlude? And what were the biweekly dinners at Merry's apartment all about? Why was she so intent on currying favor with Dara's clients, her donors, her family? What was her end game?

Dara's first inclination was to confront her assistant, show her the pictures, demand an explanation. But then, she thought better of it. Merry still had information that could destroy Autism Vanguard. She could tell the world Brooke had embezzled the charity's funds—even though her pal, "Carl the Copy," had no doubt helped her cook the books to make it look like Brooke had been stealing long before Merry's coaxing.

Plus, if she could turn AV's accounts upside down, what else was she capable of? She had access to buyers' and renters' confidential information—bank account numbers from statements showing proof of funds for cash purchases, social security numbers to run renters' credit histories. She managed all of Dara's social media for both her realty business and Autism Vanguard. Dara prickled at the thought of the potential damage this interloper could wreak, from her clients' finances to her own hard-earned reputation...and how her influence had led to the death of Dara's best friend.

Clearly, Dara had to play it cool. Pretend nothing had changed. Meanwhile, investigate and collect enough damning information to gain whatever leverage was necessary to coerce Merry to resign and remove herself from Dara's life, and preferably from Rock Canyon as well.

Celeste concurred. Meryl Rafter had picked the wrong mark to con.

She finally arrived home and turned to pull into her driveway and... *What the f—k?*

Merry's red Audi convertible blocked the entrance to her bay of the garage, distinguished by a new, less-than-professional bumper sticker that read, "If you're going to ride my ass, at least pull my hair."

Dara parked on the street and marched in anger up the walkway, mentally squashing her assistant beneath every step, and threw open the door. She found Merry and Jason on the couch in the living room, deep in conversation. Ava had curled up on Merry's lap, sucking her thumb, while Merry stroked her hair.

The two grew quiet when Dara strode into the room. "Oh, thank goodness you're back, Dara. There's been an incident with Khai. Jason and I were just discussing what to do."

Dara gave Jason a hard look as her stomach dropped at the thought of something happening to her son. "An incident? What kind of incident? Where is he?"

Jason held out his contorted hands, gesturing for Dara to calm down. "It's okay, it's okay. Khai's upstairs in his room, where he'll stay for the next two weeks, other than when he's at school—"

"We thought that was best," Merry interrupted.

Dara raised her eyebrows. "*We* thought?" she repeated, her words tinged with incredulity.

"Well, Dara, as usual, you weren't here, and decisions had to be made—"

Dara couldn't contain her fury any longer. "What the f—do you have to do with any of this? Get the hell out," she shrieked.

Merry made no attempt to leave, but instead, a tiny victory smile danced

109

on her lips, visible only to Dara.

Jason interceded before the intercourse heated up further. "Easy, Dara. Hear me out. The manager at Kreisel's Jewelry called about ninety minutes ago. Apparently, Khai and his buddies helped themselves to a few chains and a watch that had been left out on display. He was kind enough not to call the police, for which we can all be grateful."

Dara's pulse quickened further. She took a deep breath and tried to get her mind around what Jason was saying. Her stepson shoplifting? When all he had to do was ask and she would have bought him whatever he needed? Was everyone around her a criminal?

"Okay, I get it. But that doesn't explain why Merry is here." She spat out every word like poison darts aimed to kill.

Jason looked downward, as if already anticipating his wife's reaction. "Uh...well, when the manager asked Khai who he should call to discuss this, he gave Merry's number,"

"He WHAT?" Dara's voice rang louder than intended. *She* was the person everyone went to when they needed help. That was how she'd been raised, who she was, her *raison d'être*. And when Khai needed her most, he went to...Merry??? Unacceptable. The steel wall in her brain was poised to slam shut.

"It's not a criticism of your parenting abilities per se, Dara. It's just that he thought I would be less judgmental." Her assistant's patronizing tone reeked of false sympathy. "Countless nights, he and his friends come by the apartment and play video games. They think of me, and my home, as a safe space."

It took everything in Dara's power not to leap forward and gouge out Merry's eyes. How dare she suggest Khai didn't feel comfortable enough to come to her with his issues.

Who the hell did Meryl Rafter think she was?

Jason walked over and embraced Dara. "We owe Merry a ton of thanks, hon. We're lucky Khai had someone he could call, that he's been hanging out at her place instead of some random bar or dark alley with a bunch of druggies. This could have ended far worse."

"Yes. Thank. You. Merry," she said through gritted teeth.

This was the final straw—Jason siding with Merry over her at a time of crisis.

Was her husband so blind that he couldn't see what was happening here? This was now about much more than identity fraud at work, about swindling people out of money for fake cakes and enticing Brooke into embezzlement. This was about more than making Dara believe she had ordered a hit so Merry could hold the upper hand. Merry was slowly taking over her life, usurping her role as stepmother, right down to her coif.

Dara squeezed her eyes shut, as if the force could hurl this interloper from their lives. But deep down, she knew extricating Merry depended more than ever on her own investigatory prowess. She needed to analyze what made Merry tick and then stop that clock for good.

Chapter Nineteen

After Merry finally left, graciously accepting Jason's profuse thanks and Dara's grudging recognition, Dara carried Ava up to bed, and then the two of them knocked on Khai's door.

They spent a half-hour hashing out the incident. Dara couldn't decide the source of Khai's contrition: the theft itself, getting caught red-handed, or having to defend himself for turning to Merry instead of his own family for help.

"Dara, I knew you and Dad would freak. You're like Mother Theresa with a real estate license, always off somewhere helping people or working. Dad, you have your own problems with your hands and taking care of Ava. Merry's place was like a refuge. She bakes us brownies, has all the newest video games, looks the other way if we bring in beer..."

"Beer? Khai, you're only fifteen." Dara's face heated, and her outrage doubled. Was it because of the alcohol or that Merry's home had become her stepson's sanctuary?

Jason pressed his palm against her thigh. "Da, safe space, remember?"

"But Jason, he's still a minor. His fifteenth birthday was only last month." She shot Khai a disapproving glance.

"I started drinking beer when I was around his age. Remember, it could be much worse." Jason turned to Khai again. "You're not drinking anything harder, are you, son? Or taking any drugs? If you are, this would be the time to let us know."

Khai shook his head, but Dara wasn't convinced.

"The point is, Merry lets us be us. No expectations. No judgment. I like it

112

there and that's why I felt I could go to her when I got into trouble. Please don't be mad, at least not about that. It doesn't mean I love either of you any less."

"Fine, we understand," said Jason. "You're still grounded for the next two weeks, but as long as you promise never to pull something like this again, we won't demand you stop seeing your friends or going to Merry's house to hang out."

Dara started to protest, but Jason pressed her thigh again, and she bit her tongue. It was pointless trying to argue with her husband right now about Merry. He was under the woman's spell and didn't know half of what Dara knew. Things she couldn't tell him because she'd withheld the details at the time they occurred. The mock murders. The embezzlement and how it led to Brooke's suicide. Information she couldn't afford to share, lest it get out somehow and poison their lives further.

Merry was a danger to everything Dara held dear. Once she had tangible evidence, Jason would surely be more willing to believe that.

For hours afterward, Dara lay in bed in the dark, staring at the ceiling and fending off an existential crisis. This catastrophe was everything her mother had predicted, that if she chose real estate—where she actually found validation of her talents and fulfillment—she would lose her family and fail her charities. And that's exactly what had happened. While she had thrown herself into her two biggest projects, The Fortress on the Hudson and Birthday Parties for All, an opportunist had supplanted her as the family's caregiver. Her need to get ahead by building a team had blinded her to the countless red flags wrapped around Merry like a beacon. It had created an opening for the woman to infiltrate their lives, encouraging Brooke to embezzle and Khai to seek comfort outside the home. She couldn't bear to revisit the betrayal she felt at the moment when Ava referred to Merry as "Mama."

Dara knew in her heart there was still time to turn this around. She would work from home more often. Cook every night. Fire the housekeeper and dust and vacuum the house each week herself. She would take Ava to school every day and stay in the classroom as long as necessary. Trips to the aquarium, the zoo, whatever the little girl would enjoy. She would become Mother of the Year.

Right after she dealt with Merry.

Dara switched from soul-searching mode to contemplating her plan of attack.

She knew her opponent was a cunning manipulator who thought three steps ahead and who had a cadre of criminals to enlist at any moment. She needed to be equally shrewd. She spent the rest of the night playing out various scenarios and by dawn, Dara was prepared to set "Mission Merry Dismiss-mas" into action.

Chapter Twenty

Step one was to discover the true identity of her assistant. During her sleepless night, Dara realized she'd never vetted Merry when she first hired her, being so strapped for help, and so dazzled by the cake rescue. No reference checks. She also didn't have a photo handy. She needed to rectify both issues immediately.

She texted her assistant during breakfast and asked her to be a dear and stop by the Multiple Listing Service office first thing, pick up a carton of new lockboxes, and tell them to charge her account. The MLS was located in the county north of Rock Canyon, which would buy Dara time to poke around without interruption.

She gingerly searched Merry's desk, careful to leave everything in its place. Other than two half-completed contracts for clients whose names she didn't recognize, Dara saw nothing that raised any alarms. She turned on her assistant's computer and scanned the files for anything that didn't belong. There was one file named "Laundry" that stood out as odd, and when she clicked to open it, the computer asked for her password. A password-protected file on an office computer? Not permitted. She'd have to speak to her tech guys and ask if there was a way to gain access.

Dara pulled Merry's file from the cabinet, found her employment application, and typed the listed social security number into her cell. She couldn't afford to write anything down in case her assistant rummaged through *her* papers or trash can. Rock Canyon Realty had an account with the Social Security Administration they used to verify the identity of company employees, but not independent contractors like herself nor staff members she paid directly out of her own pocket. Dara pulled up the app and ran Merry's number, chiding herself for never thinking to do this with previous employees.

The results came back instantly. Her grasp on the phone tightened into a death grip as she stared at the results. Merry's social security number linked back to someone named Paisley Harwood. *Who the hell was that?*

Dara realized she'd received two gifts. First, Merry hadn't bothered using a pseudonym that matched the social security number she'd borrowed. And second, she'd chosen poorly; there were unlikely to be many Paisley Harwoods around. If the real Paisley had received any press or owned a social media account, she'd be fairly easy to locate.

Dara pulled up Google and searched for this new name. Limited hits popped up, mostly from the Manhattan Social Register Times, which published news pertaining to the city's rich and famous. Paisley Harwood, born to Garrison and Chiara Harwood and big sister Alana, ten years ago. Baptized at St. Patrick's Cathedral, two years after that. Christened at St. Matthew's January 15, last year. Good, they were still local.

Luckily, as a member of the social register herself, thanks to her parents and their "old" money, Dara had no problem looking up the Harwoods' Manhattan address. Upper East Side. *No surprise there.* She typed the information into her phone.

With the clock ticking, she had one last task to complete before Merry returned and they met for their daily morning pow-wow. She needed a copy of her assistant's image. Dara phoned the Real Estate Board and asked for a replacement copy of Meryl Rafter's license, claiming her employee was too busy to call herself. Being the top-selling agent in the entire MLS had its perks; the Board bent their rules and promised to email a temporary copy until they could messenger over the physical license, which they printed in batches, based on demand. Unsure of whether or not Merry had access to her personal email, Dara offered to stop by later that morning and pick up a photocopy instead.

Just as she disconnected the call, Merry arrived, lugging a carton of lockboxes that must have weighed over thirty pounds. Dara's mouth turned sour at the sight of her and her tight, lavender pantsuit over a white silk blouse buttoned low enough to reveal ample cleavage. The longer Merry worked there, and the more she eased herself into Dara's life, the more seductive the attire she wore, as if she knew she no longer had to fake a professional appearance. Or maybe she just wanted to rub it in, that Jason had sided with her the previous evening, and the next place she planned to appropriate was Dara's place in her husband's bed.

Or was that her imagination talking?

When Merry immediately began regurgitating the previous evening's fiasco, Dara redoubled her original suspicion about her assistant's real intentions.

"Oh, Dara. How is Khai? I hope you and Jason were gentle with him when you hashed things out. He's a fragile boy, so lost after his mom died. That's what Jason and I were discussing when you finally got home last night. But look who I'm telling. Who would know better about Khai's issues than his stepmom?"

The sarcasm was so subtle, the average listener might not have noticed it, but Dara heard it loud and clear. She mentally counted to ten. No way would she allow her assistant to goad her into an argument and give away her hand. She walked over and hugged her instead.

"Merry, Merry, Merry. What would Jason and I do without you? You were right to give Khai a safe harbor when he most needed it. With me so busy at the Fortress, I just haven't been there for him and Ava as much as I'd like. I'm truly blessed to have a friend like you as a support system, both at work and at home."

She stopped. Any more praise would have been suspect. She wanted Merry to think she'd turned a corner, not grown wise to her ruse.

Merry took the accolades in stride, smirked, and returned the embrace. "Not to worry, Da. I'll always be there for you. BFFs till the end."

Yes, that's exactly what we are, thought Dara. *Bogus fake friends. Forever.*

It was mostly a one-sided conversation, Dara enduring her assistant yattering on about how she'd charmed Mr. X into listing his summer home and persuaded Mrs. Y into making an offer that was $50,000 over asking to win a bidding war. *I, I, I. Me, me, me.* Anyone listening would have been convinced Meryl Rafter had singlehandedly saved Dara's business from certain collapse.

After escaping from their meeting, Dara drove her Volvo north to the Board of Realtors office, located across the hall from where Merry had just fetched her lockboxes. She needed that picture on Merry's real estate license if she was going to conduct any productive investigation. Merry might have talked her way out of appearing on the website and avoided notice by onlookers when carousing with her "merry" band of thieves, but the Department of State required a photo on each agent's license, and there was no way around that. Once Dara gained access to the ID and, with it, the picture, she could uncover the precise identity of the Meryl Rafter/Paisley Harwood wannabe.

Winding through the twisting Rock Canyon streets, Dara forced herself to concentrate on happy thoughts, like the smiles of the children at her Birthday Parties for All events, rather than the venom of the rattlesnake who had slithered into her life. Those parties were such joyous affairs…so different from the ones on Long Island where she'd grown up.

How she'd begged to have a Sweet Sixteen birthday party. A way to finally befriend all the teens in her class who thought her aloof because she never hung out with them after school. Of course, she didn't. While they were snarfing down burgers and milkshakes at Friendly's, she'd be going door to door, collecting old blankets for the animal shelter, or unwanted clothing for Dress for Success. Whatever virtuous deeds her mother had deemed essential for that week.

A party would have been something just for Dara. That never went over well in the Banks household, doing something that benefited just one child rather than the whole lot. Especially if the recipient was Dara. Their overprivileged and hence undeserving daughter. While the fosters could run rampant and commit all sorts of minor atrocities, they got a free pass because of their blemished histories. Meanwhile, her parents held Dara to a strict, unbreachable code of conduct. The reluctant role model, never allowed to relax and just be a typical teen.

But for whatever reason, this birthday was different. This time, her mother relented and said she could have the party. Dara invited everyone in class to the late May event, and most had agreed to come. Even Robbie, the boy she'd had a crush on since second grade, had RSVPed in the affirmative. She'd scoured Goodwill, searching for the perfect dress, because, despite their wealth, her parents believed in patronizing stores that supported charitable causes. That's something she changed once she moved out and earned her own money; she detested wearing other people's hand-me-downs.

After days searching, she found a lovely navy fit-and-flare that accentuated her curves and was certain to catch Robbie's eye. She couldn't remember being so excited. An entire day dedicated to her.

Until it wasn't.

Until Zahara, the foster closest to her age, the one whose behavior was the sketchiest, decided she didn't want her big sister to receive all that attention. Dara didn't imagine the resentment; the foster told her flat out, "You think you're going to be queen for a day. Back to the fireplace, Cinderella."

Dara tried to write off the comment as the empty threat of a jealous sibling, but a nagging doubt hung over her like the green-tinged grey clouds that forecast an oncoming tornado.

Somehow, and Dara was never quite sure how Zahara pulled it off, on the morning of the party, she woke up to screaming coming from the kitchen. She bolted down the stairs, two at a time, to find her terrified mother standing on the coffee table in the middle of the living room, pointing at the floor—which was covered in cockroaches. They were everywhere on the furniture, crawling up the walls, and, of course, covering the kitchen counters, including her birthday cake, its platter mysteriously no longer protected by its plastic dome.

Dara's father, also shaken from sleep by the screams, ran from room to room, waking the fosters and ushering them to safe harbor in the backyard. Dara remained behind, frozen like a statue in the living room, too numb from grief to even feel the roaches crawling over her bare feet. As Zahara passed by on her way to the back door, she snickered.

"No glass slipper for you today, Princess."

BAM. KABOOM.

Lost in the traumatic memories of that tragic day, while traveling at thirty miles per hour, Dara never saw the car in front of her stop to avoid hitting a boy who'd followed his wayward ball into the street. Her head flew back, as much from the sudden jolt of the collision as from the deafening explosion of the deploying airbag, and pain ripped across her chest and jaw. She remained immobile, the shock clouding her comprehension when the driver of the other car barreled past the crumpled metal debris of her Volvo's hood and started cursing at her through her cracked windows. She saw his lips move but all she heard was Zahara laughing and telling her to go back to the fireplace and sit among the cinders.

Chapter Twenty-One

The incessant, high-pitched buzz of the fluorescent bulbs and a distant ding, ding, ding jagged Dara back to consciousness. Her arms felt heavy, and beyond a dull ache, something tight and weird was going on in her mouth. She forced her eyes open but squinted while they adjusted to the bright light of the overheads, struggling to comprehend what was happening.

Then Merry's hovering face came into focus, her anxious expression dissolving into a smile. "Nurse, quick. She's up!" she called out. Then to Dara. "Don't try to talk, honey. They had to wire your jaws shut after surgery. The great news is that most people lose five-to-ten percent of their body weight from the liquid diet they put you on, so silver lining, right?"

Dara tried to force a question through her imprisoned teeth, but no sound emerged. She searched past Merry for a glimpse of Jason, came up short, and squeezed her eyes shut to push back tears. When she heard footsteps, she drew them open again to find a man in a white coat, who looked barely older than Khai, standing beside her bed.

"Mrs. Banks, Welcome back. I'm Dr. Fitzpatrick, your surgeon. Glad you finally woke up while I was here, doing morning rounds. Can we chat for a moment so I can update you on your condition and prognosis?"

"Yes, Dara, this is important. Please pay attention to your doctor, hon"

Dara shot daggers at her assistant and her patronizing tone, then shifted her gaze back to her physician.

"Mrs. Banks, first off, are you able to understand me? Blink once for yes, twice for no."

She blinked once.

"Good. Comprehension seems to be intact. I'm afraid you've been in quite a bad car accident. Do you remember anything about it?"

Dara nodded slightly; her range of motion limited by the brace around her neck. She vaguely recalled something about a sudden stop.

"You crashed into the car ahead of yours. The impact was pretty substantial, forcing your head backward. That gave you a bad case of whiplash, hence the brace. But, it was the deployment of the airbag that caused the most damage. You have four broken ribs, two broken arms, and a fractured jaw, which we've wired shut until it heals. Beyond that, the CT scan indicated possible brain damage. I'm afraid we see this too often: injuries made worse by airbags. But the good news is, they often prevent fatalities."

Oh God. This was too much information for Dara to parse in her barely coherent state. She tried to glance down at her arms, hidden from view by a sheet. Following her line of vision, Merry pulled back the fabric with a Vanna White-style flourish, revealing both limbs encased in full casts with only her fingers peeking through, rendering her hands even less useful than Jason's.

"Can you make any sort of noise? A grunt or a hum?" the doctor asked.

Dara attempted to vocalize as the doctor requested, but as before, she remained mute.

"Okay, you can relax...Unfortunately, the brain damage we saw on the scan can sometimes result in a condition called acute aphasia. We'll have to conduct further tests but from what I can see, your receptive language capabilities appear to be in working order. It's the expressive language that's impaired. You may not be able to vocalize for a while."

Terrific.

"It's likely temporary," the doctor continued. "Following an injury like this, tremendous changes occur in the brain, which help it to recover. As a result, people with aphasia often see dramatic improvements in their language and communication abilities in the first few months, even without treatment. Which is good, because you won't be able to participate in speech-language therapy until the wires come off your jaw."

"Da, they say you may be discharged in a few days and can recuperate at home. Won't that be great?"

Dara ignored Merry and her saccharine reassurances and swung her focus back to her doctor, widening her eyes to ask if there was more information he wanted to share.

"That's true," said Dr. Fitzpatrick. "The ribs may heal in as few as three weeks as long as you don't move around too much, and the arm casts should come off in about six. It's the jaw recuperation that will take the longest. We should be able to remove the wires by the beginning of March, earlier if you're a quick healer. Until then, I'm afraid you'll be sipping your liquid diet through a straw."

"Just in time for spring!" added Merry, Dara's self-appointed Pollyanna. "Who wants to be out in the snow, anyway? But, don't you worry, Dara. I'm going to be there for you. I've moved my things into the guest room, and I'll be taking care of you, the real estate business, and Jason and the kids while you recover. I can even supervise BPA over the next few months. All you have to do is concentrate on getting better."

Oh really? We'll see about that.

Dara looked past Fitzpatrick and Merry, again searching for Jason.

Merry narrowed her eyes, then nodded with comprehension. "Jason? He's home with Ava. We both decided that seeing you in the hospital would be too jarring for her. I'll head home and watch her while he Ubers over. After I cook for the family tonight, I'll be right back. You're going to get through this, Dara. *We're* going to get through it together."

Merry. Living in her home, cooking, and caring for her family, running her business and charity. If hell existed, she'd certainly found it. No way to fight back. No way to communicate to the world that Merry was an imposter who colluded with criminals and was likely one herself.

She closed her eyes tight, effectively ending the conversation, and willed herself back to sleep because now, dreams were the only place where she still had any control over her own life.

Chapter Twenty-Two

And hell, it was. Merry Rafter in Dara's life twenty-four hours a day, seven days a week. At least, during her four days in the hospital, there'd been a reprieve, thanks to limited visiting hours. But at home, no escape.

Gone were the days of reigning over the rental office at the Fortress and negotiating complicated real estate deals. Dara's life now consisted of adjusting to the awkwardness of the casts on her arms and attempting to ignore the incessant itching underneath. With her mouth wired shut, emergency cutters needed to be nearby at all times to release her jaw in case she couldn't breathe or started to choke. She also needed to remain vigilant if she felt a yawn or sneeze coming on, twisting her chin to support it against her shoulder to keep her jaw from wrenching. Dara required assistance to go anywhere and do anything, even use the toilet. Normally so independent, she found it both a frustrating and humbling experience.

Meanwhile, Merry appeared to revel in her own indispensability. She woke up at dawn, washing and dressing Ava, cooking breakfast, and coaxing Khai to walk his sister to her new school. Next, Merry helped Dara down the stairs and into the kitchen, giving her an unobstructed view of how she fawned over King Jason. She'd prepare Eggs Benedict or French toast or even Eggs Sardou—elaborate breakfast dishes Dara would never have had the time nor the inclination to whip up, especially first thing in the morning. Dara received less than royal treatment: a bottle of chocolate Ensure twisted open and served with a paper straw that usually collapsed when she was halfway through. Or a giant syringe filled with a blender-liquified version of that morning's breakfast, which Merry would squeeze through the wires into her mouth with condescending encouragement: "There you go, down the hatch."

No way to complain, though. Her only means of communicating was by blinking, and if someone wasn't watching closely, it rendered her mute. Merry had even hidden her cell phone so she wouldn't be tempted to text with the little dexterity remaining in her fingers.

After Jason kissed Dara and took off for his run, Merry would lead her to a recliner in the living room and tuck her in with a handmade afghan before staffing the makeshift office she'd created in the room's corner. Unfortunately, this left Dara privy to every real estate conversation, listening helplessly while her assistant made her more redundant by the day. In the late afternoons, Merry finally left for the Fortress, and Khai or Jason assumed Dara duty.

That meant that every half hour or so, from dawn until around three, Merry would check on her. She'd either brush Dara's teeth and apply dental wax over the wires so they wouldn't irritate her gums, smear balm across her chapped lips, or ask if she needed anything—help going to the bathroom, a glass of water, the temperature changed. A constant reminder that it was Merry who was in charge and Dara who was at her mercy.

Merry never missed an opportunity to twist the knife a little deeper. She'd casually mention how Ava had hugged her extra tight that morning and spoken a word or two ("Isn't that new school doing wonders for our girl?!") or how, with her urging, Khai was looking for a part-time job after school ("Aren't you glad we were compassionate and didn't break his spirit after the shoplifting incident?"). Not to mention how Jason thrived under her care ("He certainly loves home cooking. It's making him nice and strong for his upcoming operation."). Then she'd smile sweetly and murmur, "Time to get back to my other job," leaving Dara alone to stew over how her memories of Zahara had caused this totally avoidable accident and its aftermath. How they had curtailed her investigation of her assistant's identity. *Damn bitch.* Chalk up another win for her sweet foster sibling.

Occasionally, the doorbell would ring, and Merry would answer, signing for a package or shooing away someone promising eternal salvation. Dara learned to ignore the interruption until one day she heard heated chatter and recognized Esther's voice on the other side of the door. Esther! The only other person who knew the truth about Merry. Did she have additional details about her identity? Or her criminal cohorts?

"I'm sorry, sweetie, but I don't think she's up for visitors today. The whole incident has been so draining, you know."

Dara attempted to scream from her prison chair, unable to propel herself up to standing to reach the door herself. *"Errrrthhhrr!"*

Her voice! It was back! Not comprehendible, thanks to the stupid gratings on her jaw, but at least it was something!

"I'm sure that she'd appreciate a visit from an old friend, Merry."

"I'm sure you think so, but she's just not ready for visitors yet."

Not ready, my ass. Dara moaned again and searched frantically around her immediate vicinity for anything she could do to attract attention. Merry had left her a glass of water on the end table. That was it! She twisted slightly and tried to knock the glass to the floor with her cast. No go. Too awkward to propel her body with her ribs still sore. The conversation at the door continued, Esther's frustration matching her own as Dara attempted to lean sideways toward the table. Her torso would not cooperate with the lateral motion. How could she make this work? One last attempt. With deep concentration, she pressed her casts against her thighs, which gave her enough momentum to lift herself up slightly, move an inch closer, and nudge the glass to the floor. Success! Unfortunately, it smashed just as Merry closed the door on Esther and whatever information she had brought with her.

Errrrthhhrr!" Dara groaned, then slumped back in her chair, exhausted and defeated. Merry glanced over, noticed the broken glass, and smirked.

"Your voice is back? How nice! Now, how did this happen? Don't move, Dara. I wouldn't want you to cut yourself. I'll get towels and a broom to clean up this mess." And then, in a lower, taunting voice, she added, "Just like I clean up all your messes."

Dara's eyes flew open with astonishment at the audacity. Who the hell did this woman think she was? But as she sopped up the spill and swept away the shards of broken glass, Merry made her position quite clear.

"No liquid lunch for you today, honey. Maybe that will teach you to be a little less clumsy." Then she chuckled, Zahara-style, and sauntered back to her desk.

Chapter Twenty-Three

Saturday, a week later, Dara's parents drove up for a visit. Where Esther would have been a welcome distraction, admonishment from her mother was the last thing she needed. Especially when accompanied by four of their youngest fosters, aged three to six, who tore around the house like banshees, knocking the occasional priceless vase to the ground sans apology.

"I'm Angelica Crawford, and this is my husband, Quincy," her mother said to Merry when she arrived. She was clad in a red plaid suit that was at least twenty years old, since shopping for new clothes was a sin when the money could feed yet another child. Her father wore a more casual light blue cashmere sweater over a blue-plaid button-down shirt and jeans. Dara read their expression as put-upon, having driven two hours to see their only flesh-and-blood daughter when, surely, a soup kitchen could have benefited more from their presence.

"Jason's told us so much about you, how you're nursing our darling Dara back to health. We can't thank you enough," Angelica said, patting Merry's arm.

"It's truly my honor, Mrs. Crawford. Dara has done so much for me, launching my real estate career, introducing me to her wonderful family. It's a joy."

Give me a f—king break.

It was the very last thing Dara wanted, for Merry to insinuate herself further into her personal life. Her hatred for her assistant had compounded daily since the broken glass incident and now burned with the intensity of an arsonist's chef d'oeuvre. Sadly, there was no outlet for that dislike yet; nothing she could do while she still needed Merry's help with her recovery, her family's welfare, and her business.

Naturally, her assistant played the humility card to the hilt, much as she must have during her stints as a mock mourner at strangers' funerals and wakes. She gushed profusely and assured Angelica and Quincy how often Dara spoke of them (which was never) and in what high esteem she held them. She ordered Khai to take the fosters up to his room to play. She then ushered the adults right past Dara into the dining room, where she heard Merry offer them homemade pastries and exotic teas, remembering only as an afterthought to fetch Dara and escort her in to chat with her own parents.

"Dara, you never told us Merry was so charming. Her name, so befitting. You're lucky to have her," Angelica said as she sipped her jade oolong. Dara, sitting beside her mother, would have upchucked if it hadn't meant choking on her own vomit. She kept her eyerolls to herself, lest her assistant again deprive her of a meal as retribution.

Ava's wail from upstairs saved the day. All the commotion from the fosters must have triggered a sensory meltdown.

"Sit, Jason, I'll take care of it," Merry said. *Another opportunity to qualify for sainthood.* She scurried up the stairs, leaving the family alone to talk amongst themselves.

"You're looking very peaked, sweetheart, I must say." Her mother fluffed Dara's hair with her fingers. "I think you must have lost ten pounds since I saw you last. That's just not healthy, dear."

Through her dental prison, Dara slowly squeezed out the words that only someone listening very closely could comprehend: "Gee...thanks, Mom."

"Clearer, darling. I can't understand you."

Sensing her growing frustration, Jason leapt to her rescue.

"Angelica, that's as clear as Dara can get right now. And she's restricted to a liquid diet. I'm sure once the doctor removes the metalwork, she'll put the weight back on. Once I get my new hands, we'll eat at the best restaurants in town, won't we, darling? Binge out every night. Nothing's too good for the woman who stood by me through this fiasco." Jason stared at his deformed fingers.

Dara nodded weakly, appreciative of her husband's sentiment but confused as to why everyone was talking to her like she was a child. Well, her parents, she could understand. But Jason? Had Merry's brainwashing convinced him she was some kind of invalid, a charity case that needed coddling?

In any case, she resigned herself to just nodding for the afternoon to save her mother the trouble of having to decipher her muffled speech.

The chatter continued between them for an hour. Dara tuned it out, instead plotting how, post-recovery, she was going to expose Merry as the fraud she was. It was only when the conversation turned to Autism Vanguard that she refocused her attention on her guests.

"Jason, who's taking care of the charity while Dara here is waylaid?" Brow furrowed, Quincy reached for another pastry. "I imagine any children born during the winter months would be sorely disappointed if BPA missed their birthdays, especially after they had attended all the other kids' parties."

Dara felt the wall in her brain slamming down, signaling Celeste's arrival.

"The children are fine, Quincy. Merry's taken charge of that, too. She's delegated considerable responsibility to the newer volunteers and it seems to be working. At least that's what she tells me when she fills me in every night after dinner."

She fills you in? This was news to Dara, her face growing hot with fury. She had no idea what happened in the house—her house—after she was ushered into bed. How long would it be before Merry enticed Jason into returning the favor, filling *her* in? The thought of her assistant being the recipient of Jason's slowly reviving ardor was more than Dara could bear.

"How long before the casts and jaw clamps come off and Dara can get back to volunteer work?" asked Quincy.

"I think it's another two weeks until the casts are gone, slightly longer for the jaw. It will be wonderful for everything to get back to normal. Though I have to admit, I'll miss Merry's cooking."

"That reminds me," said Angelica. "I made the most delicious bouillabaisse for the fosters the other day…"

That was it, the last straw. Jason venerating Merry's culinary talents, her mother droning on about caring for her *other* children. She needed to do whatever she could to forget, to clear her head of the horror her life had become.

Dara used her cast to nudge her bottle of Ensure to the right, clearing the area in front of her. Engrossed in their conversation, no one noticed. Then she leaned forward and started banging her skull against the table. *Tap. Tap. Tap.*

"Honey, what's wrong?" her father asked, a hint of panic in his voice.

Ignoring the question, Dara continued her forehead concerto with a growing intensity that soon captured the attention of the rest of her family. *Bam. Bam. Bam.*

"Dara, what do you think you're doing? You stop this tantrum right now," chided her mother.

The comment only encouraged Dara to bang harder. *BAM. BAM. BAM.*

"Somebody, do something before she cracks her head open," Angelica yelled, just before Dara's grand finale, a pound hard enough to clear her brain of all the anguish around her and also strong enough to send a half-filled teacup flying into her mother's lap. Angelica shot up with a yelp, causing her saucer to careen to the floor and crack.

Celeste relaxed, her ire assuaged.

A crimson-faced Angelica was decidedly less at ease. "Dara Iobairt Crawford Banks, just because you got yourself into an accident is no reason to take out your frustration on your family. Especially when we sacrificed the entire afternoon to drive all this way to see you. I never—"

Merry ran downstairs and interrupted Angelica's channeling of Joan Crawford encountering wire hangers. "I heard the commotion all the way upstairs in Ava's bedroom. Everyone, I've got this under control. This visit has clearly been too overstimulating for our Dara. Let me put her to bed, and then I'll clean up and lend you an outfit to wear while I wash that suit, Angel."

"No, no, I think we'll just be leaving." Angelica rubbed her hands against her skirt to squeeze out the excess liquid. Dara was surprised it hadn't frozen, considering her mother's icy tone. "You've been wonderful, but Dara has some soul-searching to do before we come back again. When you're able to speak clearly, I'll expect an apology, young lady, both to your father and myself, as well as to Merry, for having to sweep up a broken saucer for absolutely no reason. You're an adult, Dara. You really should know better."

Well, at least thanks for acknowledging I'm an adult. Score one for Team Dara.

"Thank you for all your efforts, Merry," said Quincy sheepishly before he hurried upstairs to collect the fosters. Merry scampered into the kitchen to retrieve paper towels.

Jason, never one to deal well with conflict, attempted to mend fences. "Angelica, you have to understand, Dara's been under a mountain of stress. She's a very independent person, and this can't be easy for her, relying on everyone to take care of her, not being able to express herself except through moans, grunts, and eye blinks. At least with my accident, I could still speak. After she's made a full recovery, please come back, and we'll all go out and forget this ever happened."

Angelica huffed with indignation while the fosters chased each other around the table. "Come on, kids, let's go home, where children understand what good behavior looks like."

As if on cue, Bakari, her hair in cornrows, stuck her tongue out at Dara and then laughed. It was Zahara all over again. But this time, Dara swallowed her outrage and just willed Celeste back into confinement. There had been enough melodrama in the Banks household for one day. In two weeks, the casts would come off, and she'd escape this hell for good. If she hadn't wanted to expose Merry before, she certainly had double the reason to do so now.

Chapter Twenty-Four

A fortnight later, Dara and Jason took an Uber to Good Samaritan Hospital, where Dr. Fitzpatrick checked her jaw and sawed off both of the casts from her arms. Despite all of her charitable and real estate successes, along with her wedding to Jason, this ranked as one of her life's highlights. She crossed her forearms and ran her hands up and down her flaky, unencumbered limbs, ignoring the smell and the stiffness and, instead, luxuriating in the freedom, tenuously regaining her range of motion. While she wasn't yet able to enunciate clearly, she could finally take physical care of herself—fetch her own meals, go to the bathroom, shower, drive—and, best of all, communicate, albeit by writing or typing rather than with her still-distorted vocalizations.

Best of all, the doctor was impressed with how quickly her jaw had healed and told her the wires could come off at the end of the week.

Her first inclination was to drive to an arts supply store, purchase a massive posterboard, and, with a red magic marker, inscribe the words "You're fired!" in giant print. But she forced herself to tamp down that impulse, primarily because her plans for Merry surpassed a mere dismissal. Merry would suffer humiliation, much as Dara had over the past weeks under her care. That suffering could only begin once she discovered her assistant's actual identity and thus began exposing her past.

Though torturous, Dara allowed Merry to keep administering her special brand of home care while she bided her time, plotting away under the guise of readjusting to life post-accident.

Once the stiffness subsided, she Ubered over to a local car dealership.

Tired of buying "used" to appease her mother's ascetic sensibilities, she replaced her demolished Volvo with a new, shiny, black BMW M3. She'd earned the right and the money to purchase a luxury vehicle, and now she was going to enjoy it.

With the kids at school, Jason off on his run, and Merry at the office, Dara headed to the mall. She visited a dozen boutiques where she bought a wardrobe that fit her new, liquid-diet-induced size. She grinned, thinking of how her mother would cringe at the non-discounted price tags.

Next, she drove to the Fortress to assess the damage her absence had caused. Burton had agreed via text to meet her there and smiled broadly when she entered the rental office.

"I'm back," she announced through the metal grid.

Burton hugged her tightly. "It's good to see you, Dara; how are you feeling?"

"Itching to get back to work," she enunciated slowly so he could understand.

He broke the embrace and took a step back. "Frankly, Da, I'm surprised you wanted to come back before you recovered completely. Sort of hard to chat up buyers without being able to speak to them clearly."

She pulled out her phone and typed: *I can always communicate this way if I need to.*

Burton strained a smile. "Actually, everything is going swimmingly well as it is. We are sixty percent sold, thanks to Merry. I don't know what she promises them, but visitors come back to the rental office, chomping at the bit to sign. That's a real winner you hired there, Da."

Yeah, a winner. She probably blows them in the bathroom.

"Why don't we leave things as they are for now...just until the wires come off your jaw?"

She nodded, dejected. If Burton didn't need her, she would check what was happening back at the office.

She drove carefully, concentrating on the road this time. She'd experienced firsthand what can happen when daydreaming while behind the wheel. The Rock Canyon Realty sign never looked so good. Judy at the front desk gave her a giant hug, and while normally unreceptive to such grandiose gestures, Dara appreciated the sentiment. Less pleasing was finding Merry occupying *her* office, papers strewn across her usually pristine desk, shouting at a seller on the other end of the line.

"You signed the papers, and you're going through with the deal. Have you ever heard of a little thing called 'specific performance?' It means you listed the home, you accepted the offer, you signed the contract, and if you don't want the buyers to sue you up the ass, you'll move out when they get their mortgage and are ready to close. I don't care that you can't find another home. I've shown you twenty, and quite honestly, when you turn down a property because you don't like the location of the microwave, you really aren't taking this whole thing seriously. We're going out tomorrow, and you're going to find a house, and I don't want to hear another word about reneging." She slammed the phone down with a huff.

Dara was torn. Merry's argument was accurate, but her delivery was not. You don't swear at or threaten a seller. With all the supposed compassion Merry extended toward her mourners, you would think she understood that. But again, Dara's hands, while now free, were figuratively tied. She needed her assistant to staff the office, at least until she could speak clearly, and especially while she needed free time to conduct her investigation. She couldn't tip her hand and lead Merry to believe she was anything but grateful and beholden.

Merry noticed her boss in the doorway and explained matter-of-factly. "I needed privacy, somewhere with a door I could close to negotiate *your* deals. I'm sure you can appreciate that. As soon as you are able to work full-time again, I'll move. But really, considering all I've taken on, I'd like you to have Administration find me my own office. I think I've outgrown that little desk in the bullpen."

Dara internally chuckled at Merry's bravado. Believing herself in charge, both in Dara's office and in her home, she'd dispensed with the pretense of holding a subordinate role in either location. Dara couldn't wait to take her usurper down a peg.. or pulled down a whole rung, in one violent gesture. When the time was right...and when Celeste was ready.

Chapter Twenty-Five

U nencumbered by real estate work, Dara concentrated on her mission to finally extricate Merry from their lives. Her first stop was Autism Vanguard's office, where she could search for the name of the brunette from BPA's December event, who had alerted her to Merry's baking fraud. All she'd shared was the name of her daughter, Maisie, and her husband, Xander. Since they kept spreadsheets of all attending parents, alongside the names of their children, she knew it would be simple to find her. Then the woman could tell her what name Merry was going under in her former life.

She sat at the computer and typed in her password. Up popped the BPA December party folder—the vendor list, the invitation graphics, the invoices for food and drink. Everything but the attendance list. It was missing.

Thinking quickly, Dara searched the folders from prior months in case December hadn't been the mother and daughter's first event, but those attendance files were missing too. *What the...?* She hopped on Google and searched for 'Maisie and Xander.' Admittedly, a last-ditch effort and, unfortunately, one that came up short. This was a dead end.

She shot off a text to the volunteer who'd been there the longest and also had access to the computer data. *Hi. I'm at the office and can't find any of the attendance records for BPA. Was the file name changed?*

A minute later, a response popped up on her cell. *I couldn't tell you. Merry took over the invites, and she's the only one who's been sending them out since the accident. So glad you're back.*

Well, that sucked. She couldn't ask Merry about it without her assistant questioning why. She'd have to leave this line of inquiry alone and move on.

Next stop, up north to the Board of Realtors, her intended destination before crashing her car. Someone must have told the decorator that bright colors made Realtors happy and that money was their only motivation because the office walls depicted rainbows leading to houses surrounded by lawns of dollar bills rather than pots of gold.

The admin knew her well, thanks to her high production, and greeted her profusely when she entered. "Dara, we're so sorry about the accident. I hope you got the floral arrangement. It's wonderful you're back."

"I did, and the flowers were beautiful. Thank you." Determined to be understood, Dara spoke as slowly as she had with Burton. "Before the crash, I was intending to pick up a copy of my assistant's license. Her name is Meryl Rafter. Do you have it for me?"

The admin cocked her head, attempting to decipher. Dara had grown used to this. Even though her speech grew clearer each day, the muffled tones still confounded listeners. She pulled out her phone, typed the same message, and held it out for the clerk to read.

"Oh yes. When you didn't show up that day, we didn't know what to do. We mailed it."

Dara's stomach fell. She'd specifically asked them to hold the license for her. During her absence, chances were Merry had rifled through every piece of her mail. The last thing she wanted was for her assistant to start asking questions. But she couldn't worry about that right now; she'd check later to see if, by some miracle, it was still waiting, unopened on her desk. Right now, she needed that photo, and since she was already at the Board offices...

It must have gotten lost in the mail because I didn't see it, she typed. *Could you possibly print me out another copy?*

"I'm afraid the ID cards take time to manufacture; we create them in batches when enough new agents join. But I can print out a temporary copy from the computer if that would suffice. Have a seat, and I'll take care of that now."

The admin wandered into the back room, and Dara perused her phone while she waited. The longer she scrolled, the more depressed she became.

Not one text or email from clients, or even donors. Merry had effectively made her superfluous in both spaces—for the time being, at least.

"Here we go, Dara." The admin returned to the waiting room and handed her a manila envelope. "I blew it up to eight by ten, so you'd have a nice, clean copy for your files. We'll get the real one to you as soon as we can."

Just call me when it's ready, and I'll come pick it up, she typed. *I'll probably need another supply of Sold riders by then anyway.*

The admin read the missive and nodded. "Great. We're always happy to see our top agents."

Dara swallowed the urge to rip open the envelope right there in the office. Pulse racing, she carried the document to her car, where she could review it in private. This is what she needed. A photo of her assistant to show around, along with the pictures of her cohorts that Esther had left behind—all securely hidden in a locked drawer in her desk at home—so she could get the answers she needed. Take off for the city, meet Paisley Harwood's family, and find out why Merry was using their daughter's social security number. It wasn't much of a lead, but it was all she had right now.

Dara ran her finger against the seal, relishing the anticipation, and when she could no longer stand the wait, she slipped a fingernail underneath, tore it open, and pulled out the photocopy.

And then her jaw dropped...at least figuratively.

It was Meryl Rafter's license, all right, with the name and address of the correct real estate firm, but the picture was not Merry. Instead, an older schoolmarm-type, with a tight bun and a scolding expression, stared back at her from the page.

It was true agents didn't use their licenses very often, and placing photos on their business cards or For Sale signs was optional. Merry may have never needed to show the ID to anyone. And New York didn't require fingerprints for licensing the way New Jersey did. Dara supposed it was conceivable that anyone who possessed a fake driver's license and birth certificate or passport with their own photo, but reflecting the name of the person who had passed the real estate exam, could pose for the license picture. Especially someone who had Carl Vonderman, aka Carl the Copy, as part of their criminal team.

Another lead gone bad. Thank goodness Dara had one last trick up her sleeve. She revved up her new BMW's engine and headed for the mall. Best Buy would have exactly what she needed.

Chapter Twenty-Six

When Dara knocked on the door of 83 New Mill Road the next day, shopping bag in hand, her client Vivian Hunsicker met her with a hug and then escorted her into the dining room. On the table, amid a sea of garbage, were crystal glasses filled with homemade lemonade, complete with straws.

"Thank goodness you're okay, Dara. When we heard about the accident, Noah and I were devastated, absolutely devastated. How awful. But Meryl has been very communicative, and we're sure your absence has nothing to do with the fact we haven't sold the house yet...what do you think is stopping people from buying?"

Dara took another look around. It was clearly a hoarder's home and Vivian had done none of the decluttering she had recommended before they went on the market. Dara had hoped the dearth of properties in the neighborhood would guarantee a quick sale, in spite of the piles of papers, boxes, and collections filling every corner of the house. Now, the muddle played right into her plans.

"Viv, I can't imagine." To her surprise, her client seemed to comprehend every carefully uttered syllable. "That's why we're going to hold an open house this weekend, and I want you to hear everything people are thinking as they walk around. And that's why I brought these."

Dara reached into the shopping bag and pulled out three nanny cans, which she placed on the table, along with a supply of lithium-ion batteries. "These are going to record everything. We're going to place them in strategic areas of the home and then review them together next week. This one, disguised as a vase? I'd like that by the front door. This one looks like a cookie jar, so we'll put that in the kitchen. And this last one, the teddy bear? That will go in Bess's bedroom. Sound good?"

"That's a wonderful idea. I can't thank you enough."

Dara leaned in closer, as if imparting a secret. "There is one thing I'd like you to do for me. I know you're impressed with Merry's performance, and I'd like to capture how she handles clients so I can use that footage to train newer associates. If she realized we were taping her, she might get self-conscious, and then we wouldn't see the real Merry, would we? Could we keep the use and location of the nanny cams just between us?"

"Oh, I completely understand, Dara. I won't say a word. You can count on it. Now, let's get those buyers in here and get this place sold."

Once back in her car, Dara knew exactly what to text Merry. Nothing worked as well with that woman as praise and money. *Sorry for the short notice. Vivian Hunsicker called, upset New Mill hasn't sold. Begged for an open house this Sunday, 1-4 pm. Said she only trusted you to oversee it. I know the home's condition is a deterrent, so I'll increase your split to 35% if you find a buyer this weekend.*

The response took about a minute to appear, no doubt the amount of time it took Merry to figure out how to twist the knife deepest. *I promised Ava a trip to the zoo on Sunday, but we can do that early. I can be at New Mill by one. I'll post the OH right now on social media and call around the neighborhood to see if we can at least get some looky-loo action going.*

Ava to the zoo, eh? Dara pictured a stream of pleasant scenarios, which included a pack of escaping elephants trampling her assistant into the female equivalent of Flat Stanley, or a wayward crocodile swallowing her alive while Ava clapped with delight. The ring of her cell brought her back to the cold, harsh reality that her little girl was going to be sorely disappointed when her new friend was finally out of their lives for good.

The call was from her doctor's office, alerting her to a last-minute cancellation and asking if she could come in early to get her wires and arch bars removed. *Early? I'd be there yesterday if I could.* She parked her car at home and took an Uber to the office in case they needed to use anesthesia, and she'd be too dopey to drive herself home afterward. *One traumatic accident this lifetime was quite enough, thank you very much.*

The procedure took two hours and left her jaw still feeling tight. The nurse went over a series of exercises Dara needed to complete each day to increase oral mobility. She also recommended a soft diet for the next week or so. And that was that. Eight weeks of torture over in a single afternoon. Despite the late February chill, Dara waited outside for her return Uber, basking in the sun's rays and relishing the sweetest thing she'd experienced in months—the ability to speak and be understood. It was time to take back her life, and she had the perfect plan, ready to be set in motion.

Chapter Twenty-Seven

No one seemed more surprised than Merry when Dara asked her to remain in their home a little longer. If she wanted to, of course.

"Ava isn't good with transitions, and an abrupt departure may send her into a downward spiral. Plus, I may have to work late at AV over the next few weeks. And you know how much everyone loves your cooking. What do you say?"

"Well, I was looking forward to getting back to my life...there's a little someone in the wings, waiting, you know...but if I'm truly needed here, of course, I can stay a while longer," she replied, beaming.

A gamble? Perhaps. Merry's claws were already sunk into her family far too deep. But she needed her assistant to be completely at ease, unaware that anyone suspected her ruse. Would another few days of Merry's intrusion really make a difference? Especially when those days were going to help Dara reveal the woman for the sham she really was.

She slipped out early Sunday morning, citing an emergency at the Fortress, and headed over to New Mill, empty because Vivian and her family had flown to San Juan for a quickie weekend in the sun. She turned on each of the nanny cams, swung by the Fortress just in case anyone checked on her story, and then headed home.

While Merry held the open house on Sunday at New Mill, Dara dined with her family at one of Rock Canyon's most popular brunch spots, Eggs Over E Street. She and Jason enjoyed mimosas, and Ava got her favorite mocktail, a Shirley Temple. Even Khai seemed happy that things were finally getting back to normal. With Jason's surgery approved and scheduled for May, the family had every reason to celebrate. But Dara knew her real celebration would start the following day when she studied and printed out stills from the nanny cam footage that Merry was currently yet inadvertently providing.

The next morning, Merry appeared quite surprised to find Dara back in her own office, having unceremoniously dumped all of Merry's paperwork back on the desk she'd occupied prior to the accident. Nevertheless, if she had objections, she kept them to herself and instead handed Dara a manila envelope.

"Two offers, both from *my* open house," she said. "We'll have to figure out which is stronger. One is cash, with proof of funds. But it's slightly lower, and they plan to use Bennie, the Deal Killer, as a lawyer. So, we might want to go with the other deal, even if they are getting a mortgage. I called Vivian and explained everything, and naturally, she was thrilled. I just didn't mention the amount of the offers. I figured that was best for you to do."

"Great work," said Dara, determined to act as if unaware of Merry's machinations. "I've got an appointment this morning, but later, we'll parse these out, and you can call the lucky winner with the good news. Hold down the fort while I'm gone, okay?"

"That's all I've done for the last few months," answered Merry, dryly. "I think I can manage it for another hour or two."

Dara sped off, headed for New Mill Road. Vivian was so delighted about the offers, she didn't even ask to view the footage. Dara collected the nanny cams and returned to the quiet of her home study to review the contents of the SD memory cards.

She fast-forwarded past the footage taken before the open house commenced. Ah. There was Merry in all her glory, wearing a snug, low-cut, leopard-print sweater showing an inordinate amount of cleavage over pants so tight, they looked painted on. Dara wasn't sure if her assistant had dressed for an open house or a bordello. The clothing was secondary, though. What she needed was clear footage of Merry's face, and she got that in spades each time the assistant answered the door and then turned to begin a tour of the house. Dara stopped the footage repeatedly and printed out color stills to add to her dossier, already filled with pictures of Merry's cadre of accomplices.

Then, driven by curiosity about exactly how Merry had secured above-price offers for a hoarder's home that was clearly overpriced, Dara sat back and reviewed the rest of the footage from all three cameras.

She knew what she was hoping to see: Merry telling potential buyers that the sellers were desperate, that they should put in a lowball offer. Anything that revealed the sellers' motivation or indicated they would take less than asking would run contrary to her duties as a fiduciary—and give Dara an excuse to fire her. Or perhaps a visit from one of her partners in crime, mentioning something incriminating and exposing her end game vis-à-vis Dara and her family. But to her surprise, Merry did the exact opposite.

It was quite an eye-opening experience.

"Look past the clutter; it's actually working in your favor," she told one young couple whose disgusted expressions bespoke their horror at the home's condition. "This is an underpriced property in the county's best school district. There's literally nothing else available in the neighborhood. Consider the square footage, the architectural details, and the size of the plot. Once it's cleaned up, the value will shoot up, but that's something most less savvy buyers won't realize. This could be your big chance."

Dara blinked. Other than the school district talk, which actually violated fair housing rules, the rest of the pitch was perfect. And wouldn't you know it, right after their tour, the couple sat down at the dining room table and filled out an offer while Merry showed the house to the next group of guests—who also made an offer after she pointed out that the buyers before them were leaping at this opportunity.

It incensed Dara that she had to fire the best assistant she'd ever had. For a half-second, she wondered if perhaps she should ignore what she knew about Merry and just continue to employ her and reap the benefits. Having a second pair of competent hands meant almost twice the profit. That would go a long way toward paying off Jason's robotic prosthetics and the accompanying hospital bills.

Then she remembered the attack in the Fortress garage, the fake detective visit, the trumped-up leverage Merry held over her, the way Ava called her "Mommy," and she knew Merry had to go. Putting profit over family had gotten her into this mess in the first place.

Photos in hand, it was time to get on the road and see where it led.

Chapter Twenty-Eight

The next morning, Dara made herself a list of leads based on everything she'd learned either on her own, through Esther, and based on whatever Merry had shared with her, usually while tipsy, over the past few months.

Maisie's mom?

Paisley Harwood SS#

Extras Special

Brazen

Syracuse High School production of Chicago

Carl Vonderman, Jimmy Gordon, Tony Randazzo, Westminster Correctional

Two former marriages, two stepchildren—Tobias, dyslexic, Lina, UConn.
Pharma marketing.

At least a fraction of Merry's tall tales had to be true. The rest? That Dara needed to figure out. She doubted Merry had given her the real names of her stepkids and wished she could grab her assistant's phone and download their pictures to run through photo recognition software. How could she ever pull that off?

Dara paid a visit to Esther to hand her some ammunition and discover if the investigative assistant had learned any more about Merry and her cohorts. They met at the condo she had once shared with Brooke. Dara immediately noticed the widow's garb—still black—and her gaunt face, mourning apparently continuing to dull her appetite. She also noticed a change in the condo's décor—far more minimalist, as if Esther had tossed anything that reminded her of her late wife. Even the large Limoges sugar bowl she'd gifted the couple no longer sat at the center of the dining table. Probably represented too painful a memory.

"I had to switch it up," Esther explained after Dara surveyed the room. "So many ghosts. It was either that or move, and who knows better than you that there's nothing out there I could afford on my own. At least we paid this place off."

Dara nodded and reached for one of the macarons Esther had laid out. "I was wondering if you'd been following Merry around or turned up anything else on any of her friends."

"I did try to visit you a couple of times, but that bitch would never let me in."

"Probably for the best," Dara replied. "For all I know, she has the place bugged."

"Why would she do that? Do you think she joined AV and got rid of Brooke to get closer to you?"

"Got rid of...Are you thinking that it wasn't a suicide? That Merry murdered Brooke?"

"I have my suspicions but no real proof. Not yet, anyway."

While Dara wasn't about to tarnish Brooke's name by mentioning the embezzlement, she certainly didn't mind Esther nosing into Merry's past and had no compunction about raising suspicion. Let Esther turn what looked like a suicide into a homicide case, as long as it put Merry away for a long time.

"I know you're still hurting, and this investigation can't be making things easier, but anything you could find out would be helpful. She's managed to stick her fingers in every aspect of my business and family life, and it makes me uncomfortable...What did you stop by that day to tell me?"

"It was really more of a question. I was hoping you had the social security number that Merry used when she filled out her employment application."

"Way ahead of you. I ran it through the system at our office. Came up completely phony, I'm afraid."

Dara had no problem getting intel from Esther but wasn't about to furnish her with any of her leads. This investigation, and its aftermath, were things she wanted to take care of on her own.

"Don't you run background checks before hiring?"

Dara shrugged. "Not usually for independent contractors or assistants. We only use the social security numbers for end-of-year tax reporting. She must have figured that out somehow. However, maybe this will help. It's one of the reasons I came over today." Dara pulled a nine-by-twelve-inch manila envelope from her purse. "This is a blow-up of the photo that appeared on Merry's real estate license. It's definitely not Merry."

Esther opened the envelope and glanced at the printout. "No, it most definitely is not. I'll run this through the same program I used for the others and see what name comes up. To answer your initial question, I haven't found out anything more. Once you had the accident, Merry's only trips outside the home were to take care of you and your family—go to the supermarket, the pharmacy, your office, the Fortress. She pretty much devoted herself to your recovery."

"That's admirable…I guess."

"It's more than I expected from her, I'll tell you that."

"On another note, Esther, I wanted to know if Brooke kept paper copies of any of the files in AV's computer. I need to find the name of a woman who attended a BPA event with her daughter, Maisie, but the spreadsheets have mysteriously disappeared."

Esther paused for a moment, and sadness clouded her expression. "I haven't gone through any of her private papers—I just couldn't bring myself to do it up to now—but I think there may be a box of files in the bedroom. I'll get them for you."

Dara squeezed Esther's arm in solidarity as she departed and then scrolled through her phone as she waited. The usual spam emails, an offer on her listing on Locust Court. Finally, a thank you note from Vivian indicating she wanted to take the lower of the two offers, specifically because it was cash, and that meant she wouldn't have to clean up the house for an appraiser's visit. *So much for Merry leaving it to me to help her evaluate the offers.*

She looked up when Esther re-entered the room, lugging a cardboard lateral file. "This is all I could find. Could you take a look for what you need while you're here? I don't want anything of Brooke's leaving the condo until I've finished conducting my inquiry into her death. Plus, I want to hold onto every part of her that I can."

"Of course, Esther, I completely understand...the note she left on her cell...I'm sure you dusted the phone for prints?"

"Yeah, no prints but hers. But that hardly means anything. Anyone with half a brain would use a stylus or wear gloves while faking a suicide note."

"Yes, that makes sense." Dara opened the file and thumbed through the folders. She found one labeled "Party Attendance" and scanned through the spreadsheets inside. She wasn't sure if Maisie's mom had attended a party earlier than the one where they met, but anything was possible.

Sure enough, there was a Maisie who attended the very first BPA party back in the summer. Dara ran her fingernail across from the child's name to the parents' information. The mother was listed as Ivy Andrews, but true to Dara's luck, Ivy had included neither an email nor phone number, just an address. Luckily, it wasn't far from Paisley Harwood's parents' home on the Upper East Side.

"Thanks, Esther, this is exactly what I needed." She took a photo of the attendance sheet with her phone and tucked the sheet neatly back into the lateral file. "I have to take off for the city, follow up on a lead regarding a possible project. Will you text me if you find out anything about the woman in that photo?"

"Oh, you can count on it, Dara," she said with a weak smile. "Whatever scam Merry's pulling, I'm going to put an end to it, even if it kills *me*."

Dara sincerely hoped that wouldn't be necessary.

Chapter Twenty-Nine

B ack in her car, Dara again perused her list. Three of the leads were located in Manhattan—Maisie's mom, Paisley Harwood's family, and Brazen. It seemed the most logical place to start.

She took off for the city, practicing her jaw exercises and singing along to Billy Joel on the radio. A Merry-less future loomed on the horizon and that filled her with optimism and excitement for the future. Soon, Jason would have his operation and be back to his former self. Ava's improved speech, thanks to Attwood, had translated into fewer meltdowns. Khai had researched potential colleges where he could major in animation and video game creation. All milestones that had been the result of *her* efforts, not Merry's. She had helped her family heal, and now, with this investigation, she was going to inoculate them from future harm.

In less than an hour, she reached the city and parked her car in an underground garage, deciding that with multiple stops, Ubers and taxis would be an easier way to deal with the dearth of street parking in the city. Bracing against the chill, she trudged south to the rundown brownstone on East 74th Street that Ivy Andrews had listed in the Autism Vanguard records. Dara rang the buzzer, identified herself, and entered once Ivy rang her in.

The four-floor climb, with its peeling paint and occasional missing lightbulbs, was the hardest workout Dara had endured since prior to the accident. She found herself panting by the time she reached 4J. Ivy stood by the open door and welcomed her inside. The apartment smelled of meat sauce, its furnishings, early Sears. Maisie bounced around on the couch in the center of the room, singing along with Grover, whose voice blared from the television. Ivy beckoned Dana to join her in the far quieter kitchen and asked if she wanted a cup of coffee or tea.

"I'm good," Dara responded, inviting her to sit in the chair opposite. "I don't want to take up your valuable time. The last time we met, you said something that intrigued me, and I wanted to know more. Specifically, you mentioned something about your wedding cake debacle and how my assistant was involved. You said at that time, she was known by a different name than Meryl Rafter. I was wondering what that name was."

"Oh, now I have a bigger bone to pick regarding your co-worker than just the cake thing. You weren't at the January BPA event, right?"

"No, I'm afraid I had a car crash and was out of commission for a few months."

"I'm sorry, but you're apparently better now, yes?"

Dara nodded. "Yes, happy to say I'm currently operating at one hundred percent."

"That's wonderful. Because in your absence, your "Merry" spotted me at the January party and avoided me all night. Not that I was going to create a commotion or incite an incident or anything. I just wanted Maisie to have a fun time. But for whatever reason, my invitation never arrived for February, and I'm guessing it won't show up for March, either. At first, I figured maybe you didn't run them in the winter months because of possible weather issues. But then I saw the pictures in the paper—"

"Paper? What pictures? What paper?"

"The Times ran a whole feature about BPA after the January party. You didn't know? Wait, I think I kept it...hang on."

Dara waited, fuming, while in the next room, Grover philosophized over the airways that "Where there's life, there's hope." Her hope—that she could curtail the damage her assistant had caused—had begun to dwindle.

Ivy scurried back, tabloid in hand. "It was on the front page of the lifestyle section. You're welcome to keep this."

She spread the newspaper out on the kitchen table. Dara stared at the photos. It was great publicity, and she wondered why no one had mentioned it. Then she remembered how Merry had sequestered her cell, apparently for more than keeping her from dialing out. Her assistant hadn't wanted her to see any incoming messages either. All of which had mysteriously disappeared by the time she received her phone back.

The pictures celebrated children in attendance and their parents, along with the special amenities that AV provided to those on the spectrum, such as the bubble tubes and the beanbag chairs. There wasn't one picture of Merry—no surprise there—but she was the only spokesperson quoted in the story. "We thought this, we added that..." Anyone reading it would think Dara Banks had no part in the project whatsoever.

Dara sunk her nails into her palms, determined not to let her rage destroy the rest of the interview. She needed to get Ivy's information before proceeding further.

"The only reason I mention the story is because it made me realize BPA had held a party and had excluded my daughter. I'm thinking it's because your Merry recognized me and didn't want me badmouthing her to the press, or to the other parents."

It also explained why the invitation and attendance documents had mysteriously vanished from the AV computer files.

Dara had seen enough. She folded the paper and stuck it in her purse. "I'm back in charge now, and I promise that not only will Maisie be invited to all future events, but you'll also both attend free of charge."

"That's not really necessary..."

"It is. It's the least I can do. Omitting you was inexcusable. It's another reason I need to remove Merry from our charity. Your information will help. If I can prove she's operating under a pseudonym..."

"Oh, she is. She used to call herself Amoret Prager, the Cake Queen. She'd write to folks after the local papers announced their engagement, offering a discounted wedding cake. When you responded, it turned out the discount was for a single tier. Every additional tier was $1,000 more. Ours was six tiers. Our wedding planner assured us it was a good deal because the bakery would have charged us more. But of course, the bakery might have provided a cake that was all cake, not fake."

"I don't suppose you have any promotional material she might have mailed out. Anything with a phone number or return address?"

Ivy lowered her eyes. "I'm afraid not. Just the phone call and the planner's nod. She must have had every wedding organizer in town on her payroll—why else such a glowing recommendation? And she only accepted cash, so I never had the receipt she promised she'd send. Which meant I couldn't prove anything when I complained to the Better Business Bureau."

"How about the name of your planner?" asked Dara, still hopeful.

"That I can give you—Hollis Rose. He was excellent—except for this one little glitch. I guess anyone can be taken in by a fast talker. Maybe the other brides never noticed the sheet cakes in the kitchen. My caterer was a friend, and that's how I knew."

I'm so sorry this happened to you," said Dara. "If it's any consolation, I'm going to find out this woman's real identity and why she does what she does. When this all comes down, if there's any money she's sitting on, I'm going to make sure you get your $6,000 back."

Maisie ran in, holding an empty juice box, crying, "More, More."

Dara took that as her cue to leave. She'd gotten what she'd come for—a name. And a lead she hadn't expected. This was starting to look like a particularly good day.

Chapter Thirty

From Ivy's apartment, a quick cab drive uptown brought Dara to the Harwood residence on 84th and Park. It made more sense, at least initially, to speak with someone from whom Merry had stolen a social security number than with former colleagues, like Hollis Rose or the folks at Brazen, who might or might not still be in touch.

The Harwood's apartment building was a world apart from what she had seen on 74th Street. Marble floors, chandeliers, door attendants, and elevator operators. Paisley was definitely growing up in style.

She wasn't quite sure how to have the door attendant announce her, so she went old school.

"Please tell them it's Dara Crawford Banks of the Locust Valley Crawfords and the Alpine, New Jersey Banks." When in doubt, prestige usually sealed the deal.

The elevator attendant dropped her off on sixteen, the door opening right onto the Harwoods' private floor. Like the building, the apartment reeked of opulence, a mixture of contemporary and antique, with a Picasso here, a Rembrandt there, a teal balloon dog sculpture by Jeff Koons on a pedestal against a third wall. Unlike Dara's parents, the Harwoods were definitely unapologetic about their wealth. At first glance, they wallowed in it.

A housekeeper greeted Dara at the elevator, helped her off with her coat, and escorted her into the library. She perused the bookcases while she waited, finding them stacked with classics and medical journals. When Chiara Harwood joined her, tall, blonde, and dressed in a beige silk blouse and navy wool pants, Dara wondered how to address her.

155

"Uh, Dr. Harwood?"

"I wish," she said with a smile. "No, my husband is Dr. Harwood. Just call me Chiara. I don't believe we've met, but I have heard of your parents."

She led Dara to a gold Louis XIV, carved-walnut, high-backed sofa and invited her to sit. "Would you like some coffee or perhaps a glass of wine?"

Chiara's welcoming demeanor contrasted sharply with the stiffness of the sofa's cushions, as uncomfortable as the situation. "That's very kind, but I'm afraid I'm not here on a social call."

Chiara crinkled her nose. "Well, how can I help you?"

"I don't really know how to put this. I sell real estate up north in Rock Canyon, and I've hired a woman as an assistant who gave me her social security number for tax purposes. I admit it was wrong of me not to run a background check at the time, but when I did, the number didn't belong to her."

Chiara tilted her head. "I'm confused. What does that have to do with me?"

"The number she used belongs to your daughter, Paisley."

Chiara's eyes grew wide. "How can that be? We got that number for her when she was born, but she's only ten. She hasn't ever used it."

"I thought as much. I'm wondering if you knew the woman that gave me the number. Maybe that would help us figure out how she gained access to it. I have her photo here."

Dara pulled a folder from her tote bag and handed Chiara the picture she'd printed from the nanny cam footage. "When she came to me, she had longer hair pulled back in a chignon, so please try to picture her with a different style."

Chiara's face clouded over, and she handed back the photo. "Would you please excuse me for a moment?" She rose and strode away quickly.

Dara heard angry murmurs from the next room, and her stomach dropped. Something had gone terribly wrong. Merry's face stared up at her from the photo, as if gloating. *Not as easy as you thought, huh, Dara?*

The housekeeper hurried back into the room, Dara's coat in hand.

"Mrs. Banks, I'm afraid you'll have to leave now. Mrs. Harwood has nothing further she wants to say, other than she wishes you reporters would stop harassing her."

Dara's skin prickled, and she leapt from the sofa. "Reporter? What are you talking about?"

The housekeeper brusquely handed her the coat and waited while she put it on. "Hurry, please. I don't want to call Security, but I will if I need to."

"Just one second, please. Can I at least get my bag?"

What exactly was going on here? Dara desperately needed to know. She stashed Merry's photo back into its folder, pushed it into her tote, and fumbled for her purse. She crumpled a hundred-dollar bill and slipped it to the woman who now practically pushed her toward the elevator.

"Please," she whispered. "This is not for any story. This woman is trying to destroy my life, and I have to know who she is."

The woman's expression softened. She looked at the bill and then back at Dara.

"I get off at six, and I sometimes grab some pasta at Home Kitchen for dinner." The woman's voice was so low, Dara barely caught the restaurant's name. Then she nodded and got into the elevator.

"She's not to be readmitted, Quenton. Mrs. Harwood's orders," the housekeeper said as the doors closed.

Dara stared at the elevator operator, sensing an opportunity. "What's going on here? Is Chiara Harwood out of her mind? All I wanted was the name of this woman." She reached for the folder and pulled out Merry's picture again.

Quenton took a peek, then flinched before he faced forward again.

"I wouldn't go showing that picture around here." A slight Irish brogue laced his words. "Especially around Mrs. Harwood."

Dara had finally found what apparently was a hot lead, and all doors were being shut in her face, both physically and figuratively. She found herself frantic for an answer.

"Why? Who is this woman? What did she do?"

The doors opened at the lobby level, where three people waited to enter. Quenton gestured with his head toward the lobby exit and murmured so quietly, Dara could hardly hear:

"That woman killed Mrs. Harwood's best friend. Please don't come back here again."

Chapter Thirty-One

Merry murdered Chiara Harwood's best friend?

Dara lingered in the foyer, dazed, watching the elevator doors close and attempting to process the accusation, when the door attendant shot her a nasty look. She'd clearly been labeled a pariah by either Chiara Harwood or her housekeeper, probably both. She hastened out of the building and back onto Park Avenue before another employee could escort her away.

An unexpected snow shower left Dara colder than the reception she'd just encountered chez Harwood. Staring downward to avoid the flakes clinging to her lashes, she wandered east, searching for refuge to digest what she'd just learned. Once she hit Second, she ensconced herself in a small coffee shop and ordered a hot cocoa, something to sweeten the sour taste left by the morning's encounter.

Merry was many things: a con artist, a home wrecker. But a murderer? Esther had hinted at as much—that her assistant could be responsible for Brooke's death—but Dara had chalked the accusation up to grief, a way of dealing with her own culpability in the suicide. Quenton's accusation was more concrete, a revelation she had not fully considered. And Dara had left her alone with her stepchildren. Her blood chilled. Should she rush home and throw the woman out?

No, she rationalized. She probably attacks only when she feels intimidated. Right now, there was nothing threatening her. As far as she knew, she was in the catbird seat, ruling over Dara's roost while the woman of the house and the office was away. If anything, her family was never safer than now.

159

If she left the city, quit the investigation, she'd have no leverage, nothing to use to threaten Merry and force her out of their lives. She needed to stay through dinner and get the information the Harwood housekeeper might provide.

While she sipped her hot chocolate, she debated which of the leads on her Plan B list to approach next. Brazen, where Merry used to dance and carouse with mobsters? Or the wedding planner Ivy Andrews had worked with? She took out her phone and googled contact information for the latter.

"Hello, is this Hollis Rose?"

"You got him, honey. What do you need?"

At this point, Dara knew better than to mention anything regarding Merry upfront.

"I'm only in town for the day, but I want to discuss a wedding. I'm over at Madame Bonte's on Second. Do you know where that is?"

"I'm just leaving Fleurissimo's on 86th. I can be there in ten. Do we have a date?"

"Sounds great. I'm wearing a yellow floral sweater and navy skirt, sitting along the left side of the café."

"You won't be able to miss me, doll. I'll see you soon."

True to his word, there was no missing Hollis Rose. Dara had looked up photos while she waited, and he was just as colorful and flamboyant in person as his online persona. It was as if Cinna from The Hunger Games had come to life and decided that rainbow was his favorite color. Dara was sure Lenny Kravitz never would have worn a purple suit with a matching fedora and a pink and yellow polka-dotted shirt, but on Hollis, it worked.

Being Manhattan, the arrival of this outrageously dressed man didn't evoke even a side glance from their jaded fellow diners.

"Hello, gorgeous." He hung his trench on the back of his chair. "I can already see you in a mermaid trumpet gown with a plunging neckline...and maybe a string of rhinestones woven through that beautiful 'do of yours. What do you think?"

Dara smiled. What a pleasant change of pace from what she'd encountered already that day. Hopefully, what she planned to ask wouldn't alter his mood.

The server brought over a menu.

"What can I get you? My treat," said Dara.

"Oh, I never turn down a free meal." He quickly perused the offerings and turned to the server. "I'll have the smoked salmon tartine and a Honey Oat Latte. Thanks very much."

He focused again on Dara. "So, let's talk shop. When's the wedding? Who's the lucky man?"

"I'm afraid I owe you an apology if I misled you. It's not my wedding I want to talk about. I need information, and I'm very willing to pay you for your time. What do you charge an hour?"

To his credit, the warm expression never left Hollis's face. It was as if he lived in a permanent state of optimism. "I charge two hundred dollars an hour, but let's cut that to a buck fifty since you're treating for breakfast. What do you need to know? I love to dish."

This was encouraging. The tension in Dara's shoulders loosened. "I understand you oversaw a wedding several years ago for Ivy Andrews and her husband, Xander?"

Hollis looked up, chewing his lower lip. "Brunette? Size ten…princess gown. I told her she'd look better in something sleeker—a sheath with a bateau neckline, but she insisted. She didn't wear it, it wore her, but some people never listen. What about her? Did she take a look at her wedding photos and decide she wanted a redo?"

"Uh, no, nothing like that. She gave you top marks. I'm here because she mentioned you recommended the woman who provided her cake. Amoret Prager?"

The mention of the baker finally wiped the perpetual smile from Hollis's face. "Oh please, that woman, that woman. I'll never do that again."

"Do what?"

"Subcontract to someone without sampling their product first. She came highly recommended by someone who knew someone who knew someone, you know?" He leaned closer and lowered his voice. "I was told she had sponsors who were connected…and it was in my best interest to use her."

Connected. Not the first time Dara had heard this. Tony Randazzo, her Detective Frank Contardi impersonator, was supposedly involved with the mob. A friendship with far-reaching benefits from her time at Brazen?

"She worked with many wedding planners, from what I understand."

Hollis's lips puckered. "You writing a story? I'll tell you anything you want to know because that bitch could have destroyed my reputation. But it's all off the record. I don't need someone throwing a Molotov cocktail through my office window."

Dara shook her head. "No story. I just want to know everything you can tell me about her."

The server brought Hollis's meal, and they remained quiet until he walked out of earshot.

"I don't know a lot, I'm afraid." He bit into his tartine. "She just kind of appeared on the scene one day. The "it" baker. No one ever mentioned she substituted fake tiers and sheet cake for the real thing. Charged them a ton, too. My brides rarely challenge the costs, you know? That's why I love working Manhattan's celebrity circuit. Open purses, anything to impress. Ivy was the first and really the only bride to complain."

All this was old news. "And after those complaints…what happened to Amoret?"

"One day, she just disappeared. Poof. Next thing I heard, her "twin sister" had taken a job as a nanny somewhere on the Upper West Side. And then she married the father, a wannabe politician and widower with a trio of kids. She didn't even hire me to handle the wedding, that *beotch*. But who cares? I was thrilled I didn't have to risk my rep by referring her anymore."

Twin sister? Right. Sure. A widower with kids? Could one of those kids have been friends with Paisley Harwood?

"Do you know what name she started using?"

Hollis pursed his lips. "No, I'm sorry. I don't remember."

Dara sipped the rest of her cocoa, paid the check, and pulled two one-hundred-dollar bills from her purse. "I have another appointment, but you've been so helpful. I hope this makes up for the disappointment of missing out on a potential client."

He reached into his pocket and pulled out a bunch of business cards. "Take these. A beautiful woman like you must know lots of friends embarking on a second or third marriage. Make sure they know I offer discounts for repeat offenders—if you know what I mean. Something to take the bite out of the heartache of that last divorce."

Dara stashed the cards in her tote. "If I hear of anyone, you'll be the first person I call."

Chapter Thirty-Two

Dara realized she had research to do, an excellent way to kill time before her meeting with Chiara Harwood's housekeeper later that afternoon. Extensive googling on her cell phone would be murder on her eyes, though. Since the snow squall had ended, at least for the moment, she wrapped her coat tight and slogged south to the Yorkville Library on nearby 79th Street.

The turn-of-the-century, beige-stone building with its Palladian-inspired architecture awaited, and she nestled into a corner cubicle where no one could stare over her shoulder at the computer screen. Dara entered "Chiara Harwood" into the search bar, and, as she suspected, found numerous photos of the surgeon's wife, her luxurious vacations abroad, and her charitable efforts scattered throughout gossip sites like TMZ and Gawker.

The photographs featured Chiara alone or posing with her tall and stylishly dressed husband and occasionally, her daughter Paisley. Dara sighed, hoping the younger Harwood would escape the world of forced sacrifice that she'd lived through.

After twenty minutes of fruitless web browsing, the term "Chiara Harwood funeral" brought up the intel for which she'd been hunting. The jetsetter was one of the more prominent mourners at the service for the late Samantha Ellingsworth, wife of renowned Manhattan attorney, Harry Ellingsworth. Dara read through the piece and then googled all she could find on the late socialite.

Former attorney at Davis & Milliken. Condo on the Upper West Side. Three children, with twins born a decade later than the first, each admitted to the elite Harrison Preparatory School. A Page Six series of articles from the New York Post mentioned divorce and scandal, but without substantive detail. Finally, the newsflash about Samantha Ellingsworth leaping in front of the 2 train just prior to Thanksgiving six years back.

That was news, thought Dara, mournful at the thought of anyone taking their own life but relieved the elevator operator's allegations had been hyperbole. Merry hadn't "murdered" Samantha per se, but personal experience made Dara suspect the socialite *had* been pushed, if only figuratively so. She needed more background.

She googled Harry Ellingsworth. Net worth $4 billion, a combination of inheritance and earnings as a renowned mergers and acquisitions attorney. Unsuccessful state senate candidate. Children Nikki and later, Daniel and Veronica. Divorce never finalized until his wife's suicide. *Yeah, that would make it pretty final.*

Remarried only months later to society newcomer Felicity Prager. *Aha!* Amoret's supposed twin sister. The pseudonym would certainly ward off any unfortunate suspicions should Harry google his fiancée. No wedding pictures online. *Natch.* That was Merry's M.O.

There were photos of the children, however. Daniel and Veronica— around six at the time—Dara didn't recognize. But she was pretty certain that the third, Nikki, resembled a younger version of Merry's beloved stepdaughter "Lina," whose photo she'd flaunted whenever Dara felt most despondent about her own stepchildren. The once wayward girl who'd graduated from UConn and was now supposedly in pharma marketing.

Merry had claimed "Lina" was from her second marriage. Whom had she married prior? Or was that a fabrication as well?

So many names—it made Dara lightheaded. She took a moment to digest what she already knew.

Manhattan socialites Harry and Samantha married, had Nikki/Lina and the twins. Six years ago, Harry attempted to divorce Samantha and, once widowed, married Merry, aka Felicity/Amoret aka Merry. Meanwhile, Samantha's bestie, Chiara Harwood, and her husband had Paisley and … what was the name of the big sister? She googled the news article she'd read a while back. Ah, yes. Alana. Perhaps Alana had been around Nikki's/Lina's age, and the two girls had been friends. If she had been as wayward as Merry claimed, maybe she could have helped her new stepmom steal Paisley's social security card. All wild speculation, but at this point, it was all Dara had.

She continued researching Harry Ellingsworth. All that remained was a short mention on Page Six of the lawyer's divorce from his wife, Felicity, after three years of marriage. That would have left her single for a bit and then free to venture north to Rock Canyon. *Right into my lap. Lucky me.*

So that was it. Merry wormed her way into a family somehow and pushed out the wife, married the husband, then divorced the husband, and made off with the settlement. That was certainly what she was trying to pull with Dara. But gaps still existed, ones she needed to fill.

She annotated her list of leads.

~~*Maisie's mom?*~~ Real name Ivy Andrews. Provided name of Amoret Prager and wedding planner Hollis Rose. Hollis provided the name of Amoret's "twin sister," Felicity Prager. Later Felicity Ellingsworth. Once divorced, aka Meryl/Merry Rafter.

~~*Paisley Harwood SS#*~~ Led to mom Chiara Harwood and her other daughter, Alana Harwood.

Extras Special: Check to see if this actually exists. Speak to owner?

Brazen: Might still warrant pursuing.

Syracuse High School production of Chicago. Worth a trip?

Carl Vonderman, Jimmy Gordon, Tony Randazzo, Westminster Correctional

Two former marriages, two stepchildren—Tobias, dyslexic, ~~Lina, UConn, Pharma marketing~~. Real name Nikki Ellingsworth, Harry's daughter, Merry's stepdaughter.

Dara checked her phone messages and email. Nothing of import. Not surprising since Merry had practically taken over her real estate practice. What now? She still had a few hours to kill before dinner with Chiara's housekeeper, if she did indeed show up. Who to speak with next?

Dara googled Brazen, the gentlemen's club where a tipsy Merry had admitted to working. Down on 28th Street, all the way on the west side.

Still in operation but not open until 7 p.m. If she did go, it would have to be after speaking to the housekeeper.

Maybe Nikki Ellingsworth? Surely, she would be faster to give up something on her ex-stepmom than Harry, who might be bitter over an expensive divorce and, therefore, more reluctant to agree to a meeting.

Dara searched on Facebook where she found scores of entries, but none with information leading to "the" Nikki she needed. *Damn.* She tried Instagram. Still nothing definitive. She turned to LinkedIn. Pay dirt. Nikki Ellingsworth, Pharma Marketing Account Exec at Mitterhof Pharma. *Score!* Location: Westminster County. Right across the river from Rock Canyon. But clearly, not somewhere she could visit today.

Nearly out of options to kill time, Dara searched for Extras Special and found a single web page announcing "Extras for your sacred and special events." She punched the number into her cell, but the call went straight to an out-of-order message. A fake website, put up solely for her benefit if she'd thought to seek a reference before hiring Merry? She bet someone would have answered that number if she'd called a year ago, but now? No need.

Unwilling to give up, she searched for *Casting Companies* and *Extras Agencies-Manhattan*. Jackpot. It was fascinating to review the list of possible jobs these organizations advertised. About half required SAG/AFTRA credentials, but the remainder were non-union. It seemed like an uncomplicated way to pick up anywhere from $50-$150 for a day's work, but then again, considering Merry's cake haul, it would have been too low a payday unless she used those weddings and funerals to target her next mark.

Dara narrowed her search to "Professional Mourners" and up popped SideHustlesforNYActors.com or SHNYA. The jobs listed ranged from professional mourners and wedding guests to being a "standardized patient" for medical students looking for bodies to practice on. *Promising.* Plus, she had time for a visit to their midtown location. Dara pulled out her eight-by-ten of Merry and snapped a picture on her cellphone. Then she packed up her things and grabbed a taxi heading south.

SHNYA's low-lit, dingy waiting room teemed with types ranging from overweight housewives to hipsters to teenagers who looked like they were playing hooky from high school to pick up a few bucks. Dara grabbed an intake clipboard and pen from the harried receptionist and located the room's only empty chair. Wedged between a little person and a bearded Willie Nelson-wannabe who smelled like sneakers left out in the rain, she completed the form. It not only asked questions about her height, weight, and gender, but also her range of interests and hobbies. *Gotta be able to fit in and converse with the crowd.*

She listed her look as "society matron/debutante," her interests as "charity work" and "cocktail parties" and handed in her form. To her surprise, the receptionist ushered her into the casting director's office shortly afterwards. The room reeked of mold, thanks to Sneakers-in-the-Rain Guy, whose interview had preceded hers. She prayed she'd be able to make it through the discussion without gagging.

The cocaine-thin guy behind the desk, whose name plate read Oliver Smith, loudly blew his nose into an overused tissue as she took the seat opposite. His sparse combover only accentuated his encroaching baldness. His cobra smile caused her flesh to prickle.

"We don't get many like you around here," Oliver started, revealing a slight Eastern European accent. "I think we could make a lot of money together." He looked down at her application and then back up at her chest. "Especially if there's no…Mr. Bannon?"

The numbers clicked into place. This was *that* kind of extras agency.

Ignoring the question, Dara asked what the job involved.

"It's simple…if you know what you're doing. Someone dies, you have between one day and one week to study up, find out as much as you can about their family, friends, life. You decide where they know you from, but that could change depending on the person you're speaking to. If you're talking to a colleague, then you're a college friend. If you're talking to a former roommate, you know the deceased from work. Hardly rocket science. Occasionally, we have guys who hire beautiful or provocatively dressed women to show up at their funerals and say nothing. Keep 'em all guessing. A final poke in the ribs from the dearly departed."

168

"I see," said Dara, feeling like a ladybug who'd accidentally wandered into a roach motel.

"For weddings, it's pretty much the same, but usually with more lead time and a nicer dress. What are you, size four? We provide the wardrobe, but judging by your outfit, I'm thinking you wouldn't need our help."

She squirmed uncomfortably, sensing him imagining what lay underneath the garments as well.

"Political rallies, we do far more of them than we used to. Size seems to be all that matters to those clients these days, and luckily, there's almost no prep. Just pretend you're a sheep. Do what everyone else does—chant the candidate's name, applaud when the others do. Hold up a banner. If you're on camera, smile and be extra bubbly. But you…I think you could get the more expensive gigs. The sexy woman at the cocktail party, fawning over the visiting celebrity or high-powered exec. You'd be perfect for that."

Dara sensed an opening and grabbed it.

"Yes, my friend said those jobs paid the best. Is that true?"

Oliver broke into a lecherous grin, no doubt assuming he'd hit her sweet spot. "We have a sliding scale, depending on the client's D&B credit report. For the lonely businessmen gigs, if they extend…overnight…you could be looking at an easy couple thousand. Less our thirty-five percent cut of course…who's your friend?"

Dara pulled out her phone and scrolled to the photo of Merry she'd captured. "She goes by a couple of different names; you know how it is"

He nodded. Of course, he understood. Who was going to use their real name around here? She certainly hadn't.

She handed him the cell. He raised his eyebrows, his lips turning downwards, and squirmed like a rat lost in a maze.

"You're friends with…Excuse me for saying this, but you don't look like the type to be mixed up with someone like Sally Malone."

"What do you mean?" Dara feigned indignance. She'd stumbled onto something important and wanted to milk the intel for all it was worth.

"You know what I'm saying. Connected." He lowered his voice so no one in the adjoining room could hear. "Again, I mean no offense. If you're associated with these people, you'll get whatever job you want as often as you want. I don't need any trouble around here. Randazzo already gets a piece. There's more than enough to go around, you know?"

Bingo.

"Tony Randazzo, you mean?" Good old Detective Frank Contardi.

"Nah, haven't seen him for ages. Not since the thing went down. Still work with his dad, Vinny. Though Bernardo manages the weekly collections. I pay on time, every time. Again, I don't need any problems."

"The thing?"

Oliver's shoulders stiffened. "You're her friend, and you don't know?"

Time to regroup. Quickly.

"*I'm* not connected. I knew her superficially and we've lost touch. Last time we spoke, she was working here. Then life happened. I met someone, left town. When that fell apart, I did the rounds and ended up back here. My bank account's a little low and I remembered she mentioned this place as somewhere you could make good money."

Oliver's body relaxed. The nonsense she'd just sprouted apparently made sense.

"Well, the way I heard it, there was a huge blow-up between Vinny and Tony, and it had something to do with Sally. Then she disappeared. So did he. I figured she was encased in cement someplace, part of the foundation of the Mario Cuomo Bridge. But there was no way Vinny was going to off his own son, no matter whose snatch he'd gotten into, excuse my language. I'm sure he's out there somewhere...but if Sally is still alive, she'd better not ever let Vinny know because he'll turn her into worm meat before she can open those legs again."

"I...I didn't know. Wow." She lowered her eyes in mock mourning, then raised her gaze again. "How long did she work for you?"

Oliver squinted at the ceiling. "I'm thinking, maybe two years before she went AWOL. She was extremely popular, too. It was a loss, for sure. But you...you could really be the next Sally Malone. Even if you're not with Randazzo, the offer stands. You could be pulling in seven, eight thou a week if you're willing to do what it takes."

Dara tamped down a shiver of disgust. There but for the grace of God and all that. "It sounds good. I just need to take care of a few things and then get back to you, okay?"

Oliver blinked when she rose to leave. Girls must not turn him down very often, especially in the face of a quick and easy payday.

"Don't think too long," he warned. "I heard a rumor the mayor isn't going to make it into next week, and they're going to need a ton of mourners at his funeral."

Now it was Dara's turn to blink. "I hadn't heard the mayor was ill."

"He isn't," Oliver smirked.

Chapter Thirty-Three

It was nearly five when Dara escaped from SHYNA's office, desperate for a shower to wash away the ick. There was still an hour before the appointment with Chiara's housekeeper at Home Kitchen, and rush-hour traffic filled the dimly lit streets, making it difficult to find a cab back uptown. She contemplated taking the subway when her cell phone rang.

"Da, it's Esther. What's all that noise?"

She raised her voice to be heard over the din. "It's a siren. I had to commute into the city for a meeting. What's up?"

"I got the information on that photo you gave me from Merry's license."

"That's great. Who is she?"

"Someone from up in Syracuse, of all places. I'm going to text you the name and last address she registered with the DMV. I ran it through my computers and there's no criminal record, just a match on the driver's license. Maybe an actor Merry found to impersonate her. Anyway, just wanted to make sure you have it."

"Perfect. You're a lifesaver, Esther. Any other news on your front?"

"I've been trying to determine the whereabouts of the three guys I saw her with. We're so busy at the station, it's been hard to find the time, but I'll keep plugging along. It's the least I can do for Brooke. And it's something to keep my mind off how empty the condo seems now."

"I'm glad that, in some small way, this investigation is helping. I'll see what I can find out about this other woman. We'll get to the bottom of this together. Thanks again."

Well, that was something. Another lead. From Syracuse. That's where Merry claimed she'd grown up. Maybe someone from her youth.

Dara now had plenty of intel on her assistant, but between the Ellingsworth marriage, her time at Brazen, her relationship with the Randazzos, her wedding cake business, her time posing as a fake mourner/wedding guest but really as an escort with SHNYA—how did it all tie together? Exactly what was Merry up to before she came to Rock Canyon? She needed something she could use to draw a timeline. Maybe a restaurant napkin would suffice.

Dara held out her hand to hail a cab when her phone rang again.

"Da, it's Merry." God, how she hated her assistant calling her that.

"Merry, hold on." A cab pulled up and she jumped inside, giving the driver the address for Home Kitchen, her hand strategically placed over the mouthpiece so her assistant couldn't hear. "Okay, sorry about that. What's up?"

"Where are you?"

The taxi driver narrowly missed a cyclist who'd strayed into his lane, forcing Dara's stomach into her mouth.

"I'm in Manhattan. What do you need?"

"We're getting listings in the city now? That would be great. I have contacts there."

Oh, yes, I'm well aware. "This is kind of an inconvenient time. Is there something important you needed to discuss?" She tapped her foot. She didn't have time for small talk.

"It's Ava. Don't freak, but, when I went to pick her up from school, she was crying hysterically, and I couldn't calm her down. Best I can figure, one of the other kids got ahold of a pair of scissors and disemboweled her favorite Elmo doll when the teachers weren't looking. Pulled off his eyes and his arms, slashed him to bits. I think it must have happened while they were waiting for their rides; that's when the monitoring seems to be at its weakest. Ava was inconsolable, gouging her fingernails into her arms, scratching me when I tried to embrace her. I decided to drive her to the emergency room to see if they could sedate her. I did what I could, but she clearly needs her mom."

"WHAT?" Dara's blood pressure practically shot through the roof of the cab. "Why am I only hearing about this now? What kind of school has sharp objects around for kids with autism to get at? What hospital is she at?"

"Relax, Da. Everything happened so fast, there wasn't time to reach you. Jason met me at the hospital, and we okayed a diazepam injection to calm her down."

Dara winced at Merry's use of the word "we."

"I'm thinking a child brought the scissors from home, but I doubt anyone really saw anything. Ava is with Jason in the living room, resting. I've done my best to restuff Elmo and stitch him back up, and I've ordered a replacement. She's okay, but she's asking for you. When do you think you'll be back?"

"I'll leave now. I'll be home in an hour."

"Okay, I'll let her know. Jason and I will keep her occupied until then."

Dara disconnected the call and asked the driver to take her to her parking garage instead of the Home Kitchen. She was torn between guilt and upset, guilt for not being there when Ava most needed her, and upset that Merry and Jason had made decisions about the child's welfare together without consulting her. No time to worry about that right now. She needed to postpone visiting the housekeeper, Brazen, and everything related to the investigation. Her family needed her, and that's all that mattered.

"That's all that *ever* mattered." Her mother's chiding words echoed in her thoughts. Maybe this time, she was right.

Chapter Thirty-Four

Dara returned home to find Ava asleep on the couch and a scene of domestic bliss in the dining room where Jason, Merry, and Khai shared a pizza.

"We're so glad you're back at last," said Merry, more of a reproach than a greeting. "We finally got her down, and I didn't want to risk waking her up by carrying her upstairs. She's fine there for now. Did you eat? There was no time to make a homemade meal, so we ordered in."

Dara looked past her assistant and straight at her husband. "Did you speak to the school? Did they have anything to say for themselves? I can't see how we can leave her there now, after this."

"Dara, don't throw the baby out with the bathwater," Merry intervened, without even the pretense of being a guest rather than the woman of the house. "Ava's made great strides at Attwood. This was just a blip, something the staff couldn't have foreseen. I'm certain that from now on, they'll check the children for anything brought from home that they could use as a weapon—"

"I. wasn't. talking. to. you," Dara growled through gritted teeth. "This is a private family discussion."

"Dara. Don't go off on Merry. She's done more for this family than anyone I could imagine. The stuffed toy incident certainly wasn't her fault. She raced Ava straight from Attwood to the ER, and stayed with her the whole time, even after I got there. We owe her more than we can repay."

Dara stood silent, staring incredulously as her husband took her assistant's side over hers. Again. *Do you know that she's a con artist, a professional escort tied up with the mob? That she drove some poor woman to take her own life?* There was so much Dara wanted to say but couldn't—not yet. Not until she had tangible evidence rather than just rumor. The one thing she knew for sure was that she wouldn't be the next "poor" suicidal woman in Merry's string of conquests. This wasn't over, not by a long shot.

"No, Jason, she's right," answered Merry, lower lip quivering, clearly for effect. "I'm going to go up to my room, pack my things. Dara's clearly doing much better now, well enough to go to the city for the day. I've outstayed my welcome. You really don't need my help here any longer."

Oh God. Pulling the martyr card. What was she supposed to do, protest? Not a chance. She wanted this toxic spill of a woman out of her home and, hopefully soon, out of her company and charity as well. Perhaps this was the silver lining to Elmo's dismemberment.

"Merry, please," Jason pleaded. "Ava's grown to count on you so much, as we all have. Especially after tonight. Won't you stay for just a couple more days, or even a week or two? At least until we can make a less abrupt transition?"

Am I in an alternative universe? The shock was like crashing her car all over again. What exactly had gone on between the two of them all those evenings when she was stuck upstairs, recovering? Why couldn't her husband see Merry for the dangerous intruder she was?

"It's really up to Dara. This is her home. I don't want to be a burden or *persona non grata*." The defiant look in her eyes belied the humility of her retort. It broadcast she absolutely planned to remain in the house for as long as she liked. What better way to languish in her triumph than to force Dara to be the one who begged her to stay?

Dara made some quick calculations. She still needed to get over to Westminster and speak to Nikki Ellingsworth. Based on Esther's intel, she might also have to make a trip to Syracuse. Back in the city, she had unresolved questions for the folks at Brazen as well as Chiara Harwood's housekeeper, in case she still might be interested in making a few bucks by spilling what she knew.

Okay, Merry. Let's play it your way. You might think you're shoveling shit in everyone's eyes, but you're actually digging your own grave.

"Yes, Merry. What was I thinking? Please, stay. It wouldn't be the same without you here."

And your life certainly won't be the same once I force you out for good.

Chapter Thirty-Five

Dara woke to find Ava curled up next to her in bed. At least that was hopeful; she didn't hold a grudge against her for her absence. She stroked the child's hair and gently ran a finger along the tiny gouges where, in her fury, she had attacked her own arm. They were a visual reminder that while the Attwood Academy had been good for Ava, if she were to remain there, Dara would need answers. Today.

Downstairs, Merry had laid out a huge spread, as if triple-underlining her role as homemaker, followed by a series of exclamation marks. Dara begged off a creamy crab and Boursin omelet in favor of black coffee, insisting she wanted to get to Attwood early, before any of the children arrived, so she could speak privately with the principal and nurse privately.

"Dara, is that such a good idea, making waves like that?" asked Merry. "I mean, it's over. They told me it happened so quickly; they didn't see anything. I don't know if anyone did; someone had crammed Elmo's limbs, eyes, and stuffing into her backpack when I picked her up. And yes, she was crying, but she's always crying. Even if they had seen something, they'd probably deny it to avoid a lawsuit, as if any court would actually take something like that seriously. Our word against theirs. I'd leave it alone."

The tension in the room grew as taut as the pressure on a sheet of substandard window glass before it imploded. Time to step lightly.

"She has a point," said Jason, using his strap-on fork to finish the rest of his omelet. "If we make a big deal, they might subconsciously take it out on Ava. It's not like they have an open policy concerning weapons like scissors that needs to be reversed. This was clearly a one-off."

Merry held a magic influence over Jason that would likely not be vanquished through argument. Best to just nod, agree, and then question the school on her own.

"That's a really great point. I'll let it lie."

Merry arched an eyebrow of skepticism, but whatever further thoughts she had on the issue, she kept them to herself. Instead, she turned the conversation to real estate. "Since you're back, could you please take over the Fortress rentals? I have a dozen buyer tours scheduled over the next few days, and I feel like I'd be neglecting the condo project without your help."

Lovely. Assigning me my own business. "That sounds like a plan, Merry. I'll get over there this morning."

That was to be her strategy, Dara decided. Agree, agree, then do whatever she wanted. Surely, when he knew the entire story, Jason would concur that the end justified the means.

They agreed Ava should stay home from school that day, take time to recover from the trauma of the incident. Jason was happy to remain with her, leaving Dara's schedule open. Yes, she would handle the Fortress clients, but not until after she visited the school and heard their side of the story.

En route to Attwood, her cell phone rang. All she needed. Her mother's frantic voice turned her own concern into panic as it accosted her from fifty miles away.

"Da, what's this I hear about Ava? Attacked with scissors? How could you let such a thing happen?"

"Mom, calm down. They attacked the stuffed toy, not Ava. She's fine now. How did you even find out about it?"

"Merry called us yesterday, looking for you. She said she couldn't reach you on your cell, and she knew you'd want to be there for your child at such a traumatic time. Thank goodness she stepped in."

Couldn't reach me? Her phone had remained on the entire day. There were no missed calls, no voicemail.

"Should you really leave her in that school, Dara? This time, it was the toy, but next time, she could be the one who's assaulted. Maybe it's time for homeschooling, like we've always talked about."

We had never discussed homeschooling. Only Angelica brought it up, ad nauseam. Dara knew that being stuck all day at home—with no listings, no sales, and no adult interaction whatsoever—would drive her insane. It was never going to happen.

"Mom, please keep this between you and me, but I'm heading over to the school right now to speak to the headmistress and get to the bottom of this."

"Is that wise, Dara? I mean, what if they hold it against her? Merry says they'll just deny everything."

"Mom, I know a little more about the school—and what's best for Ava—than my assistant. Where does she get off calling you anyway?"

"Ever since we met her at the house that day, she's checked in with us every week or so, just to keep us apprised. More often than you do, in fact. It's very comforting."

Dara's blood pressure escalated from simmer to boil. *Really? Every week? Well, that certainly had to end.*

"I'm just pulling up to the school, Mom. Remember, just between us. Promise?"

"I really don't think it's for the best—"

"I'll take that as a yes. I'll call you back when I know more. Love to Dad." *Click.*

The principal, Mrs. Yang, welcomed Dara into her office, a homey combination of maroon and gold, with plush carpet, dark cherry bookcases, and a modular sofa arrangement off to the side, where she invited Dara to sit. She appeared surprised by the visit.

"Is Ava sick? We expected to see her today."

Dara was equally surprised by the question. "I'm here about the incident yesterday with Ava's Elmo toy."

Mrs. Yang raised her eyebrows. "What incident?"

Impatience crept into Dara's voice as she recounted the event, concluding with, "I know no one saw the attack, but certainly, you heard about it. When my assistant arrived to pick Ava up, my baby was as gutted as her toy."

Alarm blazed from Mrs. Yang's eyes. "Mrs. Banks, I assure you that random attacks between students do not occur at Attwood Academy, and if they did, I would surely be on top of the situation. Let me call in Mrs. Isaacs, who supervises the children while they are waiting for their rides."

She pressed the intercom and requested her admin to find someone to watch Mrs. Isaacs's class so she could join them. Moments later, a heavyset woman with a sweet expression appeared at the door.

"Hello, Mrs. Banks, how are you? Eleanor said it was important, so I came as soon as I could."

"Please join us, Gracie. Mrs. Banks was asking what happened yesterday while the children were waiting for their rides."

Mrs. Isaacs looked taken aback. "Happened? Nothing happened. The children's rides showed up and I walked them by hand to their cars, like I always do. Donna kept an eye on the others. I believe it was Ms. Rafter who picked up Ava; isn't that right, Mrs. Banks? Though with that cut, I keep getting the two of you mixed up." She gave a short laugh.

Dara nodded, making a mental note to grow out her hairdo.

"Ava seemed happy to see Ms. Rafter. I put her in the car and then returned to the other children. Is there something I'm missing?"

Dara opened her mouth, but Mrs. Yang interceded. "Did she, by any chance, show you something wrong with her Elmo doll or act like anything was bothering her?"

Mrs. Isaacs didn't hesitate before responding. "No, I would have noticed that. One hand in mine, the other holding Elmo. She loves him so much. She carries him around all day."

Mrs. Yang turned her attention to Dara. "Mrs. Banks, is there anything else you'd like to ask Gracie while she's here?"

Dara pursed her lips and shook her head. "I'm sorry to have pulled you out of your class, Mrs. Isaacs. Thanks for taking such loving care of Ava for us."

The teacher beamed. "We all love Ava. She's a joy, and I love watching her bloom a little more each day. Have a lovely morning."

Mrs. Isaacs hurried back to her class.

"There seems to have been a misunderstanding here, but I'm going to find out how it occurred. I apologize for disrupting your day," Dara shook the principal's hand, hoping both Mrs. Yang and Mrs. Isaacs would overlook this awkward encounter.

"Mrs. Banks, never a need to apologize. Our children's welfare is of primary importance. We always want to hear any concerns you may have. Whatever happened to Elmo—and we're so sorry to hear that anything did—it did not occur on our grounds. Please give Ava our best and tell her we hope to see her at school soon."

Dara slunk back to her car and sank into the driver's seat, determined to analyze the Elmo incident logically. Yes, they'd put on a united front of unaccountability, just as Merry had forecast. But there was a ring of sincerity and truth in every word they uttered. She'd never had an issue with the school before. She had no reason to doubt their veracity.

While it was true that a percentage of children with invisible disabilities occasionally become aggressive, Dara knew from personal experience that the students at Attwood were prescreened, generally kept to themselves, and were constantly monitored. Unpredictable things happen, of course. But if one of the children had gained access to sharp scissors and randomly attacked Ava's toy, would they have had the wherewithal to hide the weapon from view afterwards?

And why wound Elmo? Of those who tolerated theme park outings, most spectrum kids loved Sesame Place, so much so that one or two of the parks advertised themselves as autism friendly.

That left Merry, who had given Dara innumerable reasons for mistrust. But why would her assistant do something to upset Ava, especially when she's trying so hard to win over Jason?

Unless...

Dara's analytical mind flew into overdrive. Unless someone she interviewed yesterday was still in contact with Merry. Informed her that someone was sniffing around. Merry needed something to drag Dara back to Rock Canyon. Something big. And while she was at it, why not make it something that called Dara's mothering skills into question? Abandoning her child in a time of need. Leaving Merry to pick up the pieces as substitute mom. Especially with a child who couldn't tell the real story of what had actually occurred.

Still. Wasn't that a massive overreach? Would Merry have decimated Ava's favorite toy and left herself open to suspicion? Especially when the admins at Attwood would have insisted that a wildly agitated child would never have escaped their notice. She appeared far too shrewd and calculated for that.

Unless…

Unless she'd wanted Dara to know it was her behind the attack. A subtle warning. Stay out of my affairs, or something terrible is going to happen to your family. A family who trusts me and to whom I have total access. Today, it was Elmo, but tomorrow? It could be Ava. Or Khai.

The Lee incident came flying back into view. How Merry had manipulated her into believing she'd arranged for a mob hit, a man's murder.

It *had* been a threat. Now, Dara had to decide how to handle it while keeping Merry in the dark and her family safe. As long as she believed she was worshiped and indispensable and on her way to forcing Dara out of the picture, Merry posed no issue. It was only when she felt vulnerable that she turned dangerous. Dara needed to find a subtle way to keep Ava safe and her investigation low-key, all while searching for the antidote to rid the world of this toxin for good.

II

Dara and Merry

Chapter Thirty-Six

Merry hated it when things took an unexpected turn. This Dara bitch was straying out of her lane. She'd purposely set her sights on the unassuming workaholic and do-gooder with whom she and Harry had crossed paths years before at some fundraiser in the city. *Stay with that, lady. Leave the Nancy Drew shit to the professionals.*

Too bad about Elmo but when she got the call, she had to think quickly. It's not like Ava would be able to articulate how her beloved "auntie" had savaged the beloved toy right in front of her eyes. She'd responded perfectly, though, just as violently as Merry had hoped. They all should count themselves lucky she'd targeted the Muppet and not the kid. This time, anyway.

This latest information about her mark poking into her past meant she needed a new game plan. It might not be enough to just push Dara out of the way. She might need to be dealt with for good. Get rid of any lingering problems, any loose ends.

Up to now, she'd been able to keep her hands clean. If they wanted to off themselves out of despair, like Samantha E, that was their decision. Better to be the metaphorical hand that pushed the soon-to-be-ex-wife off the subway platform than the physical one. But in this case, would that level of restraint be possible?

Everyone had dirty laundry, just ask Don Henley. Clearly, she'd only done superficial research on the Banks family before making her move. And they'd checked all the boxes—rich, wife preoccupied with business over disabled husband, family in need of care. That was even more than she'd done with Ellingsworth. There, she'd limited her parameters to prestigious background, society status, political connections, self-absorbed wife. Harry's jealous streak had proven a bonus as it meshed perfectly with her endgame.

Yet here, in Rock Canyon, things hadn't gone exactly as planned. She hadn't counted on Dara being so smart. So protective. One step ahead. The car accident had been a godsend, giving her unlimited access and the opportunity to prove to Jason just how perfect she'd be as the next Mrs. Banks. Too bad Wifey had been such a quick healer.

Despite the momentary setbacks, she still adored the long con. Months of enjoying the good life—nice neighborhood, elegant house, gourmet food— while torturing the wife, watching her fall deep into despair as she slowly realized she'd lost her husband to the lowly newcomer. Any con artist could make money by stealing credit card numbers. This, though, was an art. One that only she could pull off.

She won by excelling where the wife failed. Making things fresh again after years of marriages growing stale. Where the wife took the man for granted, Merry doted on him, smothering him with attention, compliments, adoration. Where the wife had grown tired of the man's most irritating habits, Merry treated them as the most adorable quirks. Wife guilty of ignoring her husband's ego and cock? Merry lifted both, in the latter case, quite literally. Just like when she was younger, competing with her brother for her parents' attention, but now, she always won. Once she understood how the game worked, she never tired of witnessing the results. It was her manna, and she feasted to excess. The moment the wife realized she'd lost…well, it was almost more satisfying than counting the money. Almost.

There was still hope here in Rock Canyon. She'd give Dara a little more rope, wait and see if the Elmo incident was warning enough to just stay quiet and play her part. Accept her imminent divorce gracefully and move on. But if not, maybe the time had come to delve into the boss's past, see what she could use as leverage. Create a tit-for-tat situation—I'll stay schtum if you do.

Dara had better pray that I unearth major dirt from her past because if there's no standoff to be had, well…she'd better have her affairs in order instead.

Merry wasn't about to give up her mission to become the next Mrs. Banks. Bleed Jason dry in a divorce settlement and then move on to the next. She would allow nothing to interfere with her plans. Nothing.

Chapter Thirty-Seven

Though it nearly killed her, Dara played it cool for the next two weeks, silently plotting away. All for Khai and Ava's sake. Jason could look after himself, especially now that his spirits were higher and surgery imminent. But Khai—oblivious to Merry's cunning and charmed by her gifts and unconditional approval—was vulnerable. As for Ava, Dara made sure never to leave her alone in the same room with Merry again.

At the end of her fortnight of planning, while Merry was off at work, Dara made a single phone call. Then, clad in a navy Brooks Brothers pinstriped pantsuit, she jumped into her M3, and headed east to Westminster.

It took a while to navigate Mitterhof Pharma's campus, but Dara finally located the building that housed administration and sales. She had an appointment, and the receptionist took her coat and quickly ushered her into a small conference room with insulated fabric walls, plush carpeting, and a boardroom table for six. More like a recording studio, thought Dara. A place where sound and secrets never escaped.

Nikki Ellingsworth joined her moments later. A tall blonde with light blue eyes, she kept her long hair tucked in a ponytail. Her outfit, a red sweater dress and blazer, accentuated her curves while still giving off a professional appearance.

"Ms. Chase, I hope I haven't kept you waiting long."

"No worries, Ms. Ellingsworth. I know your time is valuable."

She sat opposite Dara, her eyes beaming with excitement. "Please call me Nikki. I was thrilled to learn that Inc. was doing this thirty-under-thirty article that included pharma. And that you chose me to be a part of it. Will a photographer be joining us? I know the perfect setting if you want to do any portrait shots."

Dara hated to disappoint her but lying about a prospective article had been the surest way to secure an appointment. Now was her chance to test her theory about Nikki's relationship with her stepmother and see if it held water. It was a gamble, but she had to know. On her lap sat her cell phone, with the Voice Memo app open. She reached down and hit "Record."

"No photographer, I'm afraid. The truth is, Nikki, I'm here about your stepmother, Felicity. And before you even think about leaving, please be aware that I know all about how she coerced you into stealing Paisley Harwood's social security number. Identity theft is a federal crime, punishable by up to fifteen years in prison. Even though Felicity used the card, you stole it, so whether you'd be tried as the perpetrator, or as an accessory, is up for debate."

The color drained from Nikki's face. Her eyes grew frigid, and her body stiffened, but she remained silent.

Dara pushed forward, determined to get at the truth. "The thing is, none of this has to go any further than us. Your father, your employers, the FBI need never know. As long as you answer a few questions. Will you do that for me?"

"Who the hell are you?" Nikki growled.

"My identity is immaterial here. What I want to know is how Felicity came into your life and how she influenced what happened between your father and mother."

Nikki leaned back, the red returning to her cheeks. "Well, if you leave my name out of it, I have no problem turning in that shrew. She single-handedly destroyed my family's life."

Dara's pulse surged. Finally. Someone who could shed light on the situation. "Please, start at the beginning."

Nikki sighed, as if even recalling Felicity's name was painful. "She came to us as a nanny. Mom was so busy with fundraising and then with my dad's campaign for state senate. He comes from a political family, you know. With all that going on, there was no time for either one of them to spend with me or the twins. I don't know where they found her, but I remember her not being particularly nice. She wasn't there for me, though; I was already in high school. I palled around with Paisley's sister, Alana. Sometimes, her parents hired me to babysit for Paisley. Alana could have done it alone, but I'm sure they wanted to make sure she had company."

Dara nodded, waiting for the dirt to fly.

"So, I admit, I was not particularly discriminating when I was younger. Pulled a lot of shit behind my parents' backs. Dear Nanny Felicity caught me in bed with this guy and told me that she'd keep it from my parent-, but only if I did her this one little favor. And that was to grab Paisley's social security card. So, one day, when I was at their apartment, I rifled through their papers and got it. I never knew why she needed it. I just didn't want to catch hell from my parents."

"Understandable…go on."

"She never asked me to do anything like that again. Then we all went to Aruba on vacation, the six of us. And when we came back, my mother and father weren't talking. The next thing I knew, my dad moved the four of us over to the East Side and told us they were getting a divorce. Suddenly, Dad and Felicity were really chummy—I mean, sharing-a-bed chummy. They never told us what happened. Then, after Mom killed herself, Nanny Felicity became our stepmother."

"Did you ever find out? What caused the divorce, I mean."

"Kinda. Heard some rumors, snooped around. There were these pictures my dad had from Aruba of my mom with another man. They were in bed together, naked. He had them in a drawer that I'm sure he thought he'd locked, but I found them."

Another man…

"Nikki, do you think you'd recognize the guy's face if you saw it?"

"The guy who helped ruin our lives? You bet I'd recognize it. It's permanently etched into my memory."

Dara fumbled for the manila envelope she'd brought on the off chance it could be helpful. She pulled out the pictures of Merry's three criminal amigos and spread them out on the boardroom table.

"Was it one of these guys, by any chance?"

Nikki glanced over the photos of Carl Vonderman and Jimmy Gordon. When she saw Tony Randazzo, she grimaced as if her worst nightmare had returned to give her night terrors. "That's him. That's the one. Who is he? I'd like to find him and give him a taste of his own medicine."

Figures it would be Tony, thought Dara. The good-looking one. The connected guy who no one could touch.

"He's dead," Dara lied. "He pulled his schtick on the wrong jealous husband who…well, let's just say he had his weapon confiscated."

"I'm sorry, what?"

"The guy castrated him and left him to bleed out."

Why not give the kid an ironic and satisfying ending for her trouble? Plus, she didn't need anyone else poking into Merry's past right now and possibly tipping her off again. "Just so you know, I don't believe your mom ever slept with this guy. I don't know if he drugged her or what, but Felicity has a nasty habit of setting up situations to manipulate people to achieve her own ends."

"Mom swore until her dying day that she'd never seen the guy before…I wish my dad had believed her. Things might have turned out differently. Not that Felicity stayed in our lives much longer. After hanging around for three years—coincidentally, the requirement in their prenup—she suddenly gained forty pounds and became nasty, sabotaging my dad's political ambitions, basically daring him to divorce her without actually asking. So, he did. Gave her a huge settlement, just to be rid of her. We haven't seen her since. Good riddance."

So that's how she did it. At least with Ellingsworth. Made it worth his while to release her. What happened with Tony Randazzo's dad would be another interesting story. She'd have to probe deeper.

Dara turned off the voice recorder and slipped her phone back into her bag. This had been an enlightening visit. Information she could hold over Merry's head. But damning enough to get her out of their lives? Questionable. She hadn't actually pushed Samantha Ellingsworth in front of the moving subway. She'd merely created an environment where jumping appeared preferable to living a life where Samantha had lost her husband, her children, and her reputation.

She rose and gave Nikki a sympathetic smile. The kid had had a tough life, and Dara felt bad for resurrecting long-buried memories.

"I'm sorry about your mom, Nikki, I really am. Believe me when I say your secret is safe with me."

Chapter Thirty-Eight

On the way home, Dara thanked God for the smarts that had kept her from becoming the next Samantha Ellingsworth. But she knew uncovering Merry's game wasn't enough. She needed blackmail ammunition. Celeste, vindictive and shrewd, wanted more. Her protector wanted Merry's head on a Thanksgiving platter.

It was time to get her assistant out of her house. She'd delayed up to now for the sake of convenience and to avoid rousing further suspicion over her ongoing investigation. Still, every time she heard Ava watching Sesame Street, she worried what that harpy might do next. She'd kept them apart since the Elmo incident but with one or two fact-finding trips scheduled in the near future that would keep her from Ava's side, she needed Merry gone.

In bed that night, Dara orally "relaxed" her husband and afterward, when he was at his most blissful, she delicately broached the subject.

"Jason?"

"Mm...yes, honey?" he murmured, half-asleep.

"I've been thinking about Ava. Since that incident at school, she hasn't been the same."

Jason rolled toward her. The glow of the clock radio illuminated his furrowed brow. "What makes you say that?"

"She clings more," Dara lied. "She hesitates when I drop her off in the morning, so I have to remain in the classroom until she feels comfortable. I don't mind it, of course. I'd do anything for her. I'm just thinking that perhaps we should hire someone with a therapeutic background to spend time with her when I can't be here. A nanny with training in autism and trauma. I've made inquiries and found the perfect person. She's expensive, but for that, I don't mind dipping into savings."

Jason thought for a moment. "You checked references?"

Dara swallowed her contempt for that question. He'd had Merry prancing around the house for months, and they'd never run a background check. Much to their detriment.

"Of course. All glowing. I actually got the recommendation from one of the moms who attends the Birthday Parties for All events." At least that last part was true. The woman sounded like a dream.

Jason rolled back over. "Honey, whatever you think is best. I'll leave it to you."

"It'll mean Merry has to move out. We'll need the bedroom for the nurse. You okay with that?"

Dara held her breath. Would Jason fight for her assistant to stay on? If so, had something gone on between them, perhaps something romantic, to which she had not been privy?

"Merry served her purpose while you were recovering. It was a godsend having her here. And she's a great cook. But now you're fine and ...well, I didn't want to say anything, her being your assistant and all, but I find her annoying. So self-congratulatory. Always needing validation, that pat on the back."

A huge weight lifted off Dara's chest. "But...when I wanted her out a few weeks ago, you fought for her to stay."

"I know. I wasn't sure you'd completely recovered, and it was the easy answer. I've since determined it was a mistake. Ever since that day, she's been cozying up to me a little too closely, you know? Maybe it's my imagination. But before I say anything that might endanger your work relationship, probably best she leaves."

Despite the suggestion Merry had been putting the moves on Jason, she could imagine no sweeter words than those her husband had just uttered. With a hand on his shoulder, she pushed him onto his back, facing the ceiling, and, this time, rolled on top of him. His look of surprise soon evolved into

196

one of hunger.

"Ready for round two?" she asked with a wink.

Chapter Thirty-Nine

At breakfast the next morning, Merry hummed while she served up Eggs Benedict for Jason and banana pancakes for Dara and the kids. Can't hurt to ply the soon-to-be-ex-Mrs. Banks with a few extra calories, she smiled to herself. She knew from experience it was always easier for men to let go of wives who had let themselves go. A sad fact, but if that's how this weight-crazed society worked, why not play it to her advantage?

Tonight is going to be the night. The goosebumps on her arms saluted with anticipation. Dara's scheduled meeting with the caterers for Autism Vanguard's upcoming gala presented the perfect opportunity to close the deal with Jason. First, his favorite dinner, Coq au Vin, accompanied by a $96 bottle of Domaine Serene Evenstad Reserve Pinot Noir. A splurge, true, but she knew he appreciated good wine, and she wanted him tipsy and in the most receptive mood when she pressed her advantage. She practically salivated at the thought of her future conquest.

She served everyone their breakfast and then joined them with her coffee and cottage cheese. That's when the witch broke the news that shattered her plans.

"Merry, we need to discuss something and knowing how you adore the kids, I'm sure you'll be on board," Dara started.

Already, a tug at the pit of her stomach. Nevertheless, she forced a smile. "Of course. Anything for Khai and Ava. You know that."

"Since the...incident at Attwood, we feel Ava might need specialized attention. To get over the trauma, you know?" said Jason.

Hmm...

"So, we've hired a therapeutic nurse to move in for a few weeks." Dara spoke quickly, the verbal equivalent of pulling off an adhesive bandage. "Especially since I'm going to be spending more time at work and at Autism Vanguard, we feel this will be best for everyone, especially you. Unfortunately, we only have the one guest room, as you know. But the good news is now; you can get back to your life and take on even more clients at work...if that's, in fact, something you'd like to do. You're *sooo* good at it."

Oh no, you don't. Not without a fight.

"A nurse? Someone Ava doesn't even know? How is that going to put her at ease? Will she cook? These kids deserve home-cooked meals. Khai, don't you agree? I'd hate to see this family return to eating takeout seven days a week again. Ava, that can't be what you want, is it, sweetie?"

Merry knew she was grasping at straws, but this couldn't happen. Not now. Not when she was on the verge of success.

Ava didn't look up, just kept squeezing her new Elmo—the second one Merry had bought for her. *Damn that kid.* The one time Merry needed her to at least nod, what did she get? Nothing.

"We're going to subscribe to one of those personal chef services," Jason said. "It won't be your excellent cooking, of course, but we've taken advantage of you long enough. Dara and I have been talking, and we agree that no one could have done more for us than you have over the past few weeks. We're forever in your debt. And while it won't make up for the sacrifice you've made for us, we'd like to send you on a two-week, all-inclusive trip to Paris. First class."

"It's really the least we can do," Dara added. "You can pick the dates, of course, but right now, things are slower at work. Once May hits, the summer season will be in full swing, and buyers will be coming out of the woodwork. This might be the best time to go."

Merry knew when she'd been outplayed. Turning her own plot device, the Elmo attack, against her. She jumped up and hugged each of her benefactors with as much sincerity as she could muster, all the while plotting what she might do during her supposed Paris trip. Today was not the end of this particular fight. Of that, they could be certain.

* * *

Merry moved back into her own apartment later that afternoon. Without the excitement of the coup undermining every action, the place seemed dull. No bother. Soon, she'd move into the Banks' more elegant digs for good.

Easter loomed. The anniversary of their first big dinner together. Surely, they wouldn't refuse her repeat invitation. Maybe this year, she'd invite Dara's mother and father. They'd certainly been forthcoming. Maybe they'd like an earful of whatever scandal from their daughter's past she was about to uncover. Wouldn't it be a hoot if they kicked Dara to the curb, but Merry, Mom, and Dad Crawford remained close?

Actually, maybe it wouldn't be a bad idea to pay them a visit. Find out what she could about Dara's past. Air out her childhood closet, examine any lingering skeletons. If Dara insisted on remaining resistant to her eventual ouster, Merry would need all the ammunition she could get.

Paris could wait. *Long Island, here I come.*

Chapter Forty

What a difference a few weeks made. With her recovery complete and her guestroom now occupied by a therapeutic nanny who understood boundaries, Dara had regained control of her household and her real estate practice. Ava had adjusted to the change as well as could be expected. Khai was applying himself better at school, so USC would accept him into their game design program. And Jason's attitude remained upbeat, even though the hospital had postponed his surgery until June. Though the subscription meal service wasn't up to Merry's caliber, it sufficed, especially since all they needed to do was throw the dish into the oven or microwave. Even better, neither that meal service nor Ava's new nanny tried to create a wedge between Dara and her family.

Dara contacted each of her clients and advised them Merry would be stepping back due to her well-deserved upcoming vacation in France. She even offered to drive her assistant to JFK for her Air France flight. Watching Merry wheel her suitcase into Terminal One made Dara's heart sing. *Find yourself a French family to uproot.* If only she'd fall in love with the Rive Gauche and never return. Wouldn't that be a blessing, and wouldn't "gauche" be so *apropos*? That first-class airline ticket had to be one of the best investments the Banks had ever made.

With Merry out of their hair and Ava safe, Dara asked Jason if he'd mind if she attended the regional National Association of Realtors conference up in Syracuse. It had been a while since she'd taken any work-related trips, and this would be a chance to get reinspired.

Jason didn't have any objections since his daily runs were keeping his endorphins popping, and he was spending more time with his former partner Burton Erickson. Together, they were planning for his post-surgical future, which now included the design of a follow-up to the wildly successful The Fortress on the Hudson.

What she hadn't mentioned to Jason was a detour to Manhattan before heading north to Syracuse. There was something so freeing about driving down to the city with nothing hanging over her head, no worries that someone was about to poach her husband, pilfer her children's affection, plunder her client list. Life seemed as sweet as it had before Merry parachuted into their lives. The problem was, her assistant would return in a fortnight, leaving Dara a mere two weeks to finish her investigations and build her own fortress, one of exposed lies to protect her family in the future.

Her three-fold plan: Dress inconspicuously in jeans and a button-down blouse. Visit Brazen early in the evening, before it got crowded, and gather as much intel as possible. Finally, an overnight in Scranton before making two stops in Syracuse. She hoped to visit the high school for a glimpse into Merry's early years and then visit the ominous-sounding suburb of Skunk City to spy on Vera Jones—the woman whose face appeared on Merry's real estate license. She knew she'd have to keep her distance: any woman who'd pose on Merry's behalf was probably her ally and should be approached with caution.

She found garage parking on Third Avenue near 60th Street, practically next door to Brazen's silver façade. Inside her tote, her cell phone contained pictures of all four people who had defrauded her over the past year. She also came equipped with press credentials she had ordered for $108 from a company on the Internet, along with a cover story she hoped would pass muster.

Brazen's interior was dark as melodrama and featured plush purple and beige swiveling barrel chairs surrounding a large stage where the strippers performed. An amply stocked bar ran along one wall, and overhead spots competed with lasers bouncing off mirrors and glossy table surfaces to bathe areas in alternating blues, yellows, purples, and greens. As the doors had opened just minutes before, the place was practically deserted, save a smattering of patrons who sat mesmerized by an older, emaciated stripper with tire-pumped breasts, which gyrated lackadaisically and off-tempo to the D.J.'s beat.

Dara slithered in, attempting to avoid notice, and headed directly to the coat check, where the attendant looked as downtrodden as the dancer. She handed the woman her down jacket and whispered, "Have you worked here long?"

"About five years, which I'd say is five years too long, if you know what I mean." Her accent could have emanated from any country ending in -stan.

Dara flashed her fake press credentials, which identified her as Chase Barclay, chosen because it played on her last name, Banks. Then she slipped the woman a twenty.

"Can you direct me to anyone who's been here, say, ten years or longer? I'm writing a blog post about exotic dancers and how they're not the pariahs society suggests. I'd like to get background details from someone who's been around a while."

The attendant jerked her head back, as if bribes to someone of her caliber signaled a brave new world she had yet to encounter. "Pegs has been here the longest, maybe twenty years. You've probably heard of her. She's famous for her routine with the boa constrictor, and how she sticks it up her. ..well, anyway, she gets in around ten."

Ugh. That meant three hours of sitting around watching anemic strippers, and then getting to her midway point, an overnight in Scranton, way later than she'd hoped.

"How about someone with a slightly shorter stint?"

The woman's eyes shifted to the dancer currently on stage, and she lowered her voice. "Ultima's been here at least ten years. I hear she dances to put herself through law school. I guess that's one way to study self-defense." She stifled a giggle. "Sorry, that was mean. I'm just so tired of the same old, same old, night after night."

Dara nodded. Apparently, a twenty bought you confidante status with the staff at Brazen. "Do you know when she gets off?"

"From what I understand, about ten minutes after a patron shows her a Bennie." The coat check smirked. "But for your purposes, about a half-hour from now. I'll let her know you'd like a word, okay?"

Dara holed up in a corner, requesting a diet soda, when a server of questionable age with huge knockers and a hair-trigger temper deigned to take her order. According to her research, Brazen had seen its share of scandals over the years, from having its founders accused of tax evasion and club-sanctioned prostitution to overcharging patrons by thousands of dollars. Hiring an underage server or twenty surely wouldn't have caused them any lack of sleep.

Before Dara finished her drink, Ultima sashayed over, pasties leading the way, and plopped down in the seat beside her. Dara wondered how her eyes stayed open under the weight of such heavy fake lashes.

"I understand you want to chat for some blog piece. My standard interview fee is $200. Cash."

Dara had expected nothing less. She opened her purse and peeled off three C-notes from her stack, courtesy of the Rock Canyon automated teller machine. She folded them and clandestinely palmed them to Ultima by her thigh so no one could see.

"The third hundred is a bonus for you to keep this between us. There are tons of bloggers out there, and I want to publish something original. Okay by you?"

Ultima chuckled. "You don't have to go through all this cloak and dagger shit." She spoke loudly enough for Dara to hear over the canned music, momentarily replacing the DJ until the next dancer took the stage. "This place is Bribe City, Arizona. Always something going down. So, what exactly do you want to know? And don't hand me that crap about the secret life of strippers. I'm well aware of who owns this place and who hangs out here. My guess is, so are you."

"Okay, fine. There's a woman who once worked at Brazen. She's gone by several names, so I'm not sure which one she used here. I think she dated the owner or maybe his son."

Ultima huffed. "Sounds like most women who work at Brazen. Tony's not around anymore, but in the day, both Randazzos treated the staff like liquor at an open bar—a beer here, a shot there. Sometimes, a flute of champagne. Vinny still does. You got something more for me to go on?"

"I have a picture...hang on." Dara pulled out her cell and clicked on Merry's photo. Ultima took one look and, like everyone else Dara had encountered who had known her assistant in the past, her bemused expression turned grim.

"If I were you, I'd never show that picture around here again if you want to leave here upright instead of in a bag," she whispered. "Remember what I said about the staff the Randazzos fucked? That they were like flutes of champagne? That woman was a magnum...of trouble."

Dara fought to keep her excitement in check and feigned indifference. "I've heard stories. Tell me yours. I promise no one will ever know where I heard it."

Ultima slowly surveyed the room and appeared satisfied no one was watching, especially since a younger, more curvaceous dancer had taken center stage, stripping off a nun's habit.

"She worked here years ago, before I started. Called herself Ambrosia. Wouldn't say how old she was or where she'd come from, just that she'd do whatever it took to earn some extra cash to cover expenses until her big Broadway break came through. Started as a server, but before you knew it, she was doing lap dances in the private rooms upstairs. Once the boss saw her, she didn't even have to do that. She was officially off the market."

The story was finally coming together. Dara took another sip of soda, her mouth dry from anticipation.

"They were together, I don't know, years. I started here toward the end of it. Out of nowhere, there was some huge rift between her and Vinny and Tony. The way I heard it, she'd grown bored of sleeping with Vinny and not working. Monogamy was not her thing. So, she began sleeping with Tony while, as a side hustle, doing gigs at an acting and escort agency under another name. All while continuing to *schtup* the boss. Suicidal, if you ask me, but she must have figured she was so smart and so bulletproof, she could pull it off. Or maybe, she just needed the constant validation. When Vinny found out, he flipped, threw them both out. It made him the laughingstock of the families."

"I bet," said Dara. This sounded exactly like Merry's M.O. "Any idea where they are now?"

"Nah, haven't seen or heard from either of them since. But I tell you, she must have had something ultra-damning on Vinny, or maybe connections even higher up than his because normally, pulling something like that would get you a bullet in the head faster than I can suck a dick dry. Especially because when she split, she took a shitload of the club's cash. Vinny found that part out after the fact, and I bet if he ran into her again, he wouldn't be so magnanimous. In any case, we don't mention her around here anymore. And if I were you, I'd forget everything you just heard. Don't publish a word of this because if Vinny reads it, he'll make sure you never write another word again."

"I can see where that might be true." Dara trembled, unsure if it was from excitement or fear. She stood to leave, certain she'd gotten her $300 worth.

"Before you go, for an extra hundred, I can give you something you'll never want to forget." Ultima seductively ran her tongue over her top lip as she twirled the tassel affixed to her right nipple.

"It's a kind offer, but I'm going to have to pass. Stay safe, Ultima."

"You too, ahem, Chase," said the stripper as Dara scurried toward the door. "Happy blogging."

Chapter Forty-One

While navigating I-80 W towards Scranton, Dara pieced together a timeline of what she'd learned thus far and determined what questions still remained unanswered.

Merry arrived in New York City several years back, but how and under what name is what Dara intended to discover next.

She gotten herself a job as a server/escort at Brazen as "Ambrosia" and wormed her way into mob boss Vinny Randazzo's good graces. From the sound of it, she leeched off him for years, became bored with being a trophy girlfriend, and secretly put herself back to work as extra/escort Sally Malone. And, while engaging in her side hustle, why not sleep with her sugar daddy's son as well?

Then, when she got found out, she disappeared—with Brazen's money and apparently damning dirt on Vinny—and reemerged as Amoret Prager, wedding cake designer extraordinaire. Her new persona was, no doubt, made possible thanks to a fake ID and credentials from Tony's buddy, Carl. Then, poof, she transformed into Amoret's twin sister, Felicity Prager, who insinuated herself into Harry and Samantha Ellingsworth's world as nanny to Nikki and the twins. Dara wondered if Harry's political connections spurred Merry to target that particular family, perhaps to fortify herself with extra protection against any potential retribution from the mob.

Once she forced Samantha out and the woman killed herself, Felicity Prager married and became Felicity Ellingsworth and got ahold of Paisley Harwood's social security number for future endeavors. Next, she gained weight, adopted a bad attitude, and drove Harry to divorce her for a hefty settlement. She ended up in Rock Canyon as Meryl Rafter, eager to pull an Ellingsworth on the Banks household. Befriended Dara and forced out her only friend, Brooke, so she could gain a foothold in Autism Vanguard, become indispensable to Dara's real estate clients, and present herself to Jason as the loving, stay-at-home wife, cook, and housekeeper he'd never had as a wife. The car accident? A lucky break for her, a lesson for Dara to keep the demons of the past safely tucked out of view. And when Dara became suspicious and started snooping around? Create domestic chaos to bring Mom back home and issue a subtle warning to leave Merry's past undisturbed.

Thankfully, Dara had already banished Merry from her house. This new intel was clearly enough to fire her, bar her from Rock Canyon Realty, and warn her to stay away from the Banks household forever. Exactly who was Vera Jones, the woman who posed as Merry for her real estate license? How did she tie into all of this? What happened in Skunk City when Merry was younger to set her on this path of destruction? Most importantly, how could Dara help other unsuspecting families by ensuring Merry didn't pull her special brand of homewrecking scam in the future?

One short, final trip. That's what Dara promised herself. Once she resolved these lingering questions, she could return home satisfied and resume her normal daily routine.

After a fitful sleep at a roadside Scranton motel, too hyped up to truly relax, Dara set out after breakfast for the two-hour drive to Syracuse High School, where Merry had supposedly starred as Velma in the high school production of Chicago. At least, that had been her story. From what Dara had gleaned up to now, the tales Merry told when a little tipsy and eager to impress were the ones most likely to hold a kernel of truth.

The school, home to the Syracuse Titans as the sign proudly proclaimed, consisted of a campus of red brick buildings and an auditorium situated in a huge rotunda that, from Dara's research, measured close to 9,000 square feet and could hold around 1,000 audience members. The other lovely thing she'd learned was that they rented out the space, which, as the head of a non-profit, gave her a perfect excuse to visit.

Mrs. Farnsby, the facilities director of the Davis school district, was delighted to take her on a walking tour. Once inside the rotunda, Dara oohed and aahed, explaining Autism Vanguard's fundraiser would involve a play performed by children with autism in the Syracuse area—a new market for them. After the show, AV would treat the audience to a gourmet dinner served by whatever area caterer the school recommended.

"I can only imagine the amazing productions you've put on in this theater," she said, gushing appropriately.

"They have been quite elaborate," answered Mrs. Farnsby. "Even families who don't have children in the district buy tickets. It's been a great boon to our PTA, because we share the profits with them."

"As it happens, a friend of mine starred in one of your productions—but it was quite a while ago. I don't even know what her maiden name was back then, but I'd love to see the photos."

Dollar signs flashing in her pupils, Mrs. Farnsby suggested they go over to the library and comb through old yearbooks.

"That would be so great—are you sure you don't mind?" asked Dara.

"Not at all, especially if it brings the prospect of staging a show in our auditorium into greater focus."

At the library, an elderly woman with oversized square, rhinestone-rimmed eyeglasses, and an impish smile staffed the main desk.

"Edwina, meet Mrs. Banks, a prospective client. She has a friend who starred in one of our productions, and she'd like to see photos from that year. Do you think you could help her?"

Edwina grinned. "You've come to the right place. I used to work backstage at the shows, helping with costume and set design, you name it. Who was your friend?"

Dara tightened her lips. "That's the thing. I don't know her maiden name, and I think she goes by a different first name now from the one she grew up with. But what I do know is that she played Velma in *Chicago*."

Edwina's smile dulled, something Dara had come to expect whenever she dredged up memories of the woman in question.

"Oh. You mean Georgia. Georgia Jones. She's a friend of yours?"

"Um, well, more of an acquaintance, really. But I would love to see the photos."

Enthusiasm doused, Edwina plodded to the rear of the library, shaking her head as if trying to oust a bad memory. She returned with a blue hardcover, its binding coated in dust, and flicked through the pages until she reached the drama section. She pointed to a black-and-white photo of a young Georgia Jones, aka Merry, clad in a low-cut, sleeveless, sparkly flapper outfit, arms spread wide, belting out whatever number she'd been singing at the time. No doubt about it, Merry was born Georgia Jones. Which likely meant the woman pictured on her real estate license, Vera Jones, was her mom.

"You know she skipped town the night after the production, right?" Edwina's harsh tone conveyed her disapproval. "Her brother, Ricky, had that accident, and she ran out on both him and their mom, just when they needed her most. Didn't bother graduating. Way we all heard it, she forged her mom's name on a check, emptied their bank account, and disappeared. Haven't heard from her since. Not the best legacy around here, that one. The whole community started a collection to help the mom move out of town to cheaper digs and then get back on her feet."

Dara vaguely remembered Merry talking about her brother, the golden child. The one her parents clearly preferred over her. Drama being the only way she could garner any attention or approval.

"I...I wasn't aware. No, that's not acceptable at all, is it? What kind of accident did the brother have?"

Eager to besmirch any positive impression of Georgia Jones, Edwina continued her tale with renewed vigor.

"Richard Jones was a shining star. A genius. And so nice. Everyone loved him. Then, he got into an altercation behind the school with some miscreants who were probably jealous of him and his achievements. It was after hours when the grounds were deserted, and they left him for dead. He managed to drag himself to the street and then lost consciousness. A passing driver found him, thank God, but maybe it would have been better if he hadn't. Ricky's confined to a wheelchair now, permanently disabled, barely speaks. His mom divides her time between caring for him and taking on odd jobs she can manage from home. What a waste of a brilliant mind."

"I'm so sorry. Sorry for him and for bringing up such an upsetting subject. I hope at least they caught the boys involved."

"Unfortunately, not. And once he regained consciousness, he wouldn't rat them out—that is, if he even knew who they were. I think he might have been scared they'd come back and finish the job."

Ten to one, Merry/Georgia was involved somehow, thought Dara. Maybe blowing one of the boys. Hell, probably blowing all of them. One last "fuck you" to the brother who'd been the apple of his mother's eye since birth, stealing her thunder. Then, blowing town, off to the bright lights of Broadway, which dimmed markedly once she'd seen them in person. Speculation, true. There was only one way to know for sure.

"I want to thank you both for the tour," said Dara. "I'm going to return home and urge the board to move forward with the auditorium rental. I'll likely get back to you next quarter."

"That would be wonderful." Mrs. Farnsby shook her hand. "If there's anything else you need, please don't hesitate to get in touch."

You've already given me almost everything I need. One more piece of the puzzle, and I'll be set.

Chapter Forty-Two

Shortly after eleven, Dara left the school and drove north to her final destination, the home of Vera and Ricky Jones, the address provided to her by Esther weeks before.

Their street in Skunk City had seen better days. The majority of buildings were burnt-out shells of their former selves or had fallen into disrepair, while others were in the process of doing so. A long-forgotten playground consisted of a busted see—the saw broken off—and a swing set missing its seats. This was a site ripe for regentrification, just waiting for a savvy developer with funds and vision. Dara made a mental note to mention it to Burton.

She parked across the street from the two-story, grayish house with an overgrown lawn and a station wagon way past its prime, its sides adorned with wood paneling from plastic trees. There she sat, not exactly sure why, but certain the reason would reveal itself in time.

Occasionally, someone would walk by and give her the side-eye, so she pretended to talk on her cell or check out Google Maps for the route from which she'd supposedly strayed before ending up in this sketchy neighborhood.

In reality, her Google searches sought any information she could find on either Vera, Ricky, or Georgia Jones—all of whom had mastered the art of avoiding an online presence throughout their lives. She did find one local newspaper account of Ricky's beating, assailants still at large, and the fundraisers that helped Vera pay his hospital bills. She even found one review of the *Chicago* production, which ironically gave kudos to all the actors save the attention-craving Georgia. Dara gathered she wasn't the belle of the ball even before her disappearing act.

Vera finally emerged in a floral housecoat, a cigarette dangling from her lips. Dara crouched in her seat to avoid being seen while Vera got into her station wagon and drove past.

With nowhere else to go and no other leads to pursue, Dara continued to monitor the house. Twenty minutes later, she hit pay dirt when Ricky wheeled himself out the front door and down the walkway, a plastic bag of garbage perched on his lap. He headed toward the trash cans set prominently on the side of the driveway. It was time to act on another assumption, much as she had done when speaking with Merry's stepdaughter, Nikki. It had worked then, so why not try it a second time?

"Excuse me," she called out as she approached and waved to a startled Ricky. He sat ramrod straight and motionless, a deer mesmerized by the headlights of an oncoming truck. "I don't mean to disturb you, but I'm lost, and I was hoping you could help."

Ricky's shoulders relaxed, and his glare softened. Dara's yells had been for the benefit of any snooping neighbors who might be observing, but if they put Ricky's mind at ease, all the better. Once she reached his side, however, she lowered her voice so only he could hear.

"Ricky, I'm here as a friend, and I don't mean any harm. I'm so sorry for the events that confined you to this chair, this house. I want justice for you, and for that to happen, I need to know one thing. The boys who put you in this wheelchair—were they strangers, or were they friends of Georgia's? Did she arrange for them to attack you because she was jealous of all the attention your mother showered on you growing up? This is your chance. One nod, and I'll make sure she never does anything like this to anyone else ever again."

Ricky remained silent, but his entire body began to tremble. His eyes reflected terror, whether from memory or fear of retribution. Dara assumed it was a combination of both.

"Right now, Georgia is in Paris. She'll never know I was here or that we spoke. I just need you to help me. Since the day she ran out on you and your family, she's caused pain and even death to everyone she's encountered. You have the power to put an end to it, to have the final say. Please help me," Dara implored.

"Go. Away. Never. Come. Back," said Ricky in a voice raspy from disuse. Then he swung his wheelchair around and raced back up the walkway and the ramp, slamming the front door behind him while Dara looked on.

That's about as clear an answer as I could have hoped for. Ricky, petrified of his sister and her friends, clearly had decided an unavenged silence was preferable to a painful death. Whatever Dara did next would be for the benefit of him and every future target Merry had yet to destroy. The final piece of the puzzle in place, she had her answer, and her mission was clear. Merry Rafter had to be stopped. And Dara had to be the one to stop her.

* * *

Merry was enjoying a spa day at a plush Long Island resort before visiting Dara's parents when she received the call. Annoyed at having her solitude disturbed, she nevertheless asked the massage therapist to give her a moment alone and then answered.

"Remember that woman you told me to watch out for? The one you thought was on your tail?"

She felt a chill go up her exposed spine. "Yeah?"

"There's been a woman watching the house for about an hour. I'm texting you a photo I took from the bedroom window. Is this her?"

Merry's phone dinged, announcing the text, and she downloaded the photo. Sure enough, there was Dara. Stupid woman, not even attempting to disguise herself. *She must think we're all dummies.*

"Yup, that's the bitch in the flesh." What had been a chill had now transformed into a flame of hate, burning her cheeks and igniting her venom.

"That's what I thought. Once I snapped the photo, I drove around the corner, then snuck back on foot to see what she would do. Sure enough, she approached your brother when he took out the trash."

"He didn't fucking say anything to her, did he?"

"From what I could see, he listened and then told her to get lost and headed into the house. She's back in her car now. You want me to do something?"

"Nah, Ma. I've got things under control. Thanks for keeping an eye out. When I'm done with her, she'll be scared to even talk to her own shadow, much less the police or anyone else."

"Okay then, Georgie. If you change your mind, let me know. I've still got your daddy's shotgun upstairs."

"Ma, that's old school. I have much less traceable methods of damage control."

"Where are you, anyway?"

"Paris," said Merry and disconnected the call.

She invited the massage therapist back in, and they resumed her treatment. Important to get all the kinks out of her shoulders before she went out, digging up dirt. And if there was no dirt to uncover, she'd concoct some of her own, Ellingsworth-style.

The money she sent her mother each month was certainly paying off. The old sow came in handy every now and then. Who was your golden child now, Mommy Dearest? Ricky might have had all the promise, but look at him now. Useless. Meanwhile, who pays the rent, keeps the cupboards filled, puts gas in your car? The girl you ignored, except when she took the stage, gave you something to brag about to your friends.

Sure, that girl might have arranged to have your favorite child maimed, but you figured out quickly enough that money talked. And when it did, it spoke louder than Ricky's former looks, brains, and strength. Money was power. And once she convinced Jason Banks to marry and later divorce her with a hefty settlement, she'd be set. At least until the next mark appeared.

Chapter Forty-Three

On her way to the Crawford estate in Locust Valley, Merry instructed her Audi to ring Jason's phone number. Why miss out on an opportunity to instill an element of suspicion into the Banks' happy marriage?

Jason answered with a weary hello. Ava must have been especially trying that morning.

"Jason, it's Merry. Sorry to bother you, but is Dara around?"

"Merry, bonjour! How is Paris? Shouldn't you be off at a cabaret, drinking Bordeaux, instead of wasting valuable vacation time calling home?"

"Paris is incredible," she lied. "Do you miss me? What am I saying? Of course, you do. I can't thank you enough for this amazing vacation. I'm calling because I remembered something in the Ahearn file that I forgot to tell the owner. Before they can close, they'll need a pest control company to sign a declaration stating they've treated their basement for snakes. Can you put Dara on so I can explain further?"

"Merry, I'm afraid she's out at the NYSAR convention in Syracuse and won't be back for a few days."

Merry waited a beat. "Jason, you must be confused. That convention isn't until next month. She may be in Syracuse, but not for that. No biggie. I have the lawyer's phone number in my cell, and I can call him myself. Just forget I ever rang. Go back to whatever you're doing. I'm standing outside the most adorable bakery on the Left Bank, and I see a profiterole with my name on it. Gotta go." *Click.*

Merry smiled to herself while she parked her red convertible outside the

Crawford estate. Quincy and Angelica were both standing on the front steps, waving. It warmed her insides to imagine herself as the prodigal daughter returning home, not some forgettable employee whose name they'd never manage to remember.

The house was enormous, an updated Federal Revival dating back to the 1700s, with six massive columns in front, set on twelve idyllic acres of prime Long Island real estate. At ten thousand square feet, her research placed the home's value north of nine million, and from the outside, it looked like it was worth every penny. Even the Banks' home, where she had spent so many weeks caring for that ungrateful cow, would fit inside this magnificent property three times over. Maybe she had picked the wrong mark. Perhaps Quincy was the one to marry instead. Not that it was too late. Dating within the family was one of her specialties.

The Crawfords embraced her warmly and ushered her into their living room with its antique oak furniture and copious windows, which bathed the room in sunlight.

"What a beautiful home," Merry remarked.

"We inherited it from Quincy's family." Angelica scowled, as if her surroundings tarnished her. "The furnishings, the decorations, everything. We would never lay out money for such things when the funds could go to better causes. In fact, we're thinking of selling off the more expensive pieces, aren't we, dear?"

Hypocrites. If living in luxury was so abhorrent, why hadn't they offloaded these antiques long ago? Could it be they liked living to the nines and chose to be altruistic just for show?

Before Quincy could answer, three young children of varied ethnicities ran through the room with Nerf guns, screaming and laughing and nearly knocking Merry over.

"Please forgive them," said Quincy, grabbing one child, giving her a hug, and setting her down again to continue her rampage. "I'm afraid we're way too indulgent with them, but they've had such a hard life. The more they can enjoy just being children—ones finally loved and well-cared for—it's worth all the mess and the noise. Don't you agree?"

Merry forced a smile, all the while congratulating herself on the decision to have her tubes tied years ago. Children were a waste of time and resources. Yet, Quincy and Angelica had discovered a unique purpose for them, hadn't they? Housing damaged and abandoned youths to enhance their own reputations. Buying their way into heaven, one foster at a time. Or was that just Merry's cynicism talking?

With the kids off to destroy a different room, Quincy took his place on the antique couch beside Angelica and invited Merry to occupy the chair opposite. On the table between them sat a tea set and a display of scones with raspberry jam and clotted cream.

"I'm sure you and Quincy are doing a wonderful job raising them. Exactly how many children do you have?"

"The numbers are always changing." Quincy laughed. "I think we currently have…what, Angel?"

"There are nine," she snipped, clearly annoyed her husband couldn't recall. "At our height, there were eleven, but now, we've slowed down a bit."

"And Dara was your only…." She searched for the proper phraseology. "Your only biological child?"

"Yes, that's right." Angelica leaned forward and handed Merry a scone on Rosenthal china. "Once we had her, we realized that bringing more children into the world would be a crime, especially when there were so many unwanted ones out there. When she was what, one? Two?" She looked to her husband for confirmation. "When she was a toddler, anyway, we started fostering children from around the world, giving them a better life. We raised Dara to understand her stature in this world was a rare gift denied to many, and that our role was to devote our privilege to embracing those less fortunate. It wasn't always easy for her but obviously, she finally understood, which is clear from the path she's followed with her philanthropic works. We're so proud of her for that."

Merry thought about the animals at Neglect-Thee-Not that she'd worked hard to save through fundraising. She and Dara had clearly been the human equivalent—throwaway children, both of them. Secondary in their parents' eyes. *Didn't realize we had that much in common.*

218

"That's exactly why I'm here." Merry dabbed her scone with cream and jam. "I want to organize a tribute dinner for Dara. She does so much and we need to celebrate that. I was thinking of organizing a 'This is Your Life' -type event, bringing in various people from her past and having them give short testimonials—either in person or on camera. Of course, we'd do it as a fundraiser for Autism Vanguard. I think we could charge $500 or $1,000 a plate, considering how well-respected she is in the community. What do you think?"

"Did Dara say this was okay?" Quincy lifted an eyebrow.

"Of course. She gave me permission to contact you. Otherwise, I'd never come up here and presume you'd be willing to speak to me."

Merry prayed she'd convincingly masked her anticipation over their answer and that they wouldn't call Dara to check before she got what she came for. Any unearthed scandal, assuming there was one, was crucial to her plan. After that, who cared? She wanted her employer to know she'd been here, that she now had enough dirt to destroy Dara's good name and reputation. Assuming there was dirt to be found.

Quincy thought for a moment, then cleared his throat. "Well…as long as she okayed it, I guess that would be fine. Though frankly, I'm surprised she'd be comfortable with all that attention. We raised her to be humble, to give…not to look for accolades for doing the right thing."

"Maybe if we could only concentrate on the charitable achievements and not on her personally," said Angelica. "Would that be possible?"

Brother, these two were a piece of work. As much as Merry resented Dara, even she acknowledged that the woman deserved *some* praise. She had achieved quite a bit, both in her real estate work and her philanthropy. For whatever reason, the Crawfords couldn't see that. Was it that much of a crime to be born into wealth that you had to spend the rest of your life apologizing for it?

"Anything is possible, Angelica. What I need is for you to tell me everything you can remember about Dara when she was a child and then provide names and phone numbers or email addresses of people I can contact who can testify to her good works."

Angelica looked to Quincy, searching for confirmation. He shrugged his shoulders. "I suppose if it's for the charity and it helps the children, how could it hurt?"

She nodded. "Yes, for the children." She turned back to Merry, squinting while she strained her memory. "Dara was a quiet child. She did well in class, though she wasted valuable hours after school on the track team. To her credit, she spent her remaining spare time volunteering at local charities. I doubt those people would remember her, though, because that was so many years ago. She didn't have hordes of friends, but then again, she wasn't squandering her time socializing when she could be contributing. I'm not exactly sure who you could speak with."

"No ex-boyfriends who are still around?"

"Oh no, our Dara didn't date; she really didn't have the time. We thought she would remain on Long Island, volunteering at a homeless shelter here, but she insisted on applying to college. Since she promised to major in Nonprofit Management, we relented and allowed it," said Quincy.

Merry looked around the opulent living room. It was as elegant as the neighborhood she had driven through earlier that morning, miles of estate-laden lanes and no sign of poverty. "There are homeless shelters in this area of the Island?"

"Well, no. Our church, St. Paul's, operates a daily shuttle out to Hempstead, where our volunteers serve *that* community." Angelica reached for another scone. "They work at shelters, soup kitchens, wherever the need is greatest. When Dara was in high school, she'd bike over to the local nursing home in Glen Cove or take a bus out to the animal shelter in Port Washington to donate her time. I'm not sure how attending Syracuse changed anything, because after graduation, she did the same thing she would have done anyway, but down in Rock Canyon and with neurodivergent children and battered women."

She probably couldn't wait to escape from your oppressive expectations and actually have a life. Merry downed the remainder of her tea, fingers gripping the handle of her cup so tightly, she feared it might break. This fact-finding mission was going nowhere. She wasn't here to find reasons to canonize

Dara, yet that was all her parents were offering. Shrieking erupted from upstairs, more overindulged and underdisciplined children at play. The noise sparked a thought.

"How many foster children did you have while Dara was growing up?"

Angelica's face brightened. "I can't really remember the exact number, but I know we had several little ones running around at the time, just as we do now."

"Many are crack babies or suffer from fetal alcohol syndrome, but not all," added Quincy. "Some struggle with social issues that poisoned relationships at previous foster homes. We give them a chance to be themselves and thrive."

She'd clearly stumbled upon the Crawford's sweet spot. "Maybe the fosters who grew up alongside Dara might have something to contribute? A testimonial to their big sister?"

Quincy's smile disappeared, and his forehead creased. Angelica hung her head and looked down at the floor.

"I don't think that's wise. You see…we suffered a family tragedy a few years before Dara left. There was a fire…" Quincy's words lodged in his throat.

Merry engineered a gasp. "Oh my God…how awful. I hope no one was hurt."

"Dara was a hero, truly," Angelica said. "You can certainly add that to your testimonial. She ran from bedroom to bedroom, helping the children out. But when she got to the last one, the girls must have locked the door and didn't hear her shouts…the heat and the smoke overwhelmed her…"

"Afterwards, the surviving children really didn't interact with Dara…or each other," said Quincy. "This was a house of mourning and healing for a very long time. The trauma, the skin grafts, I shudder just thinking about it. If we allowed you to speak to the fosters, it would only remind them of that terrible experience. We wouldn't want that."

Merry's skin prickled. Of course, goody-goody Dara saved the day. Almost. It must have killed her that children died under her watch. Still, how did the fire start? Why did Dara get to that room last? Wouldn't a fire alarm have alerted those two girls? She couldn't ask outright; the Crawfords were in no shape for direct probing. But maybe someone else could fill in the blanks. She'd potentially uncovered something here, something hot. No time to let the embers cool.

"How dreadful." Merry quivered her lower lip as she had at the mock funerals she'd attended years before. "I can't even imagine. A heartbreak every family member shared. Still, after so many years… talking about it might prove cathartic."

All Angelica needed was that tiny moment of commiseration to nudge open a floodgate of tears. Quincy embraced her, unsuccessfully holding back his own tsunami. Merry knew from experience the best way to get what she needed was to share a calamity of her own. She gave them time to cry themselves out, handed them each some tissues from her handbag, and gently inserted herself into their sorrow.

"I know how awful it feels to lose a loved one. My own brother was beaten and left for dead when I was in my teens. You feel…so helpless. So alone. I understand…and I'm here for you."

"Your…your brother? How tragic." Angelica dabbed her cheeks with Merry's tissue; her sobs now diminished to sniffles. "We lost two girls that day, Zahara and Oksana. Two beautiful souls…"

"We've never quite gotten over it," said Quincy. "We light a candle every month for them, visit their gravesites as often as we can…"

"And Dara. That must have been devastating for her to lose two of her foster sisters. Especially since she *did* save the rest of the children."

"Yes…yes, it was. Thank goodness she and the others escaped, albeit with burns and minor physical injuries. It took years of therapy for Dara to get over the ordeal." Quincy squeezed his eyes shut, lost in his anguish.

Therapist? That's another lead, thought Merry. It was clear she wasn't going to get much more out of the Crawfords, at least not today, while they wallowed in their mutual misery. She hugged them both and made her excuses to leave.

The afternoon hadn't been a complete wash. Parents were often oblivious to what really happened in their households. The fosters might be happy to throw shade on their big sister. And she had ways to entice the therapist into sharing his findings as well. All theoretically damning details she could use to blackmail Dara into keeping her mouth shut. Money talked, and she had plenty to share in exchange for the details she needed.

Chapter Forty-Four

Merry remembered Dara mentioning her family belonged to an Episcopal church. On a hunch, she googled local houses of worship and made a quick call from her car while still parked on the Crawford estate. Then she drove the two miles to St. Paul's, a small stone, gothic-style church with arched passageways and clustered exterior columns. She briefly scanned the property, acknowledging the allure such a homey structure might have for the pious each Sunday. But now that Merry's own holy trinity—power, money, and admiration—were in jeopardy, she prayed someone inside might provide her with the means to protect all three from the clutches of snoopy Dara Banks.

The equally impressive rectory boasted inspiring stained-glass windows and elaborate wood carvings. The parish administrator greeted her at the door, apologized that the Reverend was running late, and offered her a cup of tea while she waited in his office. The woman was young, too young, in fact, to have been working there decades prior, so Merry didn't bother prodding her for information. This was a crap shoot anyway; she'd chosen the church on a hunch based on its proximity to the Crawford home. She strategically positioned her checkbook on her lap and sipped her Earl Gray, awash in excitement over what she might uncover.

Finally, Reverend Sexton, a balding, portly man with sweat dotting his brow, made his grand appearance. "I'm so sorry, Ms. Rafter. I truly apologize for my delay. I'm afraid that sometimes, ministry affairs can't wait."

He shook her hand and lodged himself in the tufted wingback chair beside her.

"It's not a problem, Reverend," Merry assured him. "Remember, I'm the one who scheduled this last-minute appointment. It's good of you to find time to meet with me on such short notice."

"We try to make ourselves available for all our congregants, current and... future? Are you hoping to join our little church?" His gaze drifted down to the checkbook perched on her lap.

You wish. "What a lovely thought. I'm afraid I live upstate so it would be too onerous a commute every Sunday. I've just come from the Crawford home. Quincy and Angelica? They're congregants of yours, correct?"

"I've known that family for nearly three decades. They've contributed greatly to our community. How do you know them?"

Bingo! "I work with their daughter, Dara." Merry watched with curiosity as the Reverend's cheeks reddened but continued without missing a beat. "She volunteered in your outreach program, I believe. She does so much for Rock Canyon...the town's leading Realtor, establishing a wonderful non-profit that helps those with autism...and I'm planning a gala dinner in her honor."

The Reverend flexed his fingers and curled them again, as if struggling to find his words. "That's...wonderful. How can *we* help, though?"

Merry considered whether his awkwardness could be due to the resurgence of an unhappy memory. After all, the blaze had diminished his flock by two. Or perhaps she had stumbled onto something more. Time to press forward.

"Until today, I didn't know about the fire. You know Dara, so modest—she'd never boast about rescuing all those children. And the Crawfords are so emotional about the incident—and rightfully so, of course. Naturally, I didn't want to pressure them for too many details. I was wondering what light you could shed on the incident, especially since I sense this church was instrumental in their recovery from that trauma. I'm hoping my donation to St. Paul's might compensate you for those efforts."

She grazed her checkbook with the side of her palm and waited.

Reverend Sexton's eyes widened in contrast to his insistent head shake. "Ms. Rafter, as I'm sure you'll agree when we do God's work, it is truly its own reward. But if you wanted to...say, contribute to our organ fund, we would be more than delighted to accept your help."

"Organ...like in organ donations? Hearts and kidneys? You get involved in that?"

The Reverend let out a chortle. "Oh no, no. We're replacing our church organ with a Gluck. Its sound quality will be magnificent...but it comes with an equally prodigious price tag, I'm afraid. Every donation helps."

Merry tapped her red polished fingernail on the checkbook and smiled. "I'd be delighted to help defray those costs a bit. So, what can you tell me about Dara, the fire, her foster brothers and sisters?"

The tongue-loosening prospect of a hefty donation tempered whatever hesitance the Reverend had initially experienced.

"It was devastating, of course. They lost Zahara, who was fifteen at the time, and Oksana, who was twelve. From what I understand, they were roommates. Dara blamed herself, of course, initially assuming that because they were the oldest fosters, they'd gotten themselves out first and that the others more desperately needed her help."

Merry nodded. A slightly different story than she'd heard from the Crawfords. "Do they know how the fire started?"

"There was no formal announcement by the authorities. In fact, the Journal kept the whole thing very low-key. Not surprising since the Crawfords were, and still are, majority shareholders. The rumor was, it was electrical. It's an older home, so it's not surprising an occasional short or spark might get out of hand."

Merry's interest piqued. When newspapers conveniently omit details, they're usually hiding something ugly. "Surely the police investigated?"

"I'm sure they must have but I'm clueless as to what they found. Probably nothing. It's not like the Crawfords disappeared from public life out of shame. They mourned, they wore black, but they still participated in the community—attending school and church, volunteering, trudging forward. After a while, the incident became nothing more than a bad memory."

"Very brave of them...are any of the fosters from that period still living in the community, would you know?"

226

"Hmm…most moved on once they aged out of the system. But Janica was living with them at that time—Janica Rivera. She recently got married, so I guess she goes by Janica Zamm now. She lives with her new husband in Bethpage. That's about twenty minutes south of here." The Reverend's voice ended on a down note, signaling his narrative was now complete.

"Janica…what a beautiful name." Merry made out a check to cash for $1,000 and handed it to the Reverend. "You've been extremely helpful; I can't thank you enough. I'll be happy to send you all invitations to the gala when it's scheduled, if you're interested."

"Err…that would be lovely."

They shook hands, and Merry took her leave. She knew from his tone that she'd never see the Reverend again, and not just because there wouldn't be a gala. The man visually ached to have nothing more to do with the Crawford fire or with Dara. She wondered why. On to her next stop to find out.

Chapter Forty-Five

A blowout was the last thing Dara needed on her way home from Syracuse, but nevertheless, that's what she had to contend with. What was it with her and cars this year? She managed to contain the spinout and hobble onto the shoulder of I-81S just north of Binghamton, where she waited for AAA to arrive. When she called, they warned her how shorthanded they were, due to an unprecedented number of accidents that day, and that the wait might be longer than usual. She told them she understood. As long as she had access to her phone charger and the Internet, she had plenty to keep her busy. With Merry safely ensconced in Paris, she had no reason to race home.

Dara was answering emails when her cell rang. Why did her mother always find the most inconvenient time to call? Then again, was there ever an opportune moment for your parents to remind you that everything you did came up short?

"Hi, Mom, what's up?"

"Hello, Da. Your father and I are just so delighted about this gala Merry is planning in your honor. We forgot to get the date from her, and we wanted to put it in our calendar, so we don't double-book. I tried reaching out, but the calls just kept going to voicemail. We figured you might know?"

Dara scrunched her brow. She had to have misheard.

"Mom, what are you talking about? When did you speak to Merry?"

"Just earlier today, dear. Over tea and scones. She told us all about the arrangements, asked how much we thought she should charge per plate. What a great idea for a fundraiser, bringing together everyone who knows you to give testimonials. Why, your friends will no doubt invite their friends too, and you'll have a sellout."

Merry had been there today? *What the f—k.* She'd personally dropped her off at JFK a few days before. She was supposed to be staying at the George V, sampling foie gras at La Tour d'Argent, and catching a burlesque show at the Crazy Horse Saloon, not rummaging through Dara's past.

"Mom...what exactly did you tell her?"

"Not a lot. I mean, you didn't have any friends we knew of. So, we didn't have names to share with her."

Thank God for that.

"We told her how you volunteered after school..."

Please, not the fire, not the fire, not the fire.

"...and even though we didn't initially intend to, we even shared what a hero you were, the night of the fire."

Shit. Dara's blood pressure ignited like a match lit near a gas leak. She took a series of deep breaths to force herself to calm down before she had a stroke.

Think, Dara, think, urged Celeste. *It's an accident from over twenty years ago. All the fosters have moved on. No one blames you for the two who perished. The police certainly don't; they closed the case almost before it was opened. Merry might have the bare details, but that's where it ends. What's the worst she could tell people...that you failed once in your teens? That a locked door and a wrongful assumption prevented you from rescuing all the children?*

"Dara, are you still there?" her mother asked.

"Yeah, I'm here. It's just that...you know how hard I've tried to block out memories of that night. Dr. Dimitri said—"

"Yes, we all know what your therapist said. Forgive yourself. Forget that awful night. But don't we owe it to poor Zahara and Oksana to think of them as often as we can, so they can live on through our memories?"

God forbid we consider the needs of the living before those of the deceased. Dara rolled her eyes, grateful she wasn't on FaceTime where her parents could see. For the moment, she thought it best to play along and keep her parents out of her private skirmish with Merry.

"Mom, the answer to your original question is, I have no idea of the date of the event. Or if it will actually come to fruition. When I find out, I'll let you know. I'm afraid I have to go now, but thanks for reaching out."

She disconnected the call, her brain shifting into overdrive. Merry was not in Paris. Instead, she was on Long Island. Maybe she wanted to extend one final warning that Dara wasn't the only one who could rattle skeletons from the past. In other words, stay out of her affairs. But at least this meant she wasn't in Syracuse and didn't know Dara had been nosing around. This amplified her need to get back home. If Merry somehow found out about her latest excursion, it could put her entire family in danger and lead to devastating results. Time to bring in a little extra assistance.

She placed a call to Esther who, while still busy in the station house, promised to return her call in ten. When the phone rang twenty minutes later, Dara had already phoned AAA twice, begging them to move her up in their list of service calls due to an emergency at home.

"Hey, Da, what's up?"

"Not a lot, hon. How are you doing?"

"Same old. Some days are better than others, you know?"

"I *do* know. Anything new with your Merry investigation?"

"I was actually going to call you about that. Would it be okay to stop by your office later today and dust for Merry's fingerprints? I'm sure she must have touched her desk or her chair or even the receiver of a landline if she uses one. That way, I can have a friend at the FBI run them through their computers, see if we get any hits. Anything to link her with those reprobates she hangs out with might help."

"Um, sure. I don't think that would be an issue. I'll call Judy at the front desk, let her know you might be stopping by."

"That would be great. But won't you be around? We could have an early dinner. I've been feeling down, and some time with an old friend would really help."

"I feel you. I'm at a real estate convention but I should be back soon. If I'm around when you stop by, I'd love to grab something to eat and help cheer you up."

Dara paused, second-guessing her original reason for calling. If Merry didn't find out she'd been up north, spying on her mother, chatting with her brother, visiting her old school, then mentioning anything to Esther might be unnecessarily stirring the pot. There would always be a later time to share intel if it were necessary.

"Dara, was there something else?"

"No, sorry. Brain fart. Too many boring sessions. How often can you listen to the intricacies of the 1031 Property Exchange, right? I'll see you back home. Stay strong, okay?"

Dara disconnected the call, then saw the repair truck in her rearview mirror. "I don't have time to be towed," she told the driver. "Just stick on the donut, and I'll be fine."

But would she be fine? That depended on whether she got home before Merry could act upon any news she might receive from Syracuse.

Chapter Forty-Six

Merry left Janica Zamm's small split-level home with a smile on her face and two new contacts in the Notes section of her iPhone. Once she returned to her Audi, she placed a call to her on-again, off-again lover, Tony Randazzo. Triple-Play Tony, she liked to call him because if you got him into bed early enough, he was good for three rounds. All highly satisfying.

"Hey TP, you got a few minutes?"

"For you, babe, you know it. You coming round anytime soon? I got a hard-on just hearing your voice."

Merry smiled. His thick Brooklyn accent was right out of Thugsville, USA, but it belied an intellect that far transcended the rest of his hoodlum buddies. Not that they'd set that high a bar.

"Soon, TP, soon. You got any connections at police stations out on the Island, particularly in Nassau County?"

"I got connections everywhere. And where I don't got 'em, I'll make 'em."

"Excellent. Have a pen handy? I need you to write something down."

She heard shuffling, and then he came back on the line. "Okay, shoot."

"There was a fire around 2000 or 2001 in Locust Valley at 1550 Oak Hollow Lane. I want you to get me the name of whatever detective they assigned to the case and where he or she is today. Then, I need you or someone you trust to do a little reconnaissance work at the office of Dr. Peter Dimitri. He's a psychiatrist in Muttontown, and he specializes in trauma victims. I want a copy of everything in Dara Crawford's files. He would have treated her shortly after that fire. Got it?"

"She's the mark who thought Detective Frank Contardi was investigating her, no? Speaking of which, how's Project Marry Merry coming along?"

"Dead in the water, I'm afraid, thanks to this bitch's predilection for playing Miss Marple. Months invested for nothing. Stupid throwing good money after bad, so I'm going to move on. What I'm asking for today will help me buy an insurance policy, got me?"

"Yeah, got you. Wouldn't it just be easier to off her?"

"No, she's found out things from my past—possibly our past—and I don't know who else she's shared them with. Murdering her could spell suicide for me and my future "projects," and I'm not looking to die anytime soon. Better to find out enough to create a Mexican standoff. Which brings me to my third request. You still have the key to my apartment?"

"Yup. I've been raring for a chance to use it. Especially after last time..."

"Down, boy. I need you to get your crew over there and clean it out. Put all my things in storage, wipe down the surfaces, leave no trace. I'm not going back to Rock Canyon."

"Never?"

"Not if I can help it, no. Which is a pity because I was going to steal all of Dara's clients and have myself a thriving real estate practice. Easy money and almost legit." She let out a snigger.

"Where are you headed instead?"

"No idea. I might hole up at the Plaza for a bit. Feel free to stop by." The thought of him roughing her up and taking her from behind brought a smile to her lips and her hand to her crotch.

"You got it, babe. What name you gonna use this time?"

"I haven't decided yet. I still have a ton of driver's licenses and credit cards that Carl gave me last time. I've managed to steal socials here and there. I'll choose one and let you know. In the meantime, please email me whatever you dig up. Use the secret account."

"Yup. I'll get you the docs and make sure we empty out your apartment by tomorrow evening. We good?"

"We're great, babe. I'll show my thanks the next time you come to visit, k?"

"Heh. Better buckle up. You're in for a bumpy ride."

Merry smiled and disconnected the call. It was good to have people in this world you could count on. Sex, brains, and cash—that's really all you needed to get by. She had one more stop on her fact-finding mission. Soon, she'd have all the goods she needed on Dara to put this fiasco behind her and move on to more lucrative pastures.

Chapter Forty-Seven

Merry found O'Malley's Tavern crowded, dark, and quaint—everything she expected from an old Irish pub. A long oak bar flanked the right side of the saloon, the shelves stacked heavy with a predominance of brands like Jameson, Redbreast, and Bushmills, interspersed with colorful bottles of lesser-known varieties. Clad in tight jeans and a clingy, white silk blouse buttoned two buttons short of business casual, she leaned into the bartender and asked for a Dead Rabbit and to make it a double.

If she'd been searching for the ultimate stereotype of a broken former detective, Merry had found one in Kevin O'Doherty. Complete with buzz cut and a week's worth of grizzle he'd been too lazy to shave from his chin, he looked just like the photo TP had emailed earlier in the day. The detective who'd headed the investigation into the Crawford fire. He sat at a corner table with a couple of his buddies, guzzling a pint of Guinness and occasionally emitting a belly laugh loud enough to be heard over the pub's chatter. From his sagging posture and dazed expression, Merry surmised his current drink hadn't been his first. She dropped a twenty on the bar, grabbed her whiskey, and ambled over.

"This table looks like it could use a dose of estrogen." She pulled a chair from a nearby table and placed it directly opposite O'Doherty. He lifted a brow, settled his eyes on her cleavage, and grunted his assent.

"I'm Sally Malone. To whom do I have the pleasure of joining for a pint or two?"

It was just easier to go back to Sally, at least for tonight. She wouldn't be stupid enough to use Sally's old credit card, though. She didn't need Vinny breathing up her ass. Instead, she had Carl make her a copy of Dara's, thanks to her always leaving her bag lying around unattended. It wouldn't hurt to have Dara discover the charge on her Visa and realize Merry could hurt her finances as well as her reputation.

They introduced themselves as Sean, Conor, and, of course, Kevin. Sean and Conor each sported thick red beards and wore plaid flannel shirts, their vibe more lumberjack than detective.

She batted her eyelashes and ran her finger slowly along the spine of the menu that lay on the table. "So, boys, what's good here...other than the company?" So corny and yet with these guys, it seemed to work.

"The shepherd's pie is their specialty," Conor said. "I mean, if you're looking for something hardy that will keep you filled for the rest of the evening." While his brogue was adorable, subtlety was clearly not his forte.

"What are you having, Kevin?" She stared directly into his glazed eyes.

O'Doherty gave her a bemused look. "I'm waiting until I get home to my wife and eating whatever she's cooking up."

"Well, aren't you a good boy, not eating out. Still, homecooked meals can get a bit tiresome after a while. Conor, don't you agree?"

Conor nodded like a puppy eyeing kibble.

It seemed like an opportune time to change the subject. "So, what do you guys do around here, other than charm the ladies?"

"We're ex-cops," said Sean. "I was on the force twenty-five years. The others, a bit longer."

"Ooh, I bet you have interesting war stories to share."

After five rounds—all her treat—and one order of shepherd's pie she placed for herself, the boys were all talked out, having recounted seemingly all of their anecdotes except the one in which Merry had the most interest. She needed to prod a bit before they picked up and went home—all but Conor, who'd made it clear he intended to escort her to her front door, wink, wink.

"I heard tell that one of the bigger estates in the area had a huge fire, decades back. A couple of foster kids died," she said. "Were you boys on that case?"

"Yeah," said O'Doherty, his drunken voice laden with disgust. "That was a heartbreaker. Two girls, both under sixteen. A real waste of two young lives."

"How does a blaze like that even start? Old wiring on the fritz or what?"

"Yeah, right. Old wiring," he said with a snort. "At least that's what they instructed us to write in our report, wasn't it, boys? Let's leave it at that. I think it's time to wrap this up." He gestured to the server for the check, at least for the rounds they had ordered before she'd arrived.

"The family involved were major league philanthropists," Conor murmured while O'Doherty handed the server his American Express. "Practically paid to renovate the entire station house. We had to tread very lightly, you know."

Merry nodded, considering how much more information he might divulge if offered the right oral incentives.

"Conor, Sean, we're all sharing an Uber." O'Doherty fiddled with the app on his phone, effectively squashing her plan and leaving Conor crestfallen. "Ms. Malone, I trust you can order one for yourself? Or drive yourself home? I couldn't help but notice you weren't drinking as heavily as we were."

She nodded and offered up a weak smile. The guy might have retired from the force, but he was still on the case; she had to give him that.

It wasn't worth making plans to meet them the following night. She wasn't going to get much more, and what she'd already gleaned from their comments meshed with what she'd learned earlier in the day. Her fact-finding mission was complete. She had her leverage. Now, it was time to return to Manhattan and apply it to her advantage

Chapter Forty-Eight

When Dara finally arrived home, her family were already in bed. She checked on Ava sleeping safely in her room before slipping between the covers next to a snoring Jason.

She was too jazzed to get any rest. All she could think about was how grateful she was to have made it home before Merry could lash out and punish her for continuing her investigation. Now, she had what she needed to keep Merry at a distance. As soon as her assistant returned from wherever she'd gone, which was apparently not Paris, she'd send her packing and hire someone new. Preferably someone who wasn't a con artist, former escort, and an all-around nut job.

There was an irony in how similar they were, she mused. Both had been victims of parental expectations and neglect: Merry with her mother, who doted exclusively on the younger brother, and she with her own parents, who spent every waking moment helping someone other than their own daughter, and insisting that to earn their love, she had to follow in their footsteps. Merry had gone on to seek validation by constantly feeding her narcissism, breaking up both business and personal relationships to make herself feel superior. And Dara herself sought approval by constantly doing the right thing—whether through marriage to a man who needed her or unceasing charity work. They were two sides of the same coin. Except in her case, she hadn't goaded anyone to throw themselves in front of a speeding subway car.

But people have died. And it was all your fault.

I don't want to think about that, Dara silently told Celeste. There's nothing

I can do about that now.

* * *

In the morning, Jason rolled over and gave her a long kiss to welcome her home.

"How was the convention?" he asked.

This was Dara's opportunity to come clean, to tell him she'd lied but for the best reasons, to protect him and the family. But if she did, he'd freak out that she hadn't told him earlier, especially after Ava's Elmo incident. He wasn't going to buy that she knew Merry well enough to understand it had just been a warning that Ava hadn't been in jeopardy herself. It wasn't worth the effort to open up an unfortunate can of worms when there was a better way.

"To be honest, I made a huge mistake. The conference is next month. Playing catch-up at work after the accident really threw me. Plus, the thing with Ava, and hiring the new therapist. You know I don't like to admit weakness, but well, I was still a bit off. And since I was away anyhow, I checked into a spa for some much-needed R&R. I hope you're not angry with me."

He let out a sigh. "Of course, I'm not angry. It's been an insane couple of months, and you deserved a respite. Money well spent. Are you feeling better now?"

"Tip top. Ready to take on the world...starting with making my family a big breakfast. How does a cheese omelet sound?"

"Perfect." He kissed her softly on the lips. "And maybe tonight...?"

"Tonight, I'll make up for all the nights I was away. Promise."

She headed to the next room over, where the new live-in, Tammy, dressed a compliant Ava. The little girl shrieked with joy, pulled away from her therapist, and ran to embrace Dara. It felt wonderful to feel such emotion from a girl who, in her earliest days, used to look stone-faced at anything in her line of vision. Attwood Academy, combined with this new one-on-one support, was doing wonders.

"I'm making breakfast this morning." She squeezed Ava tighter. "As soon as Tammy brushes your hair, we'll eat, and I'll take you to school. Sound good?"

Ava jumped up and down with excitement. Dara headed downstairs, where Khai had already prepared a pot of dark roast, leaving the kitchen smelling…well, like home. The home she'd known before Merry entered her life and turned everything rancid.

"You're up early, Khai. Missed you, honey. How's school going?"

"Aced my two tests last week. Nothing's keeping me from getting into USC."

"Great going. If there's any subject where you feel weak, let me know. I have clients who are tutors. We're going to get that GPA up to where it needs to be. I can already see you on that surfboard in between classes. You up for an omelet?"

"Yeah, sounds great. Good to have you back."

Dara smiled. He was in a good mood, her cue to press forward.

"Khai, I need to discuss something with you." She cracked eggs into a bowl, added a dash of milk, and whisked them together. "When Merry gets back, I'm afraid I'm going to have to let her go from Rock Canyon Realty. We've had ongoing differences at work, and I think it's best if I get a new assistant. It would be awkward if you and your friends kept going to her apartment, don't you agree?"

"Not a problem, Mom. I stopped hanging out there weeks ago. Spending time with those guys wasn't the most productive use of my time, especially now that I've set my sights on this major. I can play the games here, more to study the design, though. I hope you find a new assistant that works out better. Merry was wonderful, but to be honest, too often she went overboard trying to be nice. She got on my nerves."

Dara looked over her shoulder. "Me too, Khai, me too."

After a cozy family breakfast, Dara dropped Ava at school and then drove to the office. She half-expected Merry to be at her desk, or more likely, at Dara's, playing at real estate while she plotted her next move against the family. But both computers remained off, Dara's office dark, paperwork exactly as she'd left it prior to her departure.

She sat down at her desk and prepared for a day of reviewing Merry's files, contacting her clients, and letting them know that she'd be taking over due to her assistant's extended absence. Her phone dinged, and a text appeared:

I know all about the fire and Zahara and Oksana. If you don't want everyone else to know it too, keep out of my affairs. In turn, I will stay out of yours. Consider this my resignation. Have a nice life.

Dara stared at the message, torn between relief and frustration. On the one hand, she'd triumphed where others like Samantha Ellingsworth had failed. She had her life back without the messy public scene that a firing might have provoked. But, that win came at a cost: she'd been cheated out of the chance to punish Merry for infiltrating and attempting to destroy her life, her business, and her family. In the end, relief won out, washing over her like a warm summer rain.

Okay, Georgia, she texted back, unable to resist that final jab. No response. Time to get back to work.

Chapter Forty-Nine

T he next several weeks were glorious. Dara took back her clients, many who admitted they never felt great confidence in Merry, who spent as much time patting herself on the back as she did showing homes. Dara assured them that she would be the only Realtor they'd be working with in the future.

As deals closed, Dara deposited the proceeds into an account she'd set aside to help Jason with his upcoming surgery. Unfortunately, due to the lead doctor moving out of state, the hospital postponed the operation yet again. It was now set for August. Though initially disappointed, Jason's running routine kept his endorphins high, and he'd been hard at work with new plans for a follow-up to The Fortress on the Hudson called The Citadel. He'd hired an architecture student from Rock Canyon College to be his hands as he mapped out his plans, and it had gone surprisingly well.

On the charity front, Dara continued running her monthly Birthday Parties for All events, leaning more heavily on her core group of volunteers than she had in the past. She discovered ten thousand dollars missing from the organization's bank account, which she attributed to Merry's greed. Celeste rumbled, demanding repayment in blood. Dara pushed back the demand, instead making up for the discrepancies out of her own wallet, chalking the theft up to two life lessons she'd never forget: Always check references and never hire impulsively. In fact, she didn't hire her new assistant, Rodrigo, until after three rounds of interviews, with every reference interrogated as if they were on trial for murder.

Things were going so well, in fact, that her board nominated her for

National Realtor of the Year, both in recognition of superior sales in the wake of a life-endangering accident, and because of her unrelenting non-profit contribution to the community at large. To her surprise, NAR not only accepted her local board's nomination, but they also chose her as the winner from a host of impressive candidates. They'd scheduled the event for June, right in Rock Canyon this time around, and local newspapers ran a full-page article about her achievements that the local and national real estate trades picked up and published.

Her parents accepted the gala invitation as consolation for the cancellation of Dara's imaginary testimonial dinner. Angelica still blamed her daughter for her assistant's rapid departure and the ensuing cancellation of the event.

"I'm sure you were too hard on her. And gave her too much to do. And weren't supportive enough. You should have done more to hold onto her, Dara. She was so special."

Special, indeed. Dara took her mother's diatribe from whence it came. There was no point in trying to make Angelica understand; no matter what she did, it would never be enough.

Things were going well, even without her parents' approval. Merry had stayed away, just as she had promised. Still, something continued to bother Dara—Merry's unspecified location. She'd feel more comfortable knowing for certain the harpy had moved hundreds if not thousands of miles away. Plus, there were others out there who could fall for her schemes, and that didn't sit right. Dara had the power to set things straight, take her out, but instead, she'd let Merry off with barely a reprimand. That weighed on her conscience.

Esther's upset over Merry's sudden disappearance was palpable, especially since it stalled her investigation into Brooke's death. Dara decided to wait a bit longer and then feed Esther some additional information. Perhaps let her know Vera Jones' identity as Merry's mother. Or share the recent photo of her former assistant that she'd *just* realized one of her clients' nanny cams had recorded. Esther might not be able to pin Brooke's death on her, but how could it hurt to give her investigation the ammunition it needed to locate the missing woman for them both. Even if Brooke's death remained classified as a suicide, Esther could arrest Merry for fraud, identity theft, and so much more. But for now, Dara was following her original plan: wait and let Merry believe she'd gotten away with everything. The time would come, Celeste assured her, when all that would change.

* * *

Merry did not like Pittsburgh, not at all. While it served its purpose, giving her a place far from Dara's sights to live and work as a nanny until she settled on her next mark, the city lacked the excitement and sophistication of Manhattan, or even Rock Canyon. TP stopped by occasionally when he had time to make the drive, but overall, she ached from boredom. And when she got bored, she started plotting. She considered applying for a Pennsylvania real estate license. Pittsburgh must have tons of homes and apartments for sale, and she could pick up extra cash until she targeted the next Mr. Rich, Lonely, and Neglected.

The longer she thought about it, the more realistic the idea became. She didn't necessarily have to stay in Pittsburgh; Philadelphia was less than one hundred miles south of Manhattan, and if she lived there, she could make the trek whenever she wanted. Thanks to the moneyed families who called the city home, the sales price of real estate in expensive areas like Fitler Square averaged over $1 million. She could sell homes while searching for an unhappy husband in a neighborhood like that, just waiting for a mistress. Or she could take the new same-sex marriage laws out for a spin—pursue the wife and leave the husband out in the cold. Keep things fresh. At least women knew how to find her sweet spot.

Merry investigated licensing requirements and discovered reciprocity existed between New York and Pennsylvania. Still, the new agency would want to check out her original license, and they'd notice her face didn't match her mother's picture. She'd have to start fresh, but use a new name, a new social security card. Her past gigs—dancer, escort, nanny—paid in cash, so she hadn't really needed the number. For Rock Canyon Realty, she'd used a fake one, knowing that usually, real estate companies' only hiring standard was making sure the agent was breathing, which meant no background check. Still, agencies in Pennsylvania might be more diligent. She'd have to do her research.

She didn't mind her current pseudonym, Harper Van Dyke. She'd coupled it with a convincing story about her Pennsylvania Dutch upbringing when applying for her current nanny job from a middle-class couple named Pete and Stacey Cavanaugh. They'd listened open-mouthed as she recounted how she'd escaped from her Amish family and hitchhiked to Pittsburgh with only twenty dollars in her pocket, determined to make it on her own. Whether out of pity or admiration for her courage, they'd hired her on the spot.

She felt especially proud of the story since it saved her from paying friends to provide false references, like they had with the Ellingsworth scam. She'd told the Cavanaughs her former Amish employers didn't use phones and had shunned her from the community. With such a stigma, how could they expect a positive reference, even if they trekked out to Bird in Hand, PA, to inquire directly?

Since then, she'd taken loving care of their brat and given them no reason to complain or verify her story.

Merry became increasingly enamored with her plan to take the Philadelphia real estate market by storm. For once, she could make an honest living, maybe not even need another mark. Perhaps, finally, go back to using her real name and get her own social security number. Though, if her prospecting happened to connect her with a couple who were less than content, who was she to ignore an easy million or so in future alimony?

To that end, she subscribed to the national real estate trade periodicals, eager to keep apprised of happenings in the industry, and when the most recent issue arrived, that's when she saw it. The nominee for National Realtor of the Year, with the cover story titled *Dara Banks: Overcoming All Odds to Help Herself and Others Succeed.*

She rifled through the pages, eager to read how Meryl Rafter, Dara's assistant, had been instrumental in the broker's recovery, taking care of her children—one with autism, the other a wayward teen—and nurturing her clients until Dara was healthy enough to reappear on the real estate scene. She read through the four-page story twice, stunned. Not. One. Word. Not even a mention. It was as if she'd never existed. *That ingrate. How dare she.*

At that moment, Merry ditched her plans for détente. Dara wasn't going to live long enough to accept that award, and she knew exactly how to make it happen.

Chapter Fifty

While closing the last condo sale at The Fortress on the Hudson, Dara's cell rang. She excused herself from the table and wandered into one of the attorney's unused offices to take the call.

"Mrs. Parker, this is a surprise. How are you enjoying your new home? Ready to quit renting and purchase something? This would be the perfect market to do that."

"Hi, Dara. Yes, we love the apartment, but that's not why I'm calling. There was a strange charge on our Visa bill this month. We never use the card for online purchases, we don't even charge our meals when we eat out. In fact, I think the last time we shared the number was several months ago when your assistant needed it to run a credit check. Could you look into that for us? It's only a twenty-dollar charge, and we did reverse it and put a hold on the card but still, we'd like to know how this happened."

The hairs on Dara's forearm stood on end. She considered all the credit information Merry had been privy to during her sojourn as assistant. Full access to her files. Who knew what she had written down or taken with her?

"Mrs. Parker, I'm so sorry. If Visa doesn't make you whole, I certainly will. Tell me, where was the charge from? Do you remember?"

"Oh yes, it was from a liquor store in a small town outside Pittsburgh. Wait a moment. I'll check the bill." The sound of footsteps and paper rustling followed. "The bill says it's from Shots and Shooters in Aspinwall, PA."

"That's an immense help, thanks. I'll take care of this for you, Mrs. Parker.

And if it's any comfort, that assistant is no longer with me. If it turns out it was her who used the card, I will prosecute to the full extent of the law on your behalf."

"Dara, we're not looking to get anyone in trouble. It could all be a mistake. We just wanted to find out the source of the leak, that's all."

"Thank you for being so patient and understanding. I hope we can work together in the future. Please let me know if any of your friends or family are in the market." *Why not turn lemons into lemonade?*

"Will do. Have a lovely day."

Dara disconnected the call and then googled Shots and Shooters. A rifle range with a bar, just outside Pittsburgh. A great combination for disaster. Get drunk, shoot a fellow patron. Just what the Quakers intended.

Her concerns far transcended prospective accidents at an establishment she'd never heard of before. She wondered how many other of her clients might have received similar charges on their credit cards, ones that had escaped their notice…for now. She walked back into the closing, explained to her clients that there'd been an emergency, handed them a bottle of congratulatory champagne, and drove back to the office as fast as she could.

Dara spent the rest of her day doing damage control. She checked all the rental files from the past three years—she'd archived earlier transactions prior to Merry's arrival—and called each client, asking them to review their credit card bills and contact her if they found any wrongful charges.

Several clients did call back, claiming erroneous billings, though some were still pending and had not yet gone through. The amounts ranged from twenty-five to thirty dollars, small charges that an unobservant cardholder could have easily missed. And there was a pattern to the expenditures: one the first day, two the second, each day growing by one. Dara urged the couples to cancel those cards and request chargebacks. If the companies refused, she promised to make them whole. Surprise benefit: each of the four appreciated her proactive approach so much, they gave her referrals of several friends looking for homes.

Dara asked her clients for the names of the establishments involved. Restaurants and bars, all in Aspinwall, PA. A nice little roadmap pointing to Merry's current location. Could this be a trap? Luring Dara away from home to investigate? Maybe. But why? Merry had more to lose by angering Dara than by maintaining their impasse.

More likely, the charges were small enough that Merry never imagined the cardholders would notice. Maybe she got off on petty theft. But the pattern...

The thought of her former assistant taking advantage of innocent clients rubbed Celeste like sandpaper on a newborn's skin. Her assistant had asked for a standoff and now she'd gone back on her word. This was a step too far. For all Dara knew, right now, Merry could be plotting to jeopardize some innocent Aspinwall housewife's marriage, just as Samantha Ellingsworth's and hers had been. The cycle had to end.

Pennsylvania might be the birthplace of America, but for Merry, it needed to be the exact opposite.

Chapter Fifty-One

Colin Farris was one of the country's leading real estate motivational trainers, and luckily, the Connecticut stop on his East Coast tour coincided with Dara's discovery of the credit card thefts. It gave her the perfect excuse to explain to Jason why she needed to take off for another few days. Especially since Farris specialized in training agents on how to successfully hire and retain real estate assistants, a talent Dara sorely lacked.

The trip to the Pittsburgh area normally took six hours, but Dara's lead-footed driving made it in five. Her research revealed that Aspinwall was a small borough on the Allegheny River with just over three thousand residents. She figured it shouldn't be that hard to find someone who had met Merry, especially since she already had the names of establishments the con artist had frequented in the area.

She checked into a nearby motel, wearing a long blonde wig and black-rimmed glasses she'd purchased before leaving Rock Canyon to guarantee her anonymity, and then headed out to the various establishments where Merry had passed off Dara's clients' credit cards as her own. Unfortunately, no one recognized her assistant from the nanny cam photos. Only at her fourth stop, a little diner called Nell's, did she find a server able to help.

"Oh, I know Harper well," said "Mae" when she arrived at Dara's table and heard her bogus tale of how the woman had delivered her lost dog to a local shelter; their security camera having taken the photo she was displaying.

"She's always in here with the Cavanaughs' daughter, buying her burgers and milkshakes. I'm hoping her parents don't put a stop to it; Harper's a good tipper."

"I really want to find Harper and give her a reward for her efforts. From the sound of it, she'll spend the money here. Do you know where I can find her?"

Mae handed Dara a menu. "I'm sorry, I don't know her home address. But if you hang around, she usually shows up around four, right after the little girl gets out of school. Why not order a bite to eat? I can personally recommend the pepperoni roll. It's our most popular dish."

"Oh, I'm sure it is. I'll come back later, when Harper arrives, and I'll be happy to sample one. Could you not mention any of this to her? I'd like it to be a surprise. As humble as she appears to be, she might take off before I get a chance to thank her if she knows I'm coming."

Mae's wide smile revealed two missing teeth. "No problem, ma'am. I won't say a word. But don't forget—pepperoni roll. Delish."

"Got it. I won't forget." Dara slipped her a twenty-dollar bill. Mae looked down; her face scrunched into a question mark.

"I didn't want to do you out of a tip, in case I stop by after your shift ends," Dara explained, standing to leave. "Thanks again."

She parked and monitored the entrance from the rear of the lot, where she'd be less noticeable. Just as Mae predicted, right after four o'clock, Merry appeared with her small charge, a little blond girl in pigtails, holding a miniature Pooh Bear. Merry had retained Dara's red pixie haircut but looked as if she'd dropped about ten pounds.

The sight of her caused Dara's stomach to churn, and the wall in her brain that signaled Celeste's approach threatened to separate logic from emotion, reason from fury.

That's the woman who stole money from your clients and who would have appropriated your life if you'd been more gullible and if Brooke hadn't warned you early on. Put an end to this, to her. Today. Now.

"Not yet," Dara answered aloud. "Let me handle this my way. I can do it. You'll just muddle things up, like you have before."

A half hour later, Merry and the little one emerged from Nell's and drove off, with Dara trailing carefully behind, always leaving a few cars between them. When Merry turned onto Cheshire Lane, Dara noted the driveway where she parked without turning onto Cheshire herself. After Merry entered the house, Dara drove by and made a mental note of the address: Number Two. Home of the family who, thanks to Dara, would soon learn the vital importance of checking a reference before allowing any nanny to join their household.

Chapter Fifty-Two

The next morning at six o'clock, Dara parked on Cheshire Lane, across the street and two houses down from Number Two, but still with a decent view of the front entrance and driveway. Still clad in her wig and glasses, she scarfed down a granola bar and sipped a diet iced tea as she observed, eager to get a sense of the family's schedule. At eight, a tall gentleman in a grey suit emerged, grabbed the newspaper from the front porch, and went back inside. Ten minutes later, the garage opened, and that same man, driving a black Camry, rode past Dara toward the highway.

Fifteen minutes later, an older model white Impreza rolled out of the garage. The brunette driver definitely wasn't Merry. Dara followed her for several miles until she turned into the parking lot of the University of Pittsburgh Medical Center. She parked close by and walked double-speed to catch up with the woman, who wore a brown pantsuit and orthopedic shoes.

"Excuse me, Mrs. Cavanaugh?"

The woman swung around to face Dara. "Yes. Do I know you?"

"No, no, you don't. But in about an hour, you're going to be grateful we met. Is there somewhere we can speak privately? It's a matter of life and death."

The woman gave her a dubious look. "There's a coffee shop in the lobby. I've got exactly thirty minutes before I'm due in the office. I hope that's enough time to save lives because I can't afford to be late and lose this job."

Dara decided to ignore the woman's sarcastic tone. A half-hour was long enough for an introduction. She could always finish the story at lunch.

* * *

Stacey Cavanaugh listened slack-jawed as Dara recounted her history with Merry, from the day she walked in for her interview up until the moment she resigned via text. She summarized Merry's past names and professions, showed her the fake Lee and Warren news story, their mug shots, Samantha Ellingsworth's obituary. She explained how Samantha's was the first of two suicides Merry had engineered—that she knew about, anyway—how her tales of embezzlement had likely led Brooke to take her own life as well. The warning underlining the narrative couldn't be clearer: together, they had to do something to stop "Harper" before she destroyed the Cavanaughs' marriage and with it, Stacey's life as wife and mother.

"You've given me a lot to think about." Stacey's distraught tone filled Dara with hope. The woman glanced at her phone, then pushed back her chair. "I need time to digest all this. I'm busy for the rest of the day, but could we meet again tomorrow morning? I'll do whatever it takes to protect myself and my family."

"That would be perfect. I'll spend the day developing some strategies."

A sense of calm enveloped Dara as she drove back to her hotel. Stacey Cavanaugh believed her. Together, they could—and would—pull off this plan. Before she left Pennsylvania, Merry/Harper would be history, and Dara would have helped the world by ridding it of a virus in human form before it could spread further.

The next morning, Dara arrived early at the coffee shop, pen and paper in hand. Stacey showed up five minutes later and joined her in a booth at the back.

"I made an excuse to Harper about having to check in patients early. She bought it, thank God. So where are we? What are we thinking?"

Dara laid out the plan as she had visualized it. Stacey would take her daughter to her mother's house that evening so the little girl wouldn't be privy to anything that happened the following day. Stacey would ask Merry to meet her for a performance review over afternoon tea, during which she'd confront the nanny with all she'd learned. Dara would hide in the pantry, and while both women were chatting in the dining room, she'd tiptoe into the kitchen and lace Merry's mug with a powerful sleep agent. When Merry finally collapsed, Dara would transport her back to Manhattan and deliver sleeping beauty right to Vinny Randazzo's door at Brazen. Let him take care of her, extract his pound of flesh to compensate him for the money she'd stolen.

That was the plan Dara explained to Stacey, and the one she agreed to. Not being someone who trusted anything to chance, Dara's actual plan differed slightly. She couldn't necessarily depend on Vinny seeing his old paramour, ignoring any lingering lust, and still following through on his threat. But Plan B was nothing Stacey needed to know beforehand. She'd find out soon enough.

Chapter Fifty-Three

The following day, Dara parked her car three blocks south of Cheshire Lane and trampled through the woods that ran behind the houses to enter the Cavanaugh home via the back door. Stacey had left it open as requested. There was nothing to tip Merry off in advance that Dara was waiting inside, eager to ambush her former assistant, whom Stacey had sent off, as arranged, on a morning errand. She patted her purse protectively. It contained what she needed to effectively complete her mission.

That's when everything started to fall apart. The house was empty, Stacey nowhere to be found. Dara ran through the rooms, checking each one, even the basement. Then she started to panic. She'd come so far, and she was so close. She sensed the sweat beading on her forehead, her breath quickening. How could this be happening? Celeste was quick to remind her that she probably should have dealt with Merry back in Rock Canyon when she had the chance.

She fumbled for her burner and called Stacey's number. One ring, two rings. A drop of perspiration dripped past her eyelash and onto her cheek. Finally, on the third ring, the woman picked up.

Dara couldn't control her frustration. "Where are you? Do you want to wreck everything?"

"Hey, calm down," Stacey replied, matching her angry tone. "I'm right around the corner. My mother has the flu, so I had to move my daughter to a friend's house. Just check yourself; I'll be there in a few."

Dara closed her eyes, willing her pulse to slow. Maybe, just maybe, they could still pull this off. Stacey arrived five minutes later, lips pursed, but didn't offer an apology, just headed into the kitchen to start boiling water as they'd discussed.

During their last meeting, Dara had painstakingly explained that she would prepare two cups of tea and only the blue one was meant for the nanny. Only the blue mug. She made Stacey repeat the directive three times. A slip-up here, she explained, could ruin everything.

Dara grimaced as Stacey made herself a pot of coffee and added a healthy dash of Bailey's to her mug, something she explained she needed to take the edge off. *Just what I need: an accomplice who was half-blitzed on liquor.* She bit her lip, though, reminding herself that she couldn't afford to alienate Stacey further and risk the entire plan falling to pieces.

Dara placed a nanny cam disguised as a silk plant on the dining room windowsill and donned a set of ear pods. This would allow her to stream the action to her cell, which she could watch and listen to from her hiding spot. She carefully prepared the mugs near the kettle and set out the creamer and sugar bowl on the dining table. Confident everything looked as normal as possible, she slipped into the pantry, out of view. Her body hummed with anticipation. Today, Merry would realize she'd picked the wrong mark to mess with when she decided to roll into Rock Canyon.

She watched via video stream as Stacey futzed around the dining room, deciding where to place a plate of cookies. She changed the location three times before Merry's car pulled up, and the nanny joined her in the dining room. It was finally happening! Dara prayed that the Bailey's she'd earlier disparaged would do its job and keep Stacey calm, so as not to tip off the nanny that anything was afoot.

Stacey went into the kitchen and brought out the two steaming mugs Dara had prepared. She placed the blue one in front of Merry, exactly as instructed. *Perfect.*

The nanny smiled, and reached for the mug, filling Dara with certainty they were going to pull this off. Then, much to her chagrin, she drew her hand back.

"You know, Stacey, I think I'd prefer a cup of coffee. Don't get up. I'll pour it myself."

Stacey glared into the camera once Merry left, frantically mouthing the words, "What do I do now?"

Dara couldn't respond. She could only hope Stacey played it cool and trusted Dara to have things well in hand.

Merry strolled back into the room and set her coffee mug on the table.

"Stacey, you look pale. Have a cup of tea; it'll make you feel better."

"Thanks, Harper. I'm sure you're right." She added a half-teaspoon of sugar and some cream to her mug and pushed the bowl back to the center of the table. Only after Stacey took her first sip did Merry scoop her usual three heaping dollops of sweetener into her coffee, along with a dash of cream.

"That's better," Merry said with a smile. "Now we can have our little talk." Raising her voice, she added, "Dara, why don't you come out too? I know you're here because I've had someone following you since you left Rock Canyon."

Dara's stomach dropped, and she broke into a cold sweat but remained glued to her spot in the pantry.

After a minute, Merry called out again. "Dara, you really want to come out. You remember your old pal, Lee? He's outside the Attwood Academy right now. One text from me and a stray bullet is going to send Ava to autism heaven before she ever makes it to her therapist's car. And you thought Elmo's dismemberment was bad. You wanna take a chance with your stepdaughter's life, oh great helper? That's up to you."

Stacey let out a shriek, and, on the stream, Dara saw Merry reach over and slap her employer across the face. Stacey slumped back into her chair, blubbering, mascara running down her cheeks.

While skeptical, Dara couldn't take the chance that Merry was bluffing. With wobbly knees and churning stomach, she departed from her safe place and entered the dining room. After one look at her old assistant's smug expression, the gravity of the situation hit her. She doubled over with nausea, retching and spewing that morning's breakfast onto the polished hardwood floor.

"Lovely. Very elegant. You always were a class act, Boss Lady. Go sit down beside Stacey, there's a good girl. Now, excuse me while I even up our numbers." Merry picked up her phone and made a quick call. "TP, coast is clear. You can come in now."

The back door opened, and Tony Randazzo sauntered in, a pistol in his hand. "Hello, Dara. You remember me? Good old Detective Frank Contardi?" He sniggered and took his place

beside Merry, petting his gun lovingly as if it were a pet Chihuahua.

When Dara responded, it was in Celeste's voice, not her own. "Hello, Tony. How's Vinny? Oh wait, you haven't seen him since he exiled you for *schtupping* his girlfriend."

Tony's smile fell from his reddening face, and he lifted the pistol, pointing it at Dara's head. She felt nothing, sensed nothing other than the lingering acrid taste of vomit. Celeste had taken over, leaving her numb inside.

"Easy there, TP," said Merry. "There will be plenty of time for that later. I have something to say, and it might take a while. Why don't you leave me the gun and fetch yourself a cup of coffee? It's in the pot in the kitchen."

Tony handed Merry the gun, which she pointed at both ladies, alternating between Dara's head and Stacey's heart. When Tony returned, he also sweetened his brew and downed half the mug before retaking possession of his firearm.

Merry was in her element, Dara noted, center stage with the full attention of her truly captive audience. She cleared her throat and began pontificating as if she were delivering the soliloquy from Hamlet.

"First off, you two must be the stupidest women on the face of the Earth. Dara, do you really think if I'd wanted to keep hidden, I would have used your clients' credit cards for minor purchases? Didn't you think I'd have enough sense not to give away my location? But you were too busy being Realtor of the Year to consider I might be setting a trap. And you, Stacey. What did she tell you that convinced you to betray me?"

Stacey stopped whimpering long enough to respond, voice trembling. "She told me you insinuate yourself into women's lives and take over their families."

"And you believed her. You idiot. Did you ever stop to consider why I might pick someone like you if that were my game plan? You and your husband are hardly high society. You have nothing to offer me except as a way station, a place to sleep until I find my next mark. That's something you should have realized while Dara was spinning her tales of woe. A little forethought might have saved lives."

At the mention of her imminent demise, Stacey began bawling again, prompting Tony to aim the pistol at her head.

"Stacey, shut up before I give TP here the go-ahead, and we put you out of your misery."

Merry's words cut through Stacey's tears, and she bit her lip, reducing her wails to snivels.

"What you should know, Stacey, is that Ms. Dara here is cuckoo for Cocoa Puffs. Looney Tunes. Right out of her tiny little brain. Her therapist, Dr. Dimitri, wrote as much in his reports. Let me summarize."

Dara's queasiness returned as Merry lifted her phone and stared at the screen.

"And I quote, 'Exhibits signs of dissociative identity disorder when under great stress. Also suffers from White Knight Syndrome, which is why she's attracted to those she deems broken. She feeds on the approval and validation she receives by 'fixing' these damaged souls. Can't handle any challenges to her fragile self-image. Her dark side takes over. Deadly when disturbed.' If you don't believe me, let's listen to a recording of her foster sister, Janica. I have it right here as well." She waved her phone in the air, a jubilant display of taunting triumph.

Dara saw red at the mention of her former sister's name, and she jumped up, ready to charge Merry. A warning shot from Tony exploded through the ceiling, eliciting a second scream from Stacey and causing chunks of sheetrock to rain down near the women's heads. Tony turned his gun back on the two women, alternating his aim.

"The first one who makes another sound, or another unexpected movement can be assured, it will be your last. Shut up and listen. My lady has the floor."

Merry hit the playback button on her recording app and turned the sound up to maximum volume. Her voice was the first one they heard.

"Tell me about the fire. I read in the newspaper archives it was accidental."

"Accidental, my ass. I told everyone who'd listen that Dara started that fire."

"Why would she do that? Destroy her childhood home and jeopardize the lives of her foster sisters and brothers?"

"It was three weeks after Dara's sixteenth birthday party. The one that never happened, because Zahara pulled a stupid prank and unleashed an army of live cockroaches to run loose in the house the morning of. Robbie McLean was supposed to come to that party, and after it fell apart, Dara started secretly seeing him after school instead of volunteering, like she told everyone she was doing. Oksana found out and threatened to tell our parents unless Dara purchased her silence."

"Extortion, huh?"

"Exactly. Dara agreed... and the next evening, the house went up in flames. Dara made sure everyone got out except Zahara and Oksana. She claimed their door was locked, and that was confirmed by the police and the insurance people who analyzed the hardware. But those girls never bolted their door, so I'm thinking Dara locked it from the outside. She got just enough burns to make it look like she'd truly tried to help them, but, in the end, she burned them to death out of spite and to protect her own butt."

"But you said you told everyone..."

"The Crawfords wouldn't believe me. They said Dara was a hero and I should be grateful she saved as many fosters as she did. Including me. The police listened but didn't do anything. Angelica and Quincy's money doesn't just talk in Locust Valley; it shouts over a megaphone. No one was going to do anything to piss them off. So, the authorities buried my allegations. Quincy and Angelica got Dara psychiatric treatment, claiming it was for PTSD and trauma. And we were all encouraged to forget. But I never forgot. And I never will. Zahara and Oksana died because that hypocrite couldn't stand the idea that, for one moment, she'd present an image other than flawless."

261

Merry turned off the recording and spread her arms wide, palms up, as if to say, "Ta Da!"

Stacey stared, open-jawed, horrified by what she'd heard.

Dara remained silent, attempting to comprehend Janica's accusations. Her memories of that day were fuzzy, but then again, Celeste made a habit of forcing her to do things she couldn't later recall. It was as if Dara's consciousness had risen from her body and she was watching herself from above. A flesh-covered, breathing marionette whose strings were being pulled without her consent in a battle to the death between Merry and Celeste.

"What do you have to say for yourself, Little Ms. Perfect? Even with all the questionable things I've done in my life, and there have been plenty, I grant you, I never pulled anything as calculatedly evil and cold-hearted as that. And you have the nerve to judge me, investigate my life? You have the audacity, you arsonist and murderer, to accept the title of Realtor of the Year for all the good you've done for the community? And not a mention of me in that entire article. I nursed you back to health, oversaw your business, fed your husband and kids, changed your frigging bedpan, for God sakes. What the fuck do you have to say for yourself? How do you feel about your precious legacy now?"

Celeste reminded Dara that almost ten minutes had passed. "I don't know, Merry. How do *you* feel?"

Tony's pistol fell from his hand to the floor with a clunk, and his body followed, curled up on his side, twitching and convulsing. Stacey began writhing in her chair, bug-eyed, gasping for air. Merry stared at both of them, a curious look on her face, and then her hand dropped the phone and flew to her throat, where she clutched and clawed as if slowly being suffocated. Sugar laced with paraquat and a gopher-bait strychnine chaser. Worked every time. And in this case, thought Celeste, just in time.

Dara stood up and strolled serenely between them, ignoring their grunts and thrashing. She picked up Tony's gun and pocketed it, just in case. Then she grabbed a sponge and a roll of paper towels from the kitchen and calmly cleaned up her earlier vomit, disposing of the waste in a plastic garbage bag she planned to take home. She hummed to the melody of gasps and labored breathing while she wiped any trace of her fingerprints from counters, doorknobs, anywhere she had touched. When Dara had completely erased all evidence of her visit, she returned to the dining room to check on the trio. They finally lay still, though hardly resting in peace based on their distorted facial expressions.

It was a shame about Stacey, she thought. So young, and truly an innocent bystander. Dara had begged Celeste to let her spare the woman, especially since she'd come to Pennsylvania specifically to save her from Merry. But Celeste droned on about collateral damage and how you can never leave loose ends behind. Like Janica. She'd had no idea that the former foster badmouthed her to anyone who would listen. That wouldn't do. They'd have to put an end to that—something they both agreed on—very, very soon.

Dara took one last quick look at Merry, lying there, her hands still gripping her throat. She recalled her ex-assistant's rambling set of accusations. *How dare I? How dare I? I'll show you how.* With a fury emanating from deep within, she repeatedly smashed Merry's face with her three-inch heels, one stomp for every stolen ID.

"Hey Georgia, this one's for Merry." *Crack* went her nose. "This is for Sally." Her heel squashed the corpse's left eye. "Here's for Amoret. And here's for Felicity. And finally, this is for Harper Van Dyke—and all the other names I don't know about." A barrage of kicks ensued.

By the time she finished, Merry's face was almost unrecognizable, like something you might see on a slaughterhouse floor. She gave the corpse two more kicks for good measure, these to the chest. One for Samantha Ellingsworth and the other for Ricky Jones, Merry's paraplegic brother. The guy who had done nothing wrong other than earn his mother's doting praise.

Finally satisfied, Dara placidly wiped the blood from her shoes, added those paper towels to the vomit-soaked ones and, garbage bag in hand, slipped out the back door. She walked unnoticed through the camouflage of the woods to her waiting car.

She made it home in time to flush the contents of the bag, put Ava to bed, answer her emails, and watch late-night television by her husband's side. It was a good life.

Chapter Fifty-Four

June finally arrived and with it, the Realtor of the Year ceremony, this year held in the Crystal Ballroom of the Astor Hotel. Dara had purchased a stunning, jade-hued Oscar de la Renta strapless silk ballgown, the green complimenting her pixie cut, now platinum blonde. A pair of matching satin four-inch heels and a diamond bracelet completed the ensemble. Her mother would have a heart attack if she discovered the price of the outfit, but it's not every day your industry celebrates your achievements with a gala event. If she couldn't understand that, to hell with her.

Dara had worked on her speech all week, whittling it down to ten minutes of heartfelt thanks and appreciation for the honor they'd bestowed upon her. It included a mini-commercial and fundraising appeal for Autism Vanguard, about to begin its second year of Birthday Parties for All. The events had grown so large and so popular, they needed to take over additional space in the building. A good problem to have but a problem, nevertheless.

Dara shared the room's most prominent table with Jason, Ava, and Khai, her parents, Jason's parents, and Tammy, their live-in therapist. In the tenth seat sat Burton Erickson, whose trust in her to manage the exclusive leasing contract for the The Fortress on the Hudson had transformed her sales year from good to spectacular. In the eleventh seat, her new assistant, Rodrigo. She'd also saved a place at her table of twelve for Esther, but unfortunately, she'd been a no-show.

After a dinner of lobster tails and filet mignon, the president of the Board of Realtors took the podium and delivered a glowing introduction. She listed the sales records Dara had broken and included accolades from her most prestigious clients, her fellow Realtors, board members from Autism Vanguard, and even her parents. Dara's cheeks grew hot from the attention, but at the same time, she relished the applause, because she had earned the tributes based on skills her parents always warned her to bypass in favor of philanthropy. How fitting they should be here so they could acknowledge that she had known better and made it on her own terms, proving life was about more than altruism.

"And now, ladies and gentlemen, the woman of the hour. Mrs. Dara Banks."

The president stepped away from the podium to make room for Dara, and the crowd exploded into a standing ovation. She stood silently, surveying the audience, taking it all in. Her moment. The acclaim she'd earned.

As the furor died down and she cleared her voice, Dara noticed Esther in her Nigerian headdress and a matching pantsuit walking toward the podium from the back of the room, flanked by two uniformed police officers.

She leaned into the microphone. "Esther, there's a chair for you right over there at my table. Please have a seat."

Undaunted, Esther kept approaching, stopping only when she stood directly in front of Dara. One of the officers addressed her, speaking loudly enough for the front tables to hear.

"Dara Banks, you are hereby under arrest for the murder of Brooke Barnes. You have the right to remain silent; anything you say can and will be used against you in a court of law. You have the right to an attorney; if you cannot afford an attorney, one will be appointed for you."

Dara's mic picked up the entire conversation, leaving the room abuzz with murmurs and her face burning from a mixture of fury and embarrassment. The second officer walked behind Dara, attempting to handcuff her, but she pulled her hands free.

"What the hell are you doing? There's been some mistake."

"There's no mistake, Dara," said Esther. "Would you like to discuss this here in front of all your colleagues, or down at the station house, where we can do it in private?"

266

"Here will be just fine," Dara replied with an edge. "Then the audience can all hear you apologize when you realize the error you've made. Brooke committed suicide. You never wanted to admit that. I suppose you saw it as a personal affront, but that's what happened, and you have to face up to it."

"Dara, remember when you gave me permission to go to your office and search for fingerprints? I did that, gathering prints from both you and Merry. And when Merry disappeared, I had the FBI enter them into their system so that if they ever showed up anywhere, perhaps at a station house in another precinct, or in a morgue, I'd get dinged. And a few weeks ago, wouldn't you know it? The police found a dead woman poisoned in a home outside Pittsburgh with the exact same set of fingerprints."

"I'm sorry to hear that, but exactly what does that have to do with me?"

"I asked them to rush the toxicology report. It was a small town, so they were able to do it quickly. Three bodies, each found poisoned by a combination of paraquat and strychnine. The detectives discovered the poison in the victims' coffee and tea, and in the sugar bowl on the table."

Dara shrugged. "A cult? Another Jonestown that used pesticides in coffee instead of Kool-Aid for a group suicide?"

"I suppose some might think that. The thing is, Brooke's toxicology report indicated that same combination. And when I heard about the sugar bowl, I remembered that I had stored mine away after Brooke's death without emptying it. So, I had it checked. Same thing—pesticides in the sugar. If Brooke were going to kill herself, she'd have put the poison right in her drink, not have left it in the sugar bowl for others to accidentally use."

Dara frowned, growing impatient. "I still don't understand what this has to do with me, Esther. You always suspected Merry murdered Brooke. I don't know what happened in Pittsburgh, if the group you're describing had reason to kill themselves or whatever, but maybe Merry spiked the sugar bowl. I remember Brooke mentioning she used paraquat in her gardening. Perhaps that's where Merry got the idea and used it, trying to make it look like a suicide."

"I thought that was possible, at first. In fact, I repeatedly scanned the parking lot surveillance footage from the morning Brooke died, searching for Merry's car. What I hadn't done was check for yours. And when I went back to look again after Merry's death, there it was, that old Volvo sitting right there in the lot at ten in the morning, and you exiting the car and walking toward the building."

"You can't be serious, Esther." Dara's eyes blurred with tears of frustration. "You know me. You know what I do for my family, for the community. Why would I ever harm Brooke? Ask Jason. Ask my parents. I'd never do anything like that."

Dara swiveled her head toward the crowd, searching in vain for Jason's supportive face or her parents' joint show of unflagging support. It was not forthcoming. All three looked at Dara with narrowed eyes, as if finally seeing her true colors for the first time. Her parents' blatant yet familiar expression of disgust reminded her of every attempt she'd made as a child to divert their attention away from the fosters, desperate for one smattering of affection, one smidgen of praise, as absent now as it was then.

That's when the wall came down, and Celeste spoke for them both, but the explanation came out as disjointed gibberish, as Celeste often did when called upon in times of stress.

"You have to understand. Brooke was stealing from Autism Vanguard. Merry had encouraged it. I had to let Brooke go, and she planned to confront Merry and blame her for everything. I couldn't let Brooke poke the bear. Merry was vindictive. She would have gotten angry and lashed out by telling Detective Contardi about the hit. I would have gone to jail, and then who would have taken care of Jason? Or Ava? I had no choice. Can't you see?

"No one else knew how dangerous Merry could be—her mob background, the people she'd conned, the woman she practically pushed in front of a subway. No one understood except me. Ask Merry. She'll probably brag about her exploits for hours."

Esther and the officers flinched, trying to make sense of what Dara was attempting to convey.

"Dara, Merry is dead," Esther said slowly, as if talking to a toddler. "Her real name is Georgia Jones, and if you're looking for her to provide an explanation or an alibi, I'm afraid you're out of luck. We're going to sort this all out at the station.

"I don't know what hit you're talking about, but after we're done, the Pittsburgh police would like to have a word. Stacey Cavanaugh survived your little sugar holocaust. Apparently, she only had a sip or two of tea. The herbicide burnt her esophagus, but not beyond repair, and once she could speak, she told them everything. I suppose you have a denial for that as well?"

Dara couldn't answer because she could no longer hear Esther's words. The crowd ceased to exist. She was back in Locust Valley, sitting in a highchair at the dining table of her family's home. She reached for her spoon, but it toppled to the floor. She called for her mother to help retrieve it. Her mother ignored her, too busy feeding the other three fosters in her care.

"Mommy," she cried, "Mommy. Spoon. Soup. Hungry. Spoon."

Her mother kept her back turned to Dara. "The Lord helps those who help themselves. And for those he can't help, He put us on Earth to assist. As the privileged, that is our job, our calling. You'll get the spoon after I've helped feed the others. Until then, be quiet and keep yourself occupied."

At that moment, Celeste made her debut. She looked exactly like Dara's mother but was kind and attentive. She gave the toddler all her attention—an angel the Lord had sent from Heaven to help her help herself. She suggested to Dara the best way to get what she needed was to fling her bowl of soup at one of the fosters. Enchanted by the stranger, the toddler complied.

The beating that followed was worth it. Dara Crawford had found her protector for life. And had made her first best friend.

Acknowledgements

Thanks to my beta-readers for this novel: Betty Hirsch, Donna Hagedorn, Ken Grant, S.L. Manning, and Emilya Naymark. Your remarks helped shape this book in ways I didn't originally anticipate. And special thanks to Lori Robbins, who made sure the right people took notice.

Much appreciation to Shawn Reilly Simmons and everyone at Level Best Books for making this novel possible.

And thanks, as always, to the authors at Hudson Valley Scribes, Sisters in Crime, and Mystery Writers of America, who continue to inspire me. And to my long-suffering family…thank goodness for meal services and housekeepers because without them, my husband and children would be dust-covered skeletons. Hmm…that might be a great title for my memoir.

Alphabetical List of Characters (Warning: Spoiler Alert!)

- **Ambrosia:** Alias for Merry as stripper/escort
- **Amoret Prager:** Alias for Merry, wedding cake provider
- **Angelica Crawford:** Dara's mother
- **Ava Banks:** Dara's stepdaughter with autism
- **Bakari:** One of the Crawford's foster children
- **Brooke Barnes:** Dara's friend, college roommate, co-volunteer at Autism Vanguard
- **Burton Erickson:** one of Rock Canyon's leading real estate developers (Fortress on the Hudson) and Jason's former partner at RC Architects.
- **Carl Vonderman, aka Carl the Copy:** Thug, real name of Warren Feder
- **Celeste:** Dara's internal voice, guardian, and protector
- **Chase Barclay/Ms. Bannon:** Aliases for Dara Banks
- **Chiara Harwood:** Paisley and Alana's mom
- **Dara Iobairt Crawford Banks:** Realtor/protagonist
- **Dr. Peter Dimitri:** Psychiatrist
- **Emily:** Dara's caterer
- **Esther Okoro:** Brooke's wife, Police investigation researcher
- **Felicity Prager/Felicity Ellingsworth:** Merry's alias when nanny to Harry Ellingsworth's children, future wife
- **Mrs. Farnsby:** Works with **Edwina** at Syracuse High School as Facilities Director
- **Dr. Fitzpatrick:** Dara's surgeon

271

- **Det. Frank Contardi:** Homicide Detective (alias for Tonito/Tony/TP Randazzo)
- **Garrison Harwood:** Chiara's doctor husband, Paisley and Alana's dad
- **Georgia Jones:** Merry's real name
- **Gracie Isaacs:** works at Attwood Academy
- **Harry Ellingsworth:** Samantha's husband before marrying "Felicity Prager" (Merry)
- **Harper Van Dyke:** Alias for Merry when she took up residence outside Pittsburgh.
- **Hollis Rose:** Wedding planner
- **Ivy Andrews:** Autism mom, mother of Maisie, wife of Xander
- **Janica Rivera Zamm:** Former Crawford foster
- **Jason Banks:** Dara's husband
- **Jimmy Gordon:** Thug, real name of Lee Eastwick
- **Judy:** Rock Canyon Realty receptionist
- **Kevin O'Doherty:** Police officer with Sean and Conor on the Locust Valley police force.
- **Khai Banks:** Dara's teenage stepson
- **Kylie:** Dara's departing assistant
- **Lee Eastwick:** Insurance salesperson (alias for Jimmy Gordon)
- **Lina:** Merry's alleged stepdaughter
- **Mae:** Waitress at Nell's in Aspinwall, PA
- **Maisie Andrews:** Child with autism, daughter of Ivy and Xander
- **Meryl (Merry) Rafter:** Dara's assistant, antagonist
- **Dr. Mitchell:** Jason's therapist
- **Nikki Ellingsworth:** Merry's stepdaughter, Harry's daughter, sister to Daniel and Veronica Ellingsworth (twins). Works at Mitterhof Pharma.
- **Noah Hunsicker:** Vivian's husband
- **Oliver Smith:** works at SideHustlesforNYActors.com or SHNYA
- **Oksana:** One of the Crawford's foster children
- **Paisley Harwood:** Child whose identity was stolen
- **Mrs. Parker:** Dara's client, fraud victim
- **Quenton:** Elevator operator for the Harwood's building

- **Quincy Crawford:** Dara's father
- **Reverend Sexton:** Minister at St. Paul's on Long Island
- **Richard (Ricky) Jones:** Vera Jones's golden son, Georgia's younger brother
- **Rodrigo:** Dara's assistant
- **Ruben Bockleman:** Rival Realto
- **Sally Malone:** Alias for Merry when working as an escort for SHINYA
- **Samantha Ellingsworth:** Suicide victim, Harry Ellingsworth's first wife, mother to Nikki, Daniel, and Veronica
- **Stacey Cavanaugh:** Merry's Pennsylvania mark, married to Pete.
- **Tonino (Tony/TP) Randazzo:** Mobster, son of Vinny, Real name of Det. Frank Contardi
- **Tobias:** Alleged stepson of Merry (mentioned, never appears)
- **Ultima:** One of the dancers (along with **Pegs**) at Brazen
- **Vera Jones:** Georgia (Merry) and Ricky's mother
- **Vinny Randazzo:** Mobster, Merry's paramour, father to Tony Randazzo (TP)
- **Vivian Hunsicker:** Home seller and hoarder
- **Warren Feder:** Insurance salesperson whom the girls meet at Poisson, alias for Carl Vonderman/Carl the Copy
- **Mrs. Xi:** Real Estate Client
- **Mrs. Yang:** Headmistress at Attwood Academy
- **Zahara:** One of the Crawford's foster children

About the Author

D.M. Barr (Dawn) is an award-winning author who writes psychological, domestic, and romantic suspense. Her published books include *Expired Listings, Murder Worth the Weight, Saving Grace: A Psychological Thriller, The Queen of Second Chances,* and *Simple Tryst of Fate.* Dawn recently finished her second stint co-editing a Sisters in Crime NY/Tri-state chapter anthology, *New York State of Crime,* which includes her third published short story, "Orchestral Removals in the Dark." In December 2025, Down & Out Books will publish *Better Off Dead, Crime Fiction Inspired by the Music of Elton John and Bernie Taupin,* which she conceived and edited solo. A member of ITW and SinC-New England, she has served as president of Hudson Valley Scribes, vice president of Sisters in Crime-NY, and the newsletter author/board member of the NY chapter of Mystery Writers of America. Follow her at www.dmbarr.com.

AUTHOR WEBSITE: www.dmbarr.com

SOCIAL MEDIA HANDLES:
  Facebook.com/authordmbarr
  Instagram.com/authordmbarr
  TikTok.com/@authordmbarr
  authordmbarr@bsky.social

Also by D.M. Barr

Expired Listings: Revenge Begins at Home

Murder Worth the Weight

Saving Grace: A Psychological Thriller

The Queen of Second Chances

Simple Tryst of Fate

Vacations Can Be Murder, A True Crime Lover's Travel Guide to New England, writing as Dawn M. Barclay (to be released 2/4/2025)